# THE BUBBLE We're In

Library of Congress Cataloguing-in-Publication Data has been applied for.
ISBN 9798988038511 (print) | 9798988038528 (Ebook)
First Edition.

Designed by David Colón.

# THE
# BUBBLE
## *We're In*

ALEX MELL-TAYLOR

*To Arty*
*My Jelly Belly. I Love You.*

# CONTENT WARNING

*The Bubble We're In* is the story of a dysfunctional queer relationship. As such, it is filled with examples of negative self-talk, suicidal ideation, sexual assault, and physical violence.

ALEX NEIL TAYLOR

ALEX NEIL TAYLOR

# Chapter

## 1



Christian was utterly bored. He was sitting alone in the dark—firmly planted in the forest green, mid-century velvet chaise that made up his reading nook. He looked out at the vibrant city lights of downtown, beckoning him to be anywhere but inside his apartment. Christian had promised himself that he would try to get through at least a chapter of an old book his grandfather had recommended to him, *The Fountainhead* by some blowhard named Ayn Rand, but he simply couldn't do it, even with the threat of losing his financial trust hanging over every one of his grandfather's polite 'suggestions.' His eyes glazed over the words as he reread the same paragraph over and over again.

The writing might be too intellectual for him, he thought. After his fourth time working through a passage, he abandoned his valiant effort and instead retreated to his phone—to the orange haze of the gay dating app he loved. Well, tolerated anyway. He hadn't been having any luck connecting to people in the city, and he wanted a lover. A companion. A friend? Most guys only wanted to fuck, though, and even scheduling that was tedious, as last-minute cancellations were frequent.

*No one wants you*, the dark, hoarse voice in his mind taunted.

"Shut up," Christian mumbled back. It was exhausting to argue with the voice, so he ignored it most days. It sat in the back of his mind, belittling everything he did like a family member who knew you too well.

Besides, that couldn't be true. Christian, known as *RayGun* on Grindr, had an entire world of men pinging him every day. He instantly got a ping, but it was from a dude in his fifties. Christian wasn't into people that were much older than him, so he blocked him. More hits kept coming. He spent the next thirty minutes vetting various contenders: a teen several towns over (too young), a bear 'looking' (too fat), and a polyamorous couple seeking a third (too weird).

He finally found someone worth the effort. A twenty-five-year-old with a chiseled face and an even nicer cut dick, who he would later learn was named Sebastián. He was Latino, but he didn't look too brown, not that race was a thing he cared about.

Cocky Top (Sebastián)

Hey sexy.

RayGun (Christian)

Hi cutie. How are you doing?

Cocky Top (Sebastián)

Good. Horny. Looking for some fun tonite?

RayGun (Christian)

Yes! Bttm here. Can you host?

Cocky Top (Sebastián)

Top here 😈. And yes.

Cocky Top (Sebastián)

Sends location.

RayGun (Christian)

Excellent. Give me 15 minutes.

Cocky Top (Sebastián)

👍

Forty minutes later, Christian arrived outside Sebastián's condo building. It was a modern construction of glass and red brick that had popped up along the recently-gentrified Ninth Street only six months ago. It was becoming quite a respectable neighborhood—not as nice as his, but the potential was there. Even in the early evening, twenty-something joggers felt comfortable enough to run past the boutique restaurants and gourmet delis that were quickly making this place home. He didn't feel at risk here at all.

RayGun (Christian)

here.

Cocky Top (Sebastián)

the doorman should let you up. Tell him 513.

Christian dialed the buzzer for Sebastián's apartment. The front door buzzed open, and he entered through the opaque glass doors. There was a small fountain in the entryway in the shape of an abstract metal fish. The water shot out of its open mouth, splashing into a stainless-steel, rectangular basin below. There were plastic ferns in blocky ceramic pots framing it on either side. Well, at least someone in building management is trying, thought Christian with a smug eye roll.

He reached out to touch one of them but paused at the sound of someone clearing their throat. It was the doorman, another extravagance that looked strange in this cheap building. He was a Black man in an over-starched button-down, tired black blazer, and rusty red tie. He wanted to know who Christian was there to see. Christian didn't ask for his name. He felt too nervous about doing anything besides mumble awkwardly. The doorman looked at him with a mixture of what Christian assumed was sternness and boredom. It occurred to Christian that he didn't have any identifying details for Sebastián other than his face and location.

"He said you should be expecting me?" Christian replied.

"Hnh," the doorman said with a gravelly rumble, one eyebrow bouncing up ever so briefly, like a puff of air, "One of those friends, huh." Christian couldn't tell if he was being scorned or pitied. "It's open. Go right on up," he vaguely waved at the elevators, his eyes already going back down to the crossword that Christian's presence had interrupted.

"Thank you," Christian said, his indignation only thinly concealed. His doorman wasn't nearly this rude.

Christian entered the elevator, feeling ashamed but mostly vexed. When the doors closed, he flipped the doorman off from the safety of the empty elevator car and pressed the small, round button for the fifth floor. He kept his fingertip there for a moment, feeling the electrical warmth. Christian nervously considered pressing the button to return to the ground floor but thought better of it. He had made a promise to this stranger, and he wasn't going to back out now. That would be rude, and if there was one thing that had been drilled into him since birth, it was the art of keeping up appearances.

Besides, this was supposed to be fun. Christian was going to have fun.

The doors opened again, and he got off on the fifth floor. It was more cramped than the wannabe-Bauhaus lobby below. The corridor was narrow. The fluorescent tubes buzzed impersonally, half-heartedly illuminating the space with a cold, industrial glow. It smelled of the faint lemony tang of an industrial carpet cleaner. He awkwardly wandered through the maze of hallways until he found the right door.

He knocked. Sebastián opened it immediately. He must have been waiting behind it, waiting for him. Sebastián was a tall man with black hair and light, olive-tinted skin. His shirt was off, and Christian saw he had a well-defined four-pack. He looked a little more worn than in his picture, with faint dark circles underneath his eyes from what Christian assumed was a lack of sleep. Close enough for it not to be an issue. Sebastián waved him inside, though he did not say hi. Christian hesitantly entered, and Sebastián closed the door behind him. They were standing face-to-face.

"Hey," said Christian.

"Hey," Sebastián repeated back.

They eyed each other behind the front door, Christian's eyes tracing the outline of Sebastián's nicely defined shoulders and traps, his freshly-shaven pecs, and the hint of dark hair peeking out of his armpits. Christian swallowed. Yeah, more than close enough to his profile pic.

He saw Sebastián look him up and down, his big, dark eyes hungry. Sebastián's gaze landed and locked onto Christian's blue eyes, inches away from him. His generous lips pulled up into a small, hungry grin.

They locked lips. Christian thought Sebastián's were warm and firm as they gently suckled on and around his mouth. Sebastián occasionally bit down lightly, prompting small, involuntary gasps from Christian. His pale cheeks flushed with a mixture of desire and embarrassment at being so transparently needy. Sebastián didn't seem to mind, given that his arms and hands tightened around Christian's torso and ass at every gasp.

"You're so hot," Sebastián whispered into his ear. Christian didn't respond, kissing him back harder instead. He moaned as the goosebumps spread from his ear down to his neck, adding to the pleasant swirl of desire already building in his chest.

Sebastián unbuttoned the top of Christian's button-down but ran into trouble immediately after the first two. Christian took over, and Sebastián gently nudged him over to the bed, holding his back so he didn't fall to the floor. Sebastián playfully pushed Christian down on his back when they reached the bed. Christian was turned on enough that he almost didn't notice the bed was a double-stacked mattress without a bed frame. The frame was in an unpacked box leaning against the wall several feet away.

His shirt was now off, and Christian lay on his back, grinning. He even ventured to cockily stretch his arms so his hands were behind his head. Christian knew he could show off his 5-days-a-week-at-the-gym chest better that way. He saw Sebastián's eyes open slightly wider, his little grin returning as he grunted in appreciation. The grunt and the look made Christian twitch in all the right places. Christian lifted his hips off the bed, which helped Sebastián effortlessly tear off his jeans. When it came time for Sebastián to take off his own pants, they bunched up right at his feet. He had to crouch down and lift his legs one at a time to take off each end.

"The pants'll always getcha," Christian joked.

Sebastián chuckled and stood up with an even more obvious bulge straining in his now-exposed jockstrap. That shut Christian up, and his throat was suddenly dry and very thirsty. Sebastián grabbed Christian's ankles and lifted them over Sebastián's shoulders. He left Christian there for a few seconds, grinding his bulge into Christian's underwear.

"Andrew Christian, nice," Sebastián said with a chuckle as he slowly, teasingly slipped Christian's underwear up, taking every opportunity to squeeze Christian's well-sculpted legs along the way.

"Instagram's ads… work on me," Christian joked breathily in between little moans.

Sebastián got on his knees on the bed but kept Christian's legs pushed up, leaving him completely and utterly exposed. Christian wanted this so fucking bad now. And he could tell Sebastián knew it—every time he looked down, Sebastián's grin was a little wider, the top half of his face still visible past Christian's now raging erection.

"How badly do you want this, baby?" he whispered between licks and kisses. Christian tried to say something, but it came out more like a strangled groan, which only made Sebastián's face split into a full-on devilish smile, hungrily baring his white teeth.

Sebastián rubbed up against him. Christian wanted Sebastián to fuck him, but his nervousness around barebacking snapped him briefly out of his heady, horny mind space. He considered letting Sebastián do it for a moment. Christian saw men on the apps advertise this all the time, but those people were usually on the HIV-preventative PrEP, and neither Christian nor Sebastián were. God, why hadn't he gotten on PrEP yet? Now, he would have to make things awkward, and did he really want to be so difficult?

"Wait," said Christian, gathering the courage to finally say something. "Could you get a condom?"

"Are you sure? I'm very safe…" deflected Sebastián.

"I'm… sure," said Christian.

"Sure, no prob," said Sebastián, relenting quickly. He got up and walked toward his small bathroom. Christian heard the desperate hands of someone searching for something in a hurry. Sebastián seemed to rifle through one of his drawers and then another. He returned with an opened condom wrapper.

"Ready?" asked Sebastián.

"Yes," said Christian, unsure.

He wanted this. He wanted to have fun. He wanted to be fun. Christian could feel himself tightening back up, losing his cool. No, damn it!

"You're tight," Sebastián said, carefully neutral as he probed Christian.

"Sorry," Christian apologized as the bad thoughts threatened to return.

He started to spiral. Christian couldn't even have sex right, something someone with half a brain could do. Sebastián's strong forearms faded out of view as he became singularly focused on how worthless he was. How he was once again finding a stranger on the Internet rather than a match that would make his family happy, and he couldn't even excel at being a promiscuous slut because he was a worthless fuck up. Christian stared off into the ceiling, watching the slow-moving fan above him rotate around in circles again and again and again.

One hundred and eighty-four rotations later, Sebastián finally came with a roar. He pulled out, tossed the used condom on the floor, and collapsed on top of Christian. The two of them lay entangled and cuddling. This made Christian feel better, wanted. As they wrapped around each other so tightly that it felt like the world would fade away in warm bliss. All that mattered about each other was that they were two warm bodies. Christian could be that at least, and for a while, he didn't want to know anything other than that he was alive.

*Did he enjoy it, though?* the voice asked. *This could just be in your head. He might not want to see you again now that he's used you.*

Christian shuddered at this thought, pulling himself away from Sebastián's immaculate frame.

"You okay?" Sebastián asked.

"Of course," Christian lied, moving back to cuddle this hunk and capture that energy he had felt only moments before—to be happy.

"How was your day?" Christian asked, settling on the safest question he could think of—one even he couldn't fuck up.

"It was okay," said Sebastián. "I went to work. Met a cute guy."

Christian giggled. "What's he like?"

"Very hot. I met him on the apps, you know? We might even swap numbers soon," Sebastián said coyly.

They chatted some more. They both discovered that they loved Lizzo and Beyoncé. Sebastián worked in healthcare. Christian didn't want to say what his job was. Some people in the gay community tended to get judgy when you told them you worked for the military. There was also how he got the job, which was a little embarrassing. He'd have to know Sebastián a little more before getting 'that' vulnerable.

"I hear Lizzo refused to do a branding deal with Trump Hotels. She is so based."

"Hey, actually, can we not talk about politics?" Christian interjected, wanting to avoid that landmine. "It's a big no-no for me. Everyone gets so touchy."

"I know what that is like," Sebastián said. "My abuela is freaking out about some virus in China. She's going mental. And I try not to bring any of that stuff up."

"I know, what's with our parents and all these conspiracy theories?" Christian asked.

"Dunno," Sebastián sighed.

They swapped numbers and made plans to see each other soon, and less than a minute later, Christian was walking home. Several hours later, even though they had each other's numbers, Sebastián sent a message on the app.

**Cocky Top (Sebastián)**

Hey sexy. That was a lot of fun. Don't be a stranger. 😈

**RayGun (Christian)**

You too.

# CHAPTER 2



*Damnit, another email?*

Sebastián was overworked. The firm was making all junior associates pull extra hours—too many, in his opinion, though everyone told him this was normal. Young people were supposed to be overworked. It was the way of the world, and he'd be sure to pay it forward as a senior associate. The thought of handing off all these tedious slides to some young schmuck was enough to put a smile on his face.

Unfortunately, right now, he was that young schmuck, and he was fucking miserable. Yes, he'd come to the firm to get ahead in life, but he had also come to this city because he had friends here. Many of his college gays had moved here to find work, especially his rush mate Barry, who had some job Sebastián didn't understand. A job that allowed him to party every other night like some rich fuckboy on the CW. Barry's handle on Grindr was *Mr. Thick*, and he was messaging Sebastián constantly.

**Mr. Thick (Barry)**

are you coming out tonight?

**Cocky Top (Sebastián)**

Sorry

**Mr. Thick (Barry)**

boo, even lame Rick is coming out. And we all hate that snooze fest.

When he first moved here, Sebastián imagined his life would turn out like *Friends* or *Queer as Folk*. He'd picture himself hanging out with catty gay friends every Friday and Saturday night at the local gay watering hole, chatting under the neon lights about the men they had slept with recently. Yet he hadn't had much time to hang out with his friends. Barry kept sending him invites to parties, and they all sat unread on the notification bar on his phone because he was working too hard to afford this life he couldn't enjoy, not lucky enough to be born into money like the rest of his friends.

Worse, he was so fucking horny. He spent hours a week at the gym, and besides the occasional biweekly hookup, he was not having nearly as much sex as he wanted. His abuela always said he needed to expel distractions to get ahead at work, and he was undoubtedly feeling distracted. He tried to masturbate every morning before going into the office just so his fit coworkers didn't cause him to lose his damn mind. Sebastián masturbated in the morning before his first cup of coffee. He masturbated during his lunch break in the accessible stall of the office bathroom. Sebastián masturbated when he got home from work. His last task for the day would be his sticky hands checking some work emails before he passed out on his bed from pure exhaustion.

When his boss canceled a meeting at the last minute and unexpectedly freed up some time, Sebastián had to stop himself from jerking it out of habit. He had to re-mind himself that he finally had a chance to do the things he had moved here to the city to do, and of course, that brought him back to the familiar orange glow of his phone.

Cocky Top (Sebastián)

Happy Wednesday!

RayGun (Christian)

You too, what are you up to?

Cocky Top (Sebastián)

nothing actually. I'm now finishing up at work, bored.

RayGun (Christian)

Want to meet up for a coffee? We can talk about...well, anything but the news.

Cocky Top (Sebastián)

sure. I'm tragically under-caffeinated.

Cocky Top (Sebastián)

And yes. Anything but THAT

RayGun (Christian)

want to do Green Eggs & Jam in 30 minutes? They have a great rosemary & thyme latte.

Cocky Top (Sebastián)

Yes, let's do it.

Ten minutes later, his boss sent him a typo-ridden email: "i need the revisions on the Pfizer Contract in a track changes Word doc. Please sned ASAP, urgent."

Sebastián let out a groan. His hand was on the door-knob, about to head out into the cold, and now, he had to deal with this nonsense. He had already sent those to his boss more than once. He was furious, but it was better to bury those messy, imperfect feelings until after the work was done. Sebastián was the schmuck, after all, and this was a light task that he could bang out quickly. He just needed to get through these twenty minutes, and that would be it, at least for today—probably.

A buzz from his phone.

RayGun (Christian)

here.

RayGun (Christian)

I'm waiting in the back

*Fuck*, Sebastián thought to himself.

Cocky Top (Sebastián)

Sorry, I'm going to be five minutes late.

He scanned through emails to find the information he needed. He copied and pasted emails he had already sent to his boss into one clean document. Sebastián double-checked for typos, or he would hear about it later.

*Done.*

He dashed out the door, thankful they had agreed on a place close by. He arrived 20 minutes later than intended, jogging most of the way there. Sebastián gave himself a minute to breathe. His armpits were moist and sweaty, completely undoing his morning routine. He put on some deodorant that he kept in his backpack for emergencies to mask his stank. He had to be perfect, or what was the point of any of it? He might as well move back home to the suburbs if he wasn't going to live this life right.

He took in another deep breath and crossed the threshold into *Green Eggs & Jam*. It was everything its Instagram page had advertised it to be. The coffee shop had high ceilings with exposed bronze piping. There were flashy, low-hanging lights, similar to but legally distinct from the fantastical shapes of Dr. Seus's illustrations. There were artistic photos of 20-somethings drinking coffee in elaborate poses on the wall as they wore an off-brand version of the cat-in-the-hat's quintessential red hat. People were snapping pictures of everything, but mostly of themselves.

As promised, Sebastián found Christian waiting on an oversized red couch. It looked stunning, though even from a distance, it was evident that Christian couldn't quite sit up straight in it.

"Hey, so sorry I'm late, cutie," said Sebastián. He tried not to gasp. He was breathing heavily. The run here had taken a lot out of him, though he still pretended to be unhurried. "Oh, I see you don't have anything. Can I get you a coffee?" He asked.

"Yes," Christian said instinctually. He looked flustered, though Sebastián couldn't quite tell why. "Could I get a latte?"

Within seconds, a waitress approached them, wearing long black gloves that protected her skin, with a set of menus and handed one to Sebastián.

"Hi! My name's Clarissa. I'll be your server for this afternoon."

"Nice to meet you," said Sebastián cheerfully as he sat down, relieved not to be moving. "I'm Sebastián, and this is…" He trailed off as he realized he didn't know Christian's name.

"Christian," his date said dispassionately, doing his best not to sound awkward.

"Of course," the waitress papered over. "I'll be back to check in on you in a couple of moments, but feel free to wave me over if you have any questions." She then turned to Christian. "Can I get you another coffee?" She asked.

"Yes," he said as she walked away.

Sebastián looked down and saw that there was indeed a tiny cup near Christian. He had been so distracted that he hadn't seen it. "I'm so sorry. I didn't see that," Sebastián said, pointing to the cup, feeling immensely guilty for the oversight. This date was already imperfect.

"Oh, not a problem," Christian affirmed. "Besides, I can't get enough," he joked.

"Right? I'm addicted." Sebastián blushed before trying to change tack to something else. He briefly joked about how several patrons were wearing blue masks that he kept seeing advertised everywhere online.

"Some people are taking this way too seriously," said Sebastián, nodding his head toward an elderly Chinese man.

Christian looked unsettled by this comment. "Yeah," he laughed awkwardly, barely audible. "I was reading that it's not really a big deal. Not even as deadly as the flu."

Sebastián had a pang of guilt over the comment. He was fucking this date up. Maybe he had gone too far. Perhaps it sounded racist to Christian? He tried to laugh it off and quickly change the subject to something… anything, that would make him seem better in the eyes of this cute white boy he was trying to impress.

"So… tell me about you?" Christian asked, putting on a warm smile.

Maybe he hadn't fucked this up after all. He could answer a question. He did it all the time at work. The adrenaline from the run was coursing through him. He felt like he could tackle anything.

"Well, I work in healthcare."

"A doctor?" Christian mused. "Hot."

"Lobbyist, actually. Well, not technically a lobbyist, but close enough."

"So you're who I call when I need to get a hold of a hot doctor."

"Exactly. We keep all of them on speed dial."

They both laughed at this, and Sebastián began rapidly cycling through a series of subjects. He talked and talked about everything in his life: all the fun he had had in college, his best friend Barry, his upbringing in New Jersey, or as he called it, 'the suburbs of New York City.' He spoke fondly of eating his abuela's huevos a la Mexicana for breakfast and for lunch, the sandwiches his mother would always bring home from the Jewish deli after a long day of cleaning other people's homes.

"Mexican is the best goyish food, in my opinion," Sebastián smirked.

"Wait, you're Jewish?" Christian asked. The confusion on his face was palatable.

"Yes. Latino Jews, we exist." Sebastián laughed wryly and then, after a naked pause, said: "Is that a problem?"

"Oh no, no problem," Christian said defensively. "I hang out with the Jews… Jewish people all the time. And Mexicans…"

Sebastián unconsciously frowned at this. He hoped he hadn't stumbled into a date with some closeted Republican who couldn't wrap his head around the fact that his mother was a white Jewish lady from New York and his late father was a Brown Mexican from Quintana Roo.

"That probably sounded cringe as fuck," Christian continued.

"A little," Sebastián laughed, almost letting out a sigh of relief that Christian was only the typical kind of white people racist. Still wasn't great, but not something he was unused to in the dating scene. "But as a connoisseur of cringe, I don't mind," Sebastián deflected, deciding nothing was as unsexy as lecturing someone you had just met.

Sebastián moved on to another slightly less consequential subject, continuing to unload his thoughts, and thankfully, Christian listened politely in return. The two of them talked like every detail enraptured them. They stared into each other's eyes, trying to focus on the conversation when all Sebastián wanted to do was grab hold of

Christian's neck and kiss him. Sebastián loved Christian's cute, pale face, and his supple lips. He couldn't help but think how perfect they were as a match.

He wanted to skip the 'getting to know you' part of the conversation and head back to his bed, which made the dialogue between them a little stilted as they talked about everything except for the one thing they wanted to discuss: their attraction for one another. The subtext was there, but not the raw fucking he had been deprived of way too much because of his job. Sebastián would caress Christian's hand as they talked, a gentle reminder of why both of them were 'really' there.

"Yes, I love dogs too," remarked Sebastián as he rigorously massaged the base of Christian's thumb. They caressed with more intensity, and the sensuality bled into their conversation.

"And what do you do?" asked Sebastián with cool fuck-me eyes, "Besides look stunning, I mean."

Christian blushed. "It's complicated to explain. I technically work for the Navy."

"You're a seaman? I knew I liked you," winked Sebastián.

Christian blushed even harder. "I'm… I do housing management in the Navy for officers, domestically."

"What now?"

"I, when an officer is on short-term assignment somewhere, I book their lodging."

"Oh, so you know where to find all the sexy sailors then." Sebastián joked.

"That's classified…" he quipped, raising a flirtatious eyebrow.

They both laughed. "It's very hectic right now," continued Christian. "Trump is doing something with a cruise ship, and it's got all the top brass annoyed."

"That man," said Sebastián, ruffled. He was about to say more but paused. He realized the two of them hadn't swapped political preferences at all. They had both discussed a disdain for politics, which meant they hadn't shared their preferred teams. He would typically not think anything of it and assumed his partner was close enough to his side, but Christian working for the Navy gave him pause.

"Yeah," sighed Christian.

Christian looked tense again in Sebastián's eyes. Maybe he was a conservative, after all? Or perhaps this conversation was too political—something they had both mentioned disliking immensely.

"Do you want to get out of here?" asked Sebastián.

Christian smiled.

Twenty minutes later, Sebastián was back inside his tiny apartment, staring into Christian's blue eyes. Christian's legs straddled behind his back. The world seemed to mix into a swirl of sweat and musk. Sebastián could smell an aftershave emitting from Christian's recently shaved cheeks, a bit of stubble grazing him as he rubbed his lips against it. There was also something else. Perfume? Cologne?

He noticed that Christian wasn't staring directly at him but more past him, seemingly watching the blades of the fan above them spin by. Christian's moans were not as prominent as last time, as though something was amiss. This worried him. Was he doing something wrong?

Sebastián didn't want to fuck this up, except in the most literal sense. He wanted to be a good lay.

"Everything okay?" He asked.

"Easy, pause," Christian said.

Sebastián could feel Christian contracting uncomfortably. "Should I pull out?" He asked.

"No, just give it a moment."

Sebastián paused, which allowed him to refocus his gaze on his partner's face. He stared directly into Christian's blue eyes again. They were like sheets of ice floating in clear water. "God, you are so beautiful," Sebastián said.

"Thank you kindly," Christian blushed. "So are you. Okay, you can, you know, keep going."

"You sure?" asked Sebastián.

"Yes, I'm sure."

Sebastián eased into Christian. He started to go in and out slowly. Christian seemed to be enjoying the sensation. He let out another moan—louder this time, which relieved Sebastián. He wasn't fucking things up after all.

"Say something," Christian demanded in between breaths.

"Like what?"

"Call me a slut," Christian said confidently, surprising Sebastián.

"You like that, slut?" Sebastián asked, trying out the words. They felt strange coming out of his lips but not uncomfortable. It was the strangeness that came with any new experience. Sebastián realized that he liked this one. That he could get used to this.

Around this time, Sebastián's phone buzzed a ringtone he had assigned explicitly to his manager. He ignored it, but seeing it several minutes later would prompt him to clean up and leave within moments.

The alert from his boss, ironically typed out with poor grammar and in all caps, read as follows—"

> THERE ARE TYPOS IN THIS DOCUMENT. THIS S UNACCEPTABLE. AS A JUNIOR AS-SOCIATE YOUR WORK MUST BE SPOT-LESS, DO YOU HEAR ME? DO THIS OVER, & SEND IT TO MEE IMMEDIATELY."

# CHAPTER

*Christian*

For weeks, Christian had tried desperately to see Sebastián again. Maybe desperate was the wrong word. Excessively? Substantially? He had been struggling with his words recently. He had probably struggled with his words his entire life, another flaw his mind would pick at incessantly.

*Try swallowing a dictionary, next time,* the voice mocked.

Regardless, he had tried to meet up with Sebastián. He had had a lot of fun at their last… meetup? Date? Hang? Whatever it had been, it had been nice, but Christian wasn't sure if it was the smartest move to keep seeing him. In the back of his mind, his grandfather's voice clawed at him:

*You need to find a match I will approve of by 28, or you won't get your trust.*

When Christian had 'come out of the closet,' the first thing his grandfather had done was add a morality clause to the terms and conditions concerning the acquisition of his trust. Reading through the lines, the message had been clear: he could be gay, but not an embarrassing one. A normal faggot that didn't fuck his way through life.

Christian knew he should take his dating life more seriously and find the kind of gay that would make Grandfather Samuel happy. But he just wanted to have fun—to be in his twenties and have cute interactions with men he met on the Internet. And so, he split the difference and reached out to Sebastián in the in-between spaces. When he was standing in line for coffee, lying leisurely in his bed, or procrastinating at work, he would ask, 'what's up?' or 'how are you doing?' This would inevitably lead to a conversation about plans, and honing in on a time and place was challenging.

**RayGun (Christian)**

How about we meet on Wednesday?

**Cocky Top (Sebastián)**

Can't I have brunch. Does Friday work for you?

**RayGun (Christian)**

No, my brother Sammie is coming into town. He just came back from Spain.

**Cocky Top (Sebastián)**

How was that?

**RayGun (Christian)**

great. He was going to go to Italy with his mates, but everyone there was freaking out about this virus. How about next Saturday?

**Cocky Top (Sebastián)**

can't. But next NEXT Saturday, I definitely can.

They finally agreed on the last day of February, but by then, things had become, in Sebastián's words, 'more dramatic.' An American had died on US soil, making the pandemic feel more real. Christian changed his profile name to his real one. He was looking to be more authentic. Life was chaotic. Why not be honest? He changed his profile picture too. Gone was the shirtless torso. Now, he was sporting a face picture with a warm, welcoming smile he'd practiced for hours in the mirror, wearing a chunky knit sweater with his hands casually draped behind him.

*You are not fooling anyone, whore,* said the voice.

Sebastián had not changed his picture. He saw on Grindr that Sebastián had attempted to seem more aloof with a simple *S*, with no profile information other than the word 'looking.' It seemed closer to the truth to Christian, but he was still hiding behind partial anonymity. He wondered what version of Sebastián he would meet on their date today. The kind person who made him feel safe, or this new, more reserved person who seemed to be retreating into himself to fend off a more terrifying world.

As Christian returned once again to *Green Eggs & Jam*, he noticed that things were different from before. The live show for that evening had been rescheduled with an ambiguous 'TBD.' There were also one or two non-Asian people in masks, though they were still people of color, Middle Eastern men arguing with one another in a dialect Christian didn't understand. People weren't staying inside for very long either. Patrons ducked in to pick up pastries they had ordered online and immediately rushed out the door to face the unforgiving winter wind. A reality they somehow preferred to the unknown 'virus' inside.

Christian thought they were being ridiculous. Even the TV in the cafe was blasting the headline that 'this was similar to the flu,' and people didn't suspend their lives for the flu. He sat in his seat, also on a couch, but a blue one this time. It was still uncomfortable, and he slumped steadily more and more as time passed. Thirty minutes after they were officially supposed to meet, Christian received a hastily written cancellation from Sebastián.

**S (Sebastián)**

> hEy so sorry to do this, but work is pulling me into a last-minute meeting. Raincheck? Im free tomorrow.

**Christian**

> No problem! I'm not free tomorrow, but we should do next weekend! Saturday work?

**S (Sebastián)**

> Yes! Not to be one of those Type-A gays, but could I send you a calendar invite?

Christian

Sure. Does it exist if it's not
on the calendar?

They swapped emails and set up a tenuous date for the following weekend. Christian was annoyed by the cancellation, but this was a dance he was familiar with. He filed Sebastián away as a person he would never see again and started to peruse the app for other takers. Anything to take his mind off everyone freaking out over this new flu. It was a beautiful day, and surely he could get a bite!

He was receiving plenty of them. Yet people were more hesitant than even a week ago. They were more than willing to talk about their days or sext, but he couldn't get anyone to commit to seeing him in person. He was casting his net as wide as possible, and no one was jumping in.

Christian

How about we meet up now?

Sexy Rando

umm, can't today. Sorry.

Christian

How about tomorrow?

*Blocked.*

Christian

yeah pull my hair.

FukMyHole

this is so fuckin hot.

Christian

want to fuck me in
person? Even hotter.

*Blocked.*

One person even sent their address, only to block him as he was heading to their apartment. It was hit after hit of rejection, and he didn't understand why. He had never had so much trouble before!

He eventually scored a person in the area called *NoWorries*, a man he would learn was named Jon, whose profile made him out to be a skinny, white twenty-something looking to top. The app claimed he was only 534 feet away but it was closer to 800 feet at a group house around the block.

Christian

here

NoWorries (Jon)

coming.

Jon opened the door and looked exactly as advertised. He whispered, "Hey, some of my housemates are asleep, so we have to be quiet."

Christian nodded. He was instructed to take off his shoes and stand still, holding out his arms. The young man pulled out a container of Lysol and sprayed him. Christian was told to spin around as the aerosol covered his entire body.

"I know it's weird," he whispered. "But you can't be too careful."

Christian said nothing, letting the man spray him with the bottle. It smelled of artificial lemon, the smell you would get from a Tic Tac or some other store-bought candy. He kept his mouth closed tight, but the flavor still entered his mouth. He did his best not to gag.

Jon then guided him up the creaky stairs to the house's third floor. He lived in a small bedroom that fit a twin-sized mattress and a dresser, and that was about it. His room was as tidy as it could be given the circumstances, with a pile of neatly folded clothes sitting on a tiny chair in front of the dresser.

"Sorry for the mess," said Jon.

"Don't be hard on yourself. It looks great," Christian lied.

The initiation between them was perfunctory. The obligation to be quiet prevented them from being too loud. He felt like he was a kid again, sneaking away in the dead of night to meet his brother Sammie's secret boyfriend to make out on the beach. The smell of the tide intermingled with seaweed and cheap vodka from Michael's flask. Sammie would dump Michael a week later. He never told Christian why, but always suspected Sammie had found out. To this day, Sammie had remained closeted and bitter, and their relationship had never recovered.

Except here, Christian could only smell the overpowering stench of the Lysol spray washing out everything else. The medley of chemicals assaulted his sinuses: his eyes agitated and watering. The two of them kissed for several seconds before it became too much to be enjoyable. Christian started stripping off his clothes and moving to the bed to escape the stench.

"Let me get a condom," said Jon, instantly making him feel like a better choice in Christian's eyes—like he was the safer choice. He didn't have to push for it like with Sebastián. Jon's bedroom might be messy, and his hygiene choices were questionable, but he was considerate.

Jon pulled out a condom from a drawer only a foot away. He started to slip it on before realizing it was inside out.

"Oops," he said before putting it on correctly.

"Can I enter you?" Jon asked.

"Uh, yeah, please do."

Jon quietly walked over to Christian and gently pushed up against him. "Is that okay?" he asked nervously.

"Yes, it's… good," Christian said, surprisingly not lying as his voice trailed off into a pleasurable moan. Jon was a tender lover. He gingerly held the back of Christian's head and stared directly into his eyes. He then lightly kissed the crevice of his neck before pulling back to whisper a sweet platitude into his ear.

"You are so beautiful," he said.

"So are you," Christian echoed.

He believed for this brief moment that he was beautiful: that he was a person deserving of being held by this hot twenty-something with the soft blue eyes and the sweet voice. The feeling lasted only for a moment as the voice in the back of his head slowly drained that confidence away.

*You should ask him if he needs contacts*, it whispered.

Fuck. He had been so close to coming, and now nothing.

"I'm going to cum," said Jon.

"Do it," gasped Christian.

Several seconds later, he could feel Jon finish. Christian felt the pulses surge through him until they diminished into nothingness.

"Can I help you finish?" he asked.

Christian smiled and answered his question with a kiss.

"What do you like?" asked this hot guy, who already seemed to know what he wanted in life despite looking like he belonged on the Disney Channel.

"I..." Christian paused. What did he like? Surely, he had thought about it before?

*Is mediocrity a kink?* The voice in his mind chimed in.

Christian grimaced at this, trying to stay on task. He liked things. Vanilla sex certainly bored him. He liked risks. Danger? Peril? What did that translate to with sex? "I like dirty talk," Christian said at last.

"Do you now, slut?" Jon said in a firm, commanding voice without skipping a beat.

"Yes, I fucking do."

"Well, you fucking whore," said Jon as he moved his hand up and down. "That's good because I like it when the sluts I breed are compliant. Are you a compliant little slut?" he asked with a cocksure grin.

"I'm a compliant slut, yes."

"Good because I'm not done with you yet. I'm going to pound this ass so hard that you won't be able to walk for days," he stated firmly. He then grabbed Christian's chin and looked directly at him. "Do you got that?"

"Yes, sir," he said.

That was all he needed. Christian released all over his chest. Jon lessened his hold over Christian and used his hands to wipe the liquid off his face, licking it with his lips. He then rolled over on his back next to him. The two of them basked in the glow of their respective orgasms for several minutes on the cramped twin bed, enjoying the moment before it evaporated into awkwardness.

"So, how long have you been here?" asked Christian.

Jon talked a little about his life. He was addicted to social media, checking his phone several times during their short conversation. He had recently moved to the city to intern as a quality assurance something or other for a shiny tech company. He didn't like his job much and talked excitedly about the possibility of being a social media manager, but for now, at least his job paid the rent, he joked, as a forced smile formed across his face.

Christian felt weird being in the presence of someone who cared so much about their future. He had stumbled into his current profession at the insistence of an uncle during one Thanksgiving who was willing to make some introductions. It wasn't something he enjoyed, but as long as he kept at it, his grandfather would let him access a small sum every month from his trust, and what else mattered?

"At least the summer is coming," Christian comforted a sad Jon, who had become preoccupied with his lack of career prospects.

"Yay, I'm making beach plans," Jon smiled weakly, talking about hitching a ride with some friends to Provincetown.

The two swapped numbers, and less than ten minutes later, Christian was gone, walking through the semi-crowded streets of his neighborhood with a spring in his step. He moved through recently opened Sephoras and upscale fast-casual restaurants with utter glee. Sometimes, Christian still couldn't believe this was his life. He immediately opened his phone to check Grindr: 110 views and 10 messages.

Christian felt giddy with excitement. This was going to be a jam-packed afternoon in a very busy spring.

# CHAPTER

4

*S*

Sor Sebastián kept canceling and rescheduling their second date. He didn't want to, but work was simply too busy. His manager would tell him he had a weekend off, only to demand a revision at the last minute or 'jokingly' threaten him with termination if he didn't dial into a meeting. "Your ass is on the line," his boss laughed—the punchline to a joke that was never funny to begin with.

Their date kept getting pushed back, but Sebastián never canceled. The latest 'I totally will not cancel, I swear' date was set for the middle of March. Christian kept telling him that things would settle down by then. He referenced a recent *New York Times* article that declared Covid no worse than the common flu. Though he remembered Christian telling him once that he was skeptical of the *New York Times*, and so Sebastián didn't know if he felt comforted by that justification. Influenza didn't start as the common flu, after all.

Sebastián wasn't so sure about the virus going away. He hoped so, and yet the pounding in his chest told him to be worried. California had declared a state of emergency, which made him feel like he should freak out. Christian told him that 'that' was on the other side of the country, and Sebastián's boss bragged about how the US had one of the best healthcare systems in the world. The two of them were so sure that this couldn't drag on too long.

"Surely the government had procedures in place for this sort of thing," Christian had texted.

"...or at the very least private companies," his boss rejoined during one tense meeting.

Everyone in his life kept reinforcing the idea that things would clear up by the weekend—maybe not in California—but everywhere else would be fine. He needed to stop complaining, hunker down, and focus on his work. His sister Elena was even booking a trip to Las Vegas with her gal pals soon. "I need a break from the kids. A virus has nothing against a pack of restless moms," she joked over text.

By Wednesday, however, some alarming news had come in on his phone: Trump had begrudgingly declared a state of emergency. Suddenly, Sebastián's feed was filled with instructions to do something called 'social distancing' and 'flattening the curve.' The word pandemic started to appear everywhere. They were in the middle of a pandemic, a contagion, a plague. It sounded so serious, but it didn't feel like it.

Sebastián desperately wanted to cancel his date with Christian, but they had both made such a big deal about rescheduling that not even a pandemic would cause either to be the first to back out. He would not ghost with so much of his pride invested in weeks of messages. He wanted his dating life to be perfect, like in the rom-coms he adored, so they began the dance of hashing out a safe way to meet when they weren't sure such a thing existed.

**Christian**

We have to be 8 feet apart?

**S (Sebastián)**

The CDC is saying 6.

**Christian**

That's not too bad. We could meEt at a bar.

**S (Sebastián)**

the CDC says we should avoid groups of 50 or more. So it has to be a small place.

**Christian**

How do you socially distance in a small place?

**S (Sebastián)**

you can't really. We could wait a week, see if things calm down.

Christian

Why though? If it's not serious, we might as well meet now.

S (Sebastián)

screw it, let's do a park.

S (Sebastián)

Sends Location.

S (Sebastián)

Just be sure to bring your mask.

Christian

I thought you weren't supposed to buy masks cause of the shortage?

S (Sebastián)

no, you're just not supposed to buy N95 ones. Cloth ones are fine. I have extras I can give you.

Christian

It'll be fine. I'll buy one on Amazon.

He met Christian a week later at a small park in the center of a roundabout. The park was a manicured plot of grass crisscrossed with stone paths and smooth white benches. Several similarly arranged parks were within walking distance of Sebastián's place, but none were so clean and empty. They decided to sit down more or less six feet apart in the grassy section to avoid 'coughing' pedestrians—though not many people were walking much during this period of uncertainty. People darted through the streets, giving everyone a wide berth, choosing to walk into the road rather than past one another.

The few people they did see were wearing masks. Sebastián had followed the instructions in a YouTube video to cut up an old t-shirt and turn it into a makeshift mask. It did not quite fit him and was slipping ever so slightly as he adjusted his neck. Christian had not attempted to wear anything on his face, an oversight he immediately noted.

"Why no mask?" Sebastián said, pointing to Christian's face.

"All of them are out of stock everywhere. The ones I ordered are a week away."

"Here," Sebastián said, reaching out to hand him one and then paused. "How do we do this?" Sebastián asked, referring to the awkwardness of being six feet apart while wanting to hand the mask over to Christian.

"Just leave it on the bench, and then I'll pick it up," Christian said.

Sebastián did so, and then they stared at one another awkwardly.

"Gotcha. I'd hug you," said Sebastián, "But, you know."

"Same," Christian laughed.

Christian set his blanket down on the grass. It was a large quilt with a vintage image of Captain America's smiling face stitched into it. The comic book hero's iconic vibranium shield was in the background. Its round edges faded into the American flag. Sebastián hated those comic book movies. They were so crude. He loved the classics like *Sleepless in Seattle* or *Breakfast at Tiffany's*. Rom-Coms, you could swoon over.

But he decided not to say anything. Why start their meeting on such a weird note? Sebastián hadn't bothered to bring a blanket. He had spent so much time trying to get the mask right that he hadn't prepared for the rest of their picnic. In the back of his mind, he had assumed he could borrow whatever Christian brought, but now, sitting on the damp grass, he realized how shortsighted that had been.

"So… how have you been?" asked Christian.

"It's been weird," said Sebastián. "The firm has been letting us work from home over this last week and a half. I have only seen people over Teams."

"Lucky," smirked Christian. "The Admiral is still making us go into the base."

"Aren't you nervous about that?" Sebastián asked hesitantly.

"Naw," said Christian, though his voice made him sound less confident.

Sebastián would truthfully be terrified to be in Christian's position. Now that the news of the pandemic had truly sunk in, his colleagues at the firm were acting like this would be the end of the world. They were swapping horror stories about out-of-stock grocery stores and empty streets of once-crowded downtowns. They looked like movies where everyone had been raptured, or the apocalypse had started. He felt like he was Will Smith in *I Am Legend*, walking through the remnants of a civilization that no longer existed.

It annoyed him that Christian didn't take this situation very seriously. He watched as Christian scratched his nose, colonizing his face with a mountain of germs.

The sight of his masklessness made Sebastián start to have doubts that they had any chemistry whatsoever. How could you act so indifferently in the face of something that had changed their lives overnight?

"Besides, it's not serious on the East Coast yet, remember?" Christian continued. He had parroted this talking point before, and Sebastián was confident he had gotten it from a boss or coworker.

"Umm, like every governor has declared a state of emergency, I thought? And the President. Isn't your work canceling bookings yet?" asked Sebastián with the tiniest hint of condescension. "We had a health conference in June and pulled the plug on it this morning." It had been a shit show. Months of planning gone, and now his boss wanted him to make up the money with virtual sessions that required more expertise to set up and which clients wanted to spend even less money on. "It's been sort of hectic, to be honest," Sebastián added.

"Well, we are still booking rooms for the Navy. The top brass thinks this is going to be short-lived."

"We'll see," said Sebastián curtly. He decided to change the subject before he lost his mind. "Whatcha watching?" he asked, cutting off a comment from Christian about a *New York Times* op-ed on masking.

Christian, seeming to get the hint that this was not a safe topic, played ball with diverting the conversation to TV. "Anything nerdy," he said. "I love the third season of *Castlevania*. The fight scenes in it are sick."

"Is that the one about castles?" Sebastián asked, bored already. He was not a fan of what he called 'nerd shit.'

"Not quite. It's an anime based on the Konami game, but you get to see more of the vampire's perspective this time. And don't worry, it keeps to the spirit of the original."

"Oh," said Sebastián enthusiastically, trying his best to fake excitement. He wasn't into this conversation but didn't want to return to politics, so he decided to plow forward with this snooze fest. "Is that anything like the new *Thor* movie? That man can get it."

"I don't know. I'm more of a Chris Evans guy," Christian smirked.

"Well, Captain America's way hotter after Thor gained a few in Ends Game."

"*Endgame*," Christian corrected. "And yeah, when his mom told him to eat a salad in *Endgame*, I almost lost it," Christian laughed.

"Yaaas, right? I feel like she was my CrossFit trainer." Sebastián then paused after briefly dwelling on the thought that he hadn't been to the gym in days and wouldn't be in some time. He felt a profound sense of loss at the absence of tasks and experiences he could no longer do. "God, I need to go grocery shopping," he sighed.

Sebastián, not wanting to keep things dark, admitted that he was watching the Brazilian adaptation of the reality show *The Circle*, about beautiful people in isolation trying to become influencers amongst a group of contestants. He found that the people were pretty, and he loved how nice they were to each other.

"Is that the one where they are trapped inside and can only talk through social media?" asked Christian. Sebastián grimaced, realizing his partner had stepped into another landmine, or really the same one.

"Yeah," Sebastián laughed. "My life is becoming *The Circle* at this point. Given how many episodes I have binged, I almost feel like they are my friends."

They did their best not to talk about Covid, but it hung over them like a thick smog. For Sebastián, everything was a reminder of what he couldn't do. They would talk about the weather, yet going outside didn't matter. They'd mention memories of vacations and restaurants, which only highlighted where they could no longer go. Sebastián couldn't help but be depressed—he was stuck waiting.

Christian politely listened to these complaints, but it was clear that he didn't respect them. Sebastián knew from his Instagram that Christian had continued to be out in the world, and every expression he surrendered indicated he didn't understand why his date was such a bummer. He kept sharing fun times before Covid, like his last Fire Island vacation or when he got to eat at Momofuku for free because he was sleeping with the manager. They were stories told with the expectation that life would soon be like that again, and Sebastián resented the assumption. Some bloggers he followed were starting to suggest a recovery date that would take years, not months. Things didn't feel normal, and he didn't know when they would be again. The conversation was filled with this oppressive tension they both noticed and simultaneously wished to ignore.

And so they went back to TV, yet here things were still unsafe.

"What was the last movie you saw?" asked Christian.

"*Contagion*," replied Sebastián. "I'm sort of obsessed with it."

"The movie about the plague," Christian winced.

Sebastián knew Christian was clearly bracing himself for another conversation about Covid, but he was saved from further annoyance when they heard a man coughing loudly in the distance. The two of them didn't remark on it verbally, but they gestured towards it, and within thirty seconds, they both made excuses to leave.

"I'll see you around," Christian said.

"Yeah, see you around."

# Chapter

## 5

*Christian*

In April, the base finally caved and required that contractors do most of their work remotely, mandating everyone to come in only one-day-a-week. Christian was unsure if he would have stayed home if given the opportunity. He remained unconvinced of the virus' severity as his grandfather claimed to have insider information that this would all be going away soon, but it didn't matter what Christian wanted. This was what the base was doing, and the higher-ups treated the work-from-home order like a gift to their workers.

"Don't fuck it up," the Admiral warned sternly over a video call. "We are trusting you now."

The Admiral's face was impassive and impatient as he said this. Uncle Thomas was a man twice Christian's age who had outlasted more Presidents than Christian had boyfriends. He was his uncle on his mother's side and had been a fixture in his life since before he could remember. When he told Christian to do something, Christian felt like he had to do it. It wasn't just because he was related to him or because Uncle Thomas' office was across the courtyard from his own. Christian had learned early on that it was much easier to comply with the wishes of his family than to argue. When he had been sent to Hong Kong to intern for one of his family's many subsidiaries, he went without question. He had been bounced around from Belgium to Milwaukee, and now here. The Admiral, his family, wanted him not to fuck things up, so he would try his best. He would have to if he still wanted his grandfather to permit monthly withdrawals from his trust. Christian could do this. He would kill this working-from-home thing.

Christian initially didn't understand why people were even complaining about it. It seemed easy enough: go to virtual meetings, send some emails, and you were done. His boss had never been one to hover, mainly because one call from Christian could probably get him fired, so he had been given a light touch while working in person. Now, it was practically nonexistent. They would have one call a week, and that was it.

With no last-minute interruptions, Christian could accomplish more in a far shorter time. It took him less than two hours to get everything done, and best of all, no one was there to force him to pretend to work out of guilt. He could go to the gym, do laundry, clean his refrigerator, and do whatever odd job struck his fancy. He spent half his time on social media, checking in with his long-distance friends to see what they were doing. There were a lot of posts about learning a new skill or mastering a hobby. His brother's wife Rebecca was on a baking binge, constantly posting her progress on Instagram.

"Just baked some new cookies," she posted to Instagram.

"My hubby Sammie and the kids DEVOURED these scones," she wrote on another day.

*The only thing Sammie's devouring is dick*, the voice quipped cruelly.

Christian wanted to be like them, but he didn't have many hobbies, just work and the gym. He tried to seem interesting: the way his virtual friends did on the feed. He treated his calls seriously on that first day, dressed in a button-up and dress pants. Christian had even prepared some jokes and facts to seem cool on his calls.

"Did you know hummingbirds are the only birds that can fly backward," he recited during a particularly dull Zoom call.

"That's neat," his coworker Samantha said with fake enthusiasm, shouting at one of her kids off-screen moments later.

No one seemed to care. It's not that he couldn't continue to dress professionally at meetings. It's only that no one wanted to reward him for it. In his 1-on-1 the following week, he was politely instructed that he didn't have to put all this effort in and only needed to dress professionally during client-facing calls. Apparently, no one was interested in fashion over Zoom.

"I can't believe you have time to get dressed up," a haggard Samantha said one morning, and then, realizing this might be condescending, added: "Good for you."

About a week in, Christian dropped the button-up. Most days involved him hopping out of bed and making a short thirty-second commute to his desk: no bosses, no overly chatty coworkers, and the ability to binge as much TV on the side as humanly possible. It sounded fantastic, and for a short period, it was, but the allure of pantsless video calls and cereal for dinner quickly faded. There was only so much you could do inside and even less without a screen. Christian would watch so much TV that his eyes would start to glaze over, sore and droopy from staring in one direction for too long.

*Pathetic*, the voice berated.

Christian's back started to hurt, and his head and eyes were sore. He spent his days looking at the wall just to avoid losing himself in a screen. He'd listen to his coworkers prattle on, an echo in a screen that held no significance for him—just noise—chords of meaningless sound piped through a box.

He relished going into the base, if only for one day a week. He enjoyed saying hello to the receptionist and passing people in the hall. The base was only at partial capacity, so many of the people he had become used to seeing were no longer on the same shift, but still, the random connections were priceless. He would talk to people he didn't know and feel their emotions radiating from their bodies. He loved it, and walking away every day was painful because he knew it would be six days until he had those types of interactions again.

The march back to his apartment was too much. Darker thoughts began to creep back in. They would call him worthless, lazy, difficult, unlovable, and much, much worse. He felt like all his friendships were slipping away, and there was no one to lean on. How could there be? How could anyone have time for him during a pandemic? He wanted someone to talk to, to hold, but the recommendations still called for everyone to remain six feet apart, 6 feet apart;

SIX

FEET

APART.

*It will be like this for the rest of your life,* the voice said. *You are about to go through the same thing a thousand times over, every day, FOR THE REST OF YOUR LIFE.*

This thought horrified him. Christian felt numb. He tried to stay busy and improve himself, but all you could do with other people at that distance was make awkward small talk about nothing in particular. And he had few people to even do that with. Christian didn't have many friends, and none were in the city. He had no one to talk to and was tired of the stale nothingness that had made up his days.

Some days he tried to hit up two old acquaintances named Dan and Henry from his old Alma Mater, but their interactions together were always so stiff. They could only meet outside, and a lack of close interaction prevented them from making jokes or bonding. They always left early, too, as if the virus would tear into their very being if they lingered. The three would cautiously chat about the weather, the TV shows they were watching, and inevitably, how Covid had uprooted all their plans. Dan and Henry would not shut up about their canceled plans to Provincetown.

"The B&B refunded us, but CapeAir is simply refusing to budge," Dan told Christian repeatedly on the steps of their townhouse. Christian would hang over their black iron fence, thankful that the one luxury a mask provided was that he no longer had to force a smile. He watched Dan and Henry pace back and forth as they bickered. Christian rubbed his eyes, silently praying for something interesting to break up their monotonous chatter. Perhaps lightning would strike him. For a tree to crush his bones… something. He hated this interaction and hated himself for needing it.

"Don't worry, Snookums," Henry said. "We'll figure something out. We always do. You have to believe that."

"We will," Dan said.

Had all their conversations at college always been this boring? Were these his only friends here? He didn't even know them that well. Christian thought he had shared a business class with Dan, and couldn't even remember how he had met Henry. They had so little in common. That was the crux of the problem, of course. How would you find someone you can talk to in a pandemic when 'allegedly' talking to someone new could kill you? He certainly couldn't keep himself entertained with these 'friends.' Christian waited on the wooden steps until Dan and Henry eventually gave him a reason to leave, and he then returned home to a half-eaten dinner.

It was even worse online. Christian had never realized how many of his conversations on dating platforms were a pretext for fucking. He used to ask men about their lives: their hobbies, their upbringings, where they worked. Christian thought these questions were genuine, but lately, he realized that they were only ever a protracted form of foreplay. He never cared about user *Hot Time*'s job as an accountant or that *Genuine Listener* was relearning how to play the oboe. The only thing Christian wanted *Hot Time* to do was cum on his chest, and he didn't give a diddly squat about what happened after that.

"What are you doing?" had, in Christian's mind, become a pointless question because everyone in his circle was doing the same thing: waiting. There was nothing more to do than to mark another day in this tedium. Monotony? Eternity?

### Hot Time

So what are you doing?

Hot Time had asked this question for the second day in a row and five times before that.

### Christian

Oh, nothing. I just
ordered some pizza.

This quip was the truth. Christian was eating his fourth pizza of that week. Eight slices of cheese and pepperoni had been sitting in front of him for what seemed like only a minute. Then seven. Then six. Until he had gulped down every one.

**Hot Time**

Want to swap pics?

**Christian**

We already did that. Please just stop

**Hot Time**

WHy are YoU even on here then

**Hot Time**

jerk

**Christian**

BEcause I'm bored.

**Hot Time**

So its just pizza delivery for u then boi?????? You must not be such a good cocksucker if all u wanna do is eat.

Christian decided to block him before he received the same or worse, an unearned tirade about how this random stranger deserved his time and respect. Some of the responses Christian was getting on this app were growing increasingly vile, and others truly strange. One man had called Christian a bitch for posting a picture of a snail as a joke. Another man wrote that Christian's face resembled a 'mutant with an incurable form of cancer.' A more familiar user messaged him out of the blue and asked if he thought life was fundamentally meaningless. And if so, what did that say about the people who kept on living?

He had had enough of this. *Blocked. Blocked. Blocked.*

# CHAPTER 6

## Seeking Connections

Sebastián was already an anxious person, but the endless talk of masks, viruses, and social distancing shot his levels into the stratosphere. He had started social distancing at the beginning of March. He lived alone and had found it impossible to make or keep in contact with friends. Even his best friend Barry had gone MIA.

S (Sebastián)

what's your day like, Barry?

S (Sebastián)

hey

**S (Sebastián)**
hi

**S (Sebastián)**
you there?

He longed for human interaction, changing his profile name to *Seeking Connections*, hoping that maybe the name change would help fill the hole he now felt.

But nothing seemed to change for him.

Sebastián had moved into that realm of 'weird,' he knew his friend Christian seemed to be denying himself. He no longer kept a consistent sleep schedule and instead structured his life around online meetings. Sebastián would set his alarm for ten minutes before his morning stand-up, roll out of bed, talk for a few minutes, and then go back to sleep.

"What does time even mean anymore?" he would joke to anyone he encountered.

He found himself working later into the evening, which he honestly preferred. Sebastián had always been a night owl, and these last couple of years, he struggled to calibrate to his firm's prompt 9 AM workday. He spent many late nights drafting emails with a cup of coffee or even a glass of wine by his side. Sebastián sometimes felt guilty about drinking alcohol during work hours, but then he would remind himself a pandemic was going on and say "fuck it" out loud to his empty studio apartment. He felt like Olivia Pope from *Scandal*—flawless and alone.

Sebastián was finding he did not want to get out of bed. It was hard to imagine his days ever getting any better. He felt like a zombie, stuck in a constant state of inertia and deep pessimism. What was the point of putting effort into anything? He certainly wasn't going to start dating again or see friends.

On the bright side, if you could call it that, his company was doing very well, so he didn't have to worry about meeting his figures for his end-of-year bonus. His workload had skyrocketed, which he was told was reasonable given the amount of healthcare-related work the firm was getting from the pandemic, but he no longer enjoyed these busy days (did he ever?). It took him hours to get himself into the right frame of mind to work, and he spent most of his nights on the couch with his laptop on his lap, staring at the wall.

"I'm over this," he said aloud to himself over and over again, praying that his resignation would somehow lead to the pandemic being over. "I want this to end."

His one saving grace was Christian. He sent him many messages, mainly because he was one of the few people Sebastián had developed an actual relationship with pre-Covid, who hadn't abandoned him. Their messages started as sexts. Sebastián would tell Christian how much he missed his throbbing cock. They would swap pictures allegedly taken in the heat of the moment but were from months ago, all perfectly cropped and edited. The veins of Sebastián's dick would bulge in the picture, and you could see the milky cum dripping from its tip. He would stare at it before hitting the send button, fantasizing about them getting it on.

Christian

so hot.

**Seeking Connections (Sebastián)**
thanx :). How about you, handsome?

Christian would then send a picture of his erect cock, also perfectly composed, and their conversation would peter out from there. Necessity required talking about anything but sex, so they soon stopped discussing it altogether. They made witty puns and swapped articles of trending recipes. The two started watching the reality show *Tiger King* together, using a party viewing app to watch the same stream. They would joke about some of the show's crazier moments and swap fan theories. Christian was convinced that Carole Baskin had killed her husband, though Sebastián remained on the fence.

**Seeking Connections (Sebastián)**
why would she kill her husband
when she already had access to
all of his money?

**Christian**
power. She wanted to control the Tiger
Sanctuary at all costs.

**Seeking Connections (Sebastián)**
what a horrible reason. no wonder
she's not smiling.

**Christian**
naw, she's happy. She's probably even
happier than before!

**Seeking Connections (Sebastián)**
well I'm not.

The more time passed, the more comfortable Sebastián got with sharing information with Christian. There was no more planning a meet-up and no more tricks to get each other excited— just information. He shared with Christian any random thought that entered his head: Sebastián told him how fat he thought he was getting, about his loneliness, how much he hated work, and how he enjoyed their time together.

Sebastián was extremely homesick and, at one point, described in detail the one and only time his family had taken a trip to the beach. He had never gone back. His family had constant car troubles that made vacation difficult, even one as short away as the Jersey shore. He explained how much he missed strolling along the beachfront as the tide came in—the water hitting his toes, kneeling at the ocean's edge, listening to the calming rhythm of the waves. His sister Elena immediately disrupted that moment with a quick push to his back, and the two of them started fighting. His abuela had to stop the fight with a stern look and a smack to both their heads.

Christian loved the beach too and told Sebastián that he missed the ocean as well—he had apparently vacationed in Connecticut every summer at his grandfather's beach house since he was six. Sebastián sort of hated him for this. How the ocean was a regular occurrence and not one imperfect memory preserved with longing, but he held his tongue. He needed Christian as a receptacle for his pain.

One night, unprompted, he launched into a story about how he once cheated on a group project by stealing the grading rubric from the teacher's desk. The teacher found out but considered Sebastián one of the 'good' students and blamed the class troublemaker, another darker Latino student named Miguel, on whom Sebastián had an intense crush. He never confessed the truth to either the professor or Miguel. In fact, he had never told anyone about it. It was never the right moment. Sebastián had felt terrible about it for years and wondered if he should have had the courage to confess. What if he'd told the truth? He would have saved everyone a lot of trouble: all the heartache he caused his teacher and, more importantly, the trouble he had caused Miguel.

**Seeking Connections (Sebastián)**

Miguel got expelled from
school a year later.

**Seeking Connections (Sebastián)**

I know more things were probably
going on with him that led to
him getting expelled, but I
still blame myself.

**Christian**

well it's in the past now. No use
sweating over it.

This acceptance made him feel ecstatic… like he could tell Christian anything. Finally, someone understood. One particularly lonely night, after Sebastián had a bad Zoom call with his boss, he asked Christian if life was meaningless. For over two weeks, he hadn't seen another person in the flesh besides his grocery clerk and Uber Eats driver, and the loneliness was getting to him. It all seemed so pointless, and Sebastián needed to get another perspective. Christian was the only person in his life that he could talk to honestly.

There was a pause, and then briefly, Sebastián thought Christian blocked him. He was worried he had gone too far and considered sending him an apology over text—drafted it even—and then, a couple of minutes later, his account resurfaced.

Christian

> No, you are just having a hard time. We should see each other in person again. I think living by yourself is getting to you.

They spent the rest of the night chatting about inconsequential things before once again swapping photos. This time Sebastián sent one taken in the moment. His dick was imperfectly half erect. He had run out of all the others.

# CHAPTER

## 7

*Christian*

It started with a cup of coffee. Christian decided to meet Sebastián to get some caffeine at *The Silver Spoon* on the corner of 11th and F St. It was a recently renovated hot spot that had risen from the ashes of a foreclosed bodega. The owners had spent a fortune remaking the interior with bronze piping, large twinkle lights, and lots and lots of potted plants. What was with everyone using plants as a substitute for taste? It had all been an attempt to lure in wealthy millennials, Gen Xers, and boomers looking to be served $6 cappuccinos on their lunch breaks.

Of course, Christian thought, now there were no lunch breaks. *The Silver Spoon* could stay in business by offering pickup only. It technically had to serve food as well to count as an 'essential business,' a ridiculous concept, which is why three different variations of cookies had been added to the menu, mostly unordered. Patrons continued to come as they did before for their caffeine fix, but not as frequently and never for long. The indoors were still viewed as a perilous unknown, with danger lurking around every corner.

Christian and Sebastián would come in daily to pick up their coffee orders and gourmet sugar cookies, which were better than he had expected. Christian didn't like looking at the barista. He didn't know why. She would say hi, and Christian would only mumble back something inaudible in her direction. He was so nervous around her. She wore a hijab with a vibrant pink and green pattern over the blue apron that made up her uniform, and the phrase 'If you see something, say something' popped into his mind whenever he saw her. He would look away from her as he placed his order, averting his gaze and leaving the premises as quickly as possible.

Christian and Sebastián headed to a nearby park to talk aimlessly. The park was in the center of a four-way intersection—cars encircled the green oasis on all sides. It was full of shade, concrete benches, and green shrubs sprouting from every flat surface. The park was named after a Civil War general whose larger-than-life statue was situated on a broad stone platform that looked down on the enslaved people he had allegedly freed. They wore shrouds and sat beneath the general's feet at their workstations, paying their respects to him, their cause for celebration and freedom. It was the kind of place, Christian thought, where you could sit and feel like you were part of something significant—the grandeur of a respected history, something eternal that continued to endure.

You could also be safe here. Police patrolled it frequently, and the park was laid out so vagrants had no comfortable place to sleep. Overhead sections had purposeful holes to let the rain through (and make sleep difficult), and brilliant marble tiles were scattered throughout the park so that nowhere was entirely flat. Christian felt secure that in this place, he wouldn't be hassled… harangued… harassed… by these men, when all he wanted was to be left in peace with his… friend Sebastián. They would always sit on the same bench beneath the rear of the General's horse—something he joked about more than once.

"Here we meet again," Christian would laugh, dramatically tilting upwards to look at the horse's ass. "I've been waiting to see you."

Sebastián would always roll his eyes and joke about the 'wild' things that happened in the park after dark, even though the constant police presence made such a thing impossible. The two of them would sit more or less six feet apart. Uncomfortable metal bars protruded every two feet to keep the homeless from sleeping on them at night. The bars made it awkward to converse comfortably, so they always had to switch positions. Sometimes, they would be halfway turned to each other. Other times, Sebastián would stand up and talk with Christian from several yards away.

Distance was never something they regulated too stringently, though. Whenever Sebastián would violate that murky barrier of six feet, Christian never dared to correct him. He felt that asserting himself would be too awkward and too rude—besides, he wasn't sure he believed in all of this business anyway. Christian let the distance slide, millimeter by millimeter, inch by inch, until one day, they were standing right next to each other.

Sebastián had not seemed to notice his slow progression towards Christian. He was too wrapped up in his thoughts to care, but there came a moment when Christian could tell that the realization had dawned on him. He saw Sebastián's face contort like someone who had just been struck by a revelation so big it might consume him. His eyes widened, and his mouth widened, too.

Christian's entire body flooded with awareness. He could feel his legs and arms tingling with anticipation. All of his senses seemed to amplify and grow. He sensed the crisp texture of the air, the cold metal bars, the thick, earthy smell of the green shrubs, and even the bench's hard, crumbly edges. It was as though all of the sensations from his entire life had been compressed into one moment of intense clarity.

And then, just as quickly, it all receded into the background, and only he and Sebastián remained in the forefront. Sebastián's dusky skin. His surprisingly thick and supple lips. His hair. The freckles that dotted his face and arms and made it seem as if he had been splashed with a bucket of earth. Christian had not seen anyone this close, unmasked, in weeks, and here was this hot guy in his mid-twenties staring back at him with a warm smile. He didn't want to let the moment go. He couldn't.

"Do you want to sit down?" Christian asked, staring into Sebastián's eyes.

Sebastián paused. He clearly wanted to sit down, but he didn't move. His feet were planted firmly in place, the muscles in his legs tight. He was rooted there.

"But Covid, right?" he asked hesitantly.

"I have been thinking about that a lot," Christian said casually and yet also meticulously. His words were rigid, as if he had been considering this line of thought for a long time, which, of course, he had. "My brother Sammie has started hanging out with some of his friends, but only, like, a few of them. He calls it his 'Covid bubble.'"

*That's a very strange way to describe an orgy*, the voice mocked.

Christian grimaced. He had suspected that his brother was doing more than just 'hanging out' with these friends. Sammie had never come clean about hooking up with guys on his weekend trips: far too much was on the line for him, yet Christian had suspected it. However, even if it were true, Sammie wasn't seeing men outside that group and his family, so it was close enough to a real bubble to feel genuine.

The suggestion, or at least the curated one Christian had just presented, seemed to pique Sebastián's interest. "Is that safe?" he inquired.

"Yes," Christian replied with a muted expression, his heart pounding. "Sammie says they only spend time with each other and no one else. They also social distance and wear masks with everyone else, so… ," he said, letting his sentence trail off so that Sebastián's imagination could fill in the dots.

*Liar*, the voice continued.

Sebastián slowly turned to look at Christian, who felt like the Earth might open up and swallow him whole. Sebastián's eyes locked with his, and he grinned after a long moment. "I have a lot more Googling I have to do, but I think I might be down," Sebastián responded.

"Cool, cool, just let me know."

They parted ways. Christian snapped out of his reverie like he had just awakened from a dream, but it wasn't a dream. He had rehearsed and rehearsed this scenario for so long, and now, with a little nudge, he had finally gotten the words to spill out of Sebastián's mouth. A commitment. A guarantee. A promise. Sebastián would look into it, and Christian hoped that would be enough. The net had been cast, and now all he needed to do was wait.

Before leaving the park, Christian searched for 'Covid bubbles' on his phone. His first hit was for an article from the CDC urging people to keep away from those they were not working or living with, but he didn't click on it. Nor did he settle for the following three articles from concerned epidemiologists and politicians. They were too formal and dry for him to digest, more meaningless liberal banter.

He wanted to find someone who Sebastián would respect. A liberal that still had the commonsense to question this insanity with social distancing. All his coworkers at the base shared articles and videos from conservative influencers like Dan Bongino, which he suspected would not appeal to Sebastián. He wanted to find someone who knew how to talk to liberal snowflakes. Someone who could subtly break down the empty rhetoric of their arguments.

Christian googled through seemingly endless results of health Instagrammers and self-care TikTokers until finally, he found a hit. A blog post from a self-described 'former psychologist and current educator' named Dr. Angela King. The article was about managing playdates with the kids from her mommy group. "Commonsense solutions so parents can keep living their lives safely," read the italicized subheader. Christian was transfixed. Ironically enough, he read the article so intently that he almost bumped into a mother pushing a stroller.

She scoffed.

"Sorry," Christian mumbled before heading out.

"Watch where you're going, idiot." She shouted after him.

When he arrived at his apartment, he posted King's article on Facebook. "Fascinating read," he wrote above it but then deleted his entire post fifteen minutes later after one of his alleged 'friends' called him a conspiracy theorist. Christian muted that person and started to binge King's mommy podcast, *Little Rascals*. He knew he wasn't crazy.

"The trick is to pick people you trust," Dr. Angela King reassured her viewers. "It's really common sense. I've still been meeting once a week, and no one in our circle has caught it."

After that comment, Christian whipped out his phone and sent Sebastián a link to the podcast. His heart was racing from a mixture of excitement and shame. The wait for a reply was torture. He braced himself for rejection as he waited and waited. The minutes ticked by, and finally, 40 minutes later, he received a ping from him—just two words.

**Seeking Connections (Sebastián)**
I'm in.

**Christian**
That's fantastic.

**Christian**
want to meet up

**Seeking Connections (Sebastián)**
Yes.

**Christian**
Sends location.

Sebastián was at Christian's apartment less than 20 minutes later.

"Hey, stranger," he said before giving Christian a fat, wet kiss.

"Good to see you again," Christian said happily, kissing him back.

When they pulled away from each other, Sebastián looked around. "I don't think I've ever been here," he admitted as he walked inside Christian's apartment. Sebastián scrutinized the room in what seemed like awe, admiring Christian's stunning floor-to-ceiling windows that allowed him to overlook the park where they drank their coffee every morning.

They stood close, budding their foreheads against one another. "Hey," Christian whispered.

"Hey," Sebastián repeated back softly.

Sebastián stayed over that night, though they didn't have sex. They talked for hours and held each other as they drifted to sleep, thankful not to be alone.

# CHAPTER

## 8

### Feelin' Lucky

Sebastián woke up the following morning and gently tried to untangle himself from Christian's muscular arms, instinctively picking up his phone to check his notifications. He was so excited that one of the first things he did was change his profile name to *Feelin' Lucky*, which instantly resulted in a series of cheeky notifications.

"Want to get lucky?" was by far the most frequent.

He tried getting up, but Christian brought him in closer, letting out a sound that resembled a purr.

"Where are you going?" he asked, kissing Sebastián's neck.

Sebastián leaned into these kisses. He let himself enjoy his body being covered in wet, little pecks. He wanted to live in this moment forever—to be consumed by a wave of joy. He couldn't remember the last time someone knew his body this intimately. Christian was learning what part of his neck Sebastián enjoyed being nibbled on and what section of his hip drove him wild.

"Jesus, you are wonderful," Sebastián gasped.

They were both naked, and Christian started to blow him. Sebastián moaned. His eyes went wide, and then, several seconds later, his stomach growled. Christian looked up, Sebastián's now firmly engorged member still in his mouth.

"I guess I'm hungry," Sebastián laughed.

"Let's eat then," said Christian, hopping out of bed.

Christian and Sebastián walked over to his kitchen. It looked like it came out of a fucking *Home & Garden* catalog. It was a sleek, modern setup with white marble countertops and wicker fruit baskets hanging from the ceiling. A glass convention stovetop was built into the marble, so the transition between the two looked seamless, and tucked away in the corner was a sleek, retro Smeg refrigerator that Christian casually remarked was imported from Italy.

Sebastián had noticed the large windows the night before, but now that Christian had pulled the blinds to let the morning sun in, he could see a picture-perfect view of the downtown. The skyscrapers in the distance were tinted pink and gold from the sun and sky, making the glass seem like the color of a shiny piece of opal. Sebastián felt like he was in a movie or some alternate world where people's lives were as good as they seemed on TV. With the money this place costs, it might as well be floating above the clouds on another planet in some CW reboot.

"You can afford all this on a military salary?" Sebastián asked.

"Parents helped somewhat," he admitted sheepishly.

*A shit ton, if this view was any indication,* Sebastián thought bitterly.

"Are you loaded?" Sebastián joked, trying not to sound too pointed.

"We're comfortable," said Christian.

Christian's words added an air of finality to his statement, and so Sebastián dropped it. Money seemed to make him uncomfortable. It made Sebastián uncomfortable, too. He was struck by a memory he had as a kid. It was the holidays, and his family had a joint Christmas with his more well-off cousins. He had received a book, a *Captain Underpants* book he had wanted very badly, and his cousins had received two separate Nintendo 64s. Sebastián had mentioned how much they cost, which caused a similar silence in the room.

"We don't do that," his mother had told him after rushing his crying twelve-year-old self into another room. She then asked him to apologize to his cousins.

Sebastián still shuddered at the memory. During his childhood, it was a common experience not to question why his cousins were so much better off than him. They would bring over their fancy toys and wear brand-new clothes when he only got hand-me-downs, and he wasn't allowed to mention it. If they refused to share and he complained, he would have to sit in the corner for a time-out and listen to everyone else have fun.

And so, when he looked out upon the stunning vista of the city, this memory pricked at him. He had worked so hard to get a good job just to remain the poorest person in the room. He touched the glass of the window gently with his hand, wanting this life more than anything, yet that felt so pathetic. It wasn't nice to talk about other people's wealth. That's not something perfect people did.

In the distance, he could see Christian start to get out the ingredients for something breakfast-related. He pulled out eggs and milk and scrambled them together in a small saucepan. The sound of the ingredients clashing together was soothing to Sebastián. He saw Christian reach for a bottle in the fridge and then pause.

"Are you allergic to anything?" Christian asked.

"Yes, actually, to soy."

Christian looked at the bottle's label he was holding and placed it back inside his cabinet. Sebastián helped Christian chop several broccoli stems for what he learned would be a frittata. They flirted and kissed as they tossed the ingredients into the hot pan. Christian then moved behind Sebastián and directed him through the recipe.

"You're going to want to toss the spinach in like so," he said, physically directing Sebastián's hands to dump the rinsed spinach into the pan.

He had never seen Christian so forceful before. He was usually far-timider. He must be more comfortable in his own space, and Sebastián found himself liking this new side of him. Sebastián could feel himself getting hard as the two pretended to be chef and sous-chef. He could feel a bulge as Christian continued to lean into him. Maybe a nice apartment wasn't worth getting too angry over, he assured himself as he dropped to his knees.

They ended up eating at a small table on Christian's outside patio. The food was lukewarm and soggy because Sebastián had paused the cooking to blow Christian, but the experience was still lovely. Sebastián held Christian's hand and smiled as the two took in the city below. There was so much life up here: birds roosted on the roofs and poles singing unappreciated melodies; butterflies and moths flapped to the currents of the wind; seed spores elegantly descended downwards; squirrels nibbled discarded food just out of sight, and; tiny, panicked people dashed across the near-deserted streets, oblivious to it all.

All of them schmucks.

Sebastián didn't often have the time to look down on others. It was a funny feeling after months of being bossed around by the higher-ups. He was so big and powerful up here. He wondered how he had ever lived most of his life in a small town filled with hicks. He would never get tired of city life—not now after being at this height.

He felt bad for people like his sister Elena who had gotten hitched young and early to her high school sweetheart—a Jew just like his mother had wanted (though his abuela wasn't happy about this). Elena would pester him for stories whenever he came home to Jersey for a visit. "I need to live vicariously through you," she would joke, "It's so boring and sad down here, Sebas. Everyone looks the same. You know everyone, and they know even less."

But here, on this patio, he felt like someone or, at least, someone who could be someone. A person who could order around other schmucks who were smaller than him. It became typical for Christian and Sebastián to brunch on that patio on the weekends and even most weekday mornings. They would prepare some manner of eggs and coffee and take in the refreshing spring air, judging the schmucks down below. Conversations varied from work to sports to TV shows. The only things they avoided were politics and Covid. The latter of which Sebastián would secretly check on his phone. It had recently passed 100,000 deaths.

After food, they would usually go for a walk—either to the subway so Christian could go to work on the one day he was required on base or a hike of the city if it was the weekend. They would explore some new aspect of their community they had never had the time to appreciate. The glow of being in a new relationship made this exploration magical. They strolled through parks and monuments, and even as shops closed and tents were pitched, Sebastián couldn't help but feel special for being in each other's company. It was as if they were Jack and Kate discovering their love for one another in the bowels of the *Titanic*.

"Sometimes I can't believe how big this city is," Sebastián found himself remarking on a mid-afternoon stroll. "I never knew half this stuff was even here until Covid."

One day, they were in a park they had visited often. The pair had gone slightly off-path to sit on a giant boulder beside a waterfall. It hadn't rained recently, so the stream was a mere trickle of its average volume. Sebastián let his feet dangle over the edge. The mist hydrated the soles of his feet as he stared out into the horizon of this small, curated forest that bled into a gentrified metropolis.

Sebastián draped his arm across Christian's shoulders. "This is beautiful," he said.

"Not as beautiful as you," Christian replied.

It was perfect. In Sebastián's mind, the only thing ruining the moment was an encampment of tents some 500 feet away. It had steadily been growing pole-by-pole since March, with people unable to get their landlords to extend rent just one more day, but he tried to ignore it—it was not like he could do anything about it. He pushed it outside his notice so that the only thing they could see was each other.

"I like you a lot," continued Christian.

"Me too," said Sebastián, letting Christian fall into him as they stared at the water falling below. There was a pause, and then Sebastián turned his gaze towards Christian. He wanted this life, didn't he? A life where he could sit high above the clouds, looking at the city beneath him like it was something he owned. "Would you like to be, you know, together?" Sebastián asked, gulping loudly.

Please say yes. Please don't turn this *Notebook* into a *Remember Me*.

Christian stared back at him as if the world had frozen in place. His mouth was wide open.

# CHAPTER

## 9

*Christian*

The word "yes" left his mouth before even processing what he had said. The beauty of the moment was intoxicating. The waterfall was beautiful, like being at a resort during a family vacation. His eyes were lost in the landscape for a moment. The rippling blue of the waterfall below him, the shimmering white of the water above. The brisk but gentle wind. All of this together created an experience he didn't feel he could say no to.

Sebastián kissed him, overcome with joy over Christian saying yes. They continued to kiss as the water cascaded around them. "I'm so happy right now," Sebastián said. "I don't think I've ever felt so happy."

"Neither have I." Christian echoed, again simply repeating the words.

And then he pulled back. Was that true?

He enjoyed spending time with Sebastián. Their stint together during quarantine was one of the few things that had kept him sane, but was that the foundation for a relationship? His parents claimed to love one another, but it didn't sound like it when they talked. His mom and dad treated each other like an obligation. A chore. He didn't want to be like that, but was Sebastián the right choice?

More importantly, was it the type of relationship his grandfather Samuel would accept? A match that would let him administer his trust at 28? It seemed like his grandfather had only just accepted that Christian was gay, which had taken years, and the one unspoken condition was that he make this flaw as unembarrassing as possible. Would he really be comfortable with some uncultured fling Christian had picked up from an app—just to not be bored?

*You'll be an embarrassment*, the voice chided.

He had to remind himself that this was not that serious. They hadn't said they loved each other. The word boyfriend hadn't even been brought up, just 'being together,' which was effectively what they were already doing.

Love was never an emotion Christian had understood. If greater society were to be believed, it was supposedly a powerful word that could change a man. People in movies describe love as an intoxicating feeling. Yet if such a thing existed, it was not an emotion he had ever known. Whenever the topic of love came up, his grandfather would always describe his love for his first wife, Mildred, and it was a far cry from the description in the movies. She would be described as polite, and well-mannered, and always able to pull off the perfect dinner party, though she had died long before Christian was born.

This was a similar emotion. It didn't feel powerful or transformational. Christian was satisfied. Satiated. Content. Dependent. If his grandfather's love for Mildred was indeed love, then his feelings for Sebastián were similar. He liked the constant stream of attention from him. The attentiveness. The care. It felt nice.

They were just together.

He wasn't sure how strong his feelings for Sebastián were, and he didn't want to question his emotions too deeply at this point. What was the point? It would only complicate this moment. This, right now—the husky orange rays setting on Sebastián's face as he stared up at him in adoration: that was enough. It had to be.

"So together," Christian said at last. "Where do we go next?" he remarked, gesturing to the vast city beneath them.

# CHAPTER

## 10

### On Cloud 9

Sebastián stopped feeling so alone after that day at the waterfall. "Possibly off the market," he wrote in his bio. He was feeling ecstatic about everything. The dopamine hit from receiving a ping from Christian was enough to make his heart swoon. *On Cloud 9*, he wrote as his new username, feeling like his hands were on fire as he saved the handle on his phone.

This moment was perfect.

Christian had posted no new changes to his profile, mainly because he seemed to stop checking the app outside of communicating with Sebastián—or at least, Sebastián had assumed he had. When you start a new relationship, there is hardly time for entertaining other guys on the side. Christian and Sebastián were with each other nearly all the time, waking up often in the same bed and sharing most meals together. How could he have the capacity to think of someone else?

*Was he thinking of someone else?*

They still hadn't officially declared each other boyfriends. They were dating—together— but nothing else. Occasionally, Christian let slip the possibility of them sharing a future together: talking about when they would visit his grandfather for Christmas, his parent's house, or go to Southern France during his family's annual vacation. These droplets of information piqued Sebastián's interest. He wanted Christian. And also, he wanted this life he would hear during snippets of conversation: the Parisian chateaus, the gourmet meals. It sounded perfect.

The first few weeks of their relationship were beautiful because they gave him a window into that life. It was annoying that they couldn't go out to bars and restaurants anymore, and yet, at the same time, life held an almost vacation-like quality to it. They stayed up as late. They ordered as much takeout as they wanted. They fucked loudly and often. Christian and Sebastián drowned out their time in isolation with newer, brighter memories until it almost felt like a dream, suppressed so deeply that its existence seemed only visible by the absence of posts on their respective Instagram feeds.

"#sohappy," Christian wrote underneath a picture of the two of them posing in front of a hip new mural.

Sebastián liked it immediately.

Step by step, they learned their perfectly curated section of the city together. Covid had slowed down the pace of life for them, and now they could take in the sights. Every day, they would choose a direction and just walk. One day, they would be gallivanting through an ornate sculpture garden in the outside courtyard of a Marriott hotel. The next, they would be posing in front of a splashy 'Love is Love' mural for Instagram. The surroundings of their neighborhood became known to them in a way Sebastián did not realize was possible. As their trust built, they began wandering to nearby monuments and landmarks around the neighborhood. They took particular pride in the routes, walkways, and shortcuts they had learned, debating which way would be the fastest.

"See, the D Street alleyway is faster than through the park," Sebastián bragged one morning, showing the time on his phone.

"I'm still not sure," smirked Christian, trying to play his stubbornness off as a joke, even though to Sebastián, it seemed like he was only half-joking. His insistence was so hot and charming, like he could bend the world to his will.

"Fine, let's switch routes," said Sebastián, resetting the timer on his phone before retracing Christian's footsteps. "You know how much I like to prove you wrong," he joked.

Christian smiled. "You are the best b… best friend, person a guy could ask for," Christian stumbled.

Was he going to say the word boyfriend right there? Sebastián was sure of it, but Christian glossed over the comment as if nothing had happened. He moved the discussion back to their route and where they would eat after.

"What should we order for takeout?" Christian asked.

Christian had paid for everything these last few weeks—something Sebastián had never brought up. It was nice to be treated to things, and, truthfully, the restaurants were more expensive than he could budget for anyway. The kinds of places that had à la carte options and market price entrees. They would bring into Christian's apartment Korean barbecue chicken, succulent with its meat dropping off the bone; handmade squid ink pasta in a creamy vodka sauce; lamb vindaloo that sizzled and crackled with heat.

Sebastián would take pictures of these, but Christian never did. They didn't seem very special to him. Why would they? He had probably been eating this type of food his entire life. That lucky bitch.

"Thai?" Sebastián asked.

"Sure, let me pull it up," Christian said, taking out his phone.

And that was when Sebastián heard the ping of an app he knew all too well.

*Was he on fucking Grindr?*

# CHAPTER 11



Christian didn't know why he turned on Grindr again. No, that was a lie. He did. It had been two weeks since that day on the waterfall, and he wasn't feeling 'this' anymore. Christian was lethargic and bloated from all the food they were ordering. His tiny fridge—a fridge he had never realized was so small until this moment—was filled with styrofoam and plastic cartons of half-eaten takeout. His apartment was a mess because Sebastián constantly moved books, chairs, and clothes places they weren't supposed to be.

He had liked his life. It may not have been ideal, but it had at least been comfortably predictable. Chris man used to a routine. He would work out at 5:00 AM in his building's gym every day before getting ready for that morning's calls. A routine that had been chipped away with the pandemic, admittedly, but with Sebastián, that energy had sapped away completely. They would start the day cuddling and fucking, and by the time all that business was sorted, he would be thrown off for the rest of the day.

His hands had moved to open the app, almost unthinkingly, as he navigated to the one place that reliably gave him the dopamine hits he craved. There was a loud, recognizable ding. His phone was not on mute.

Shit.

*You really have the tact of three toddlers in a trench coat*, the voice mocked.

"Are you on Grindr?" Sebastián asked.

"Um, no," Christian said reflexively.

There was an icy pause as Sebastián said nothing. All Christian could think of was how much he had just made an ass of himself.

"I mean, technically, yes," Christian corrected. "Sorry. My brain just was on autopilot."

"Are you on autopilot a lot?" Sebastián asked. His words were stiff and unforgiving.

"No, baby," Christian replied. He cringed at this. He had never called Sebastián 'baby' before. "Here, I'll delete it."

"No," Sebastián said. "I don't want to force you to do that. Besides," Sebastián paused, his analytical brain kicking into high gear, "It's a pointless gesture. There would be nothing stopping you from redownloading it again."

Christian didn't know what to say to this. "I'm sorry," he said finally.

"It's fine," Sebastián said. "I haven't deleted it either. It's fine."

# CHAPTER 12

## Looking

Sebastián had accepted Christian's apology, but things still didn't feel right. He didn't understand what was happening to them. It was like a switch had flipped in their relationship. The thrill of newness seemed to be slipping, and it terrified him. While he occasionally took pictures of their trips around the city, he was doing so less and less.

And then, one day, neither of them posted anything to Instagram.

Then another.

And another.

Was this their relationship fading?

He didn't feel as if he were floating in the clouds anymore. He was falling, and he needed someone to catch him quickly. "Looking," he wrote in a huff shortly after their 'conversation,' secretly hoping that Christian would see it too and know that he had hurt him. It was also true. He did want more friends in his day-to-day life. His messages with his college friends had petered out. He still had heard nothing from Barry and needed an outside perspective to make sense of his life.

Sebastián wanted to be thrilled by everything like he had been three weeks ago, but everywhere he went was always the same: a sterile downtown where nothing felt accessible. There were only so many times Sebastián could pose for pictures or map out his steps before feeling bored. This was a sin he didn't want to admit to Christian, lest the relationship stagnate, and both of them returned to being alone, and Sebastián returned to being... less upwardly mobile.

That could not happen, yet Sebastián was also struggling to maintain the relationship too. He was invested in the idea of Christian's life, but not so much in the man himself, who he found somewhat boring.

"Did I tell you the Admiral is getting a divorce?" Christian asked Sebastián during one afternoon stroll.

"And 59 seconds... What? Yeah, your uncle? I think you said that yesterday," he responded, not looking up from his phone. "They are sick of each other's guts, right? Cause of Covid?"

"Yeah, I guess I did tell you," responded Christian wistfully.

*Fuck*, Sebastián thought bitterly. It had only been a couple of weeks, and he felt like he was already fucking this up. Sebastián could feel it drifting out of his hand, like the dirt clumps he used to play with as a child in the lot behind his apartment building. Even as he tried to keep the Earth from falling through his fingers, it always seemed to slip, staining his hands with black and brown. The only thing to do was let go and rinse the dirt away.

They spent more days on the patio, absentmindedly staring at schmucks down below. Sebastián started to be on his phone more, checking the news and Covid death numbers, which only exacerbated his anxieties, but he couldn't help it. He had to know the numbers.

"We hit 7,000 new cases this week," he rattled off.

"That's a lot," Christian remarked. "Listen, can we not talk about that."

"Sure. There's always the death numbers," Sebastián joked darkly.

"What do you want to do after this? After Covid?" Christian asked abruptly, very obviously wanting to move on to another subject.

Sebastián had to think about it for a moment, setting his phone down. "Well, I've always wanted to go to Japan."

"Me too," Christian said gleefully.

"Why do you want to go?" Sebastián asked.

"All the anime!" Christian beamed, "I want to see the country that gave us *Dragon Ball Z* and *Death Note*. Plus, I've already been to Seoul and Bangkok, and it would be nice to round out my passport with Tokyo, you know? How about you?"

Sebastián gulped. What do you even say to someone so worldly? Someone who spoke like they really could travel and not just have it be some distant pipe dream.

"I've never traveled outside the county," Sebastián admitted, "and I always wanted to go. I learned Japanese in college and haven't had many chances to use it."

"Well, we should go when this is over," Christian said, gesturing to the world and everything else with his hands.

"Only if we get to take a pit stop in Greece. *Mamma Mia* made that country seem beautiful," Sebastián demurred, hoping Christian would respect him more if he also wanted to travel on a whim. Anything had to sound less pathetic than admitting that he had never left the country. "How's your brother, by the way?" he asked, changing the subject. "He's still doing that bubble thing?"

"Sammie? Yeah, actually. For over two months now. He recently went camping with five of his closest friends in the Blue Ridge Mountains. They all rented one house in the woods for the weekend, where they drank and played games. No wives allowed. His Instagram made it seem like they were shirtless all the time. It sounded really fun."

Sebastián thought it reminded him of a fancier version of his childhood. He had spent a lot of time in the woods, though he had never rented a house to do it. They were always just around him.

"Who would you bring if you could?" Sebastián asked. "Into a Covid bubble, I mean."

"Besides, Chris Hemsworth, you mean?" Christian quipped.

"I'm serious. A handful of friends in the woods. Who'd you pick?"

"I'm not sure. I haven't been in the city for too long, and I've been a bit of a workaholic. Dan and Henry, maybe? What about you?" he said.

Sebastián couldn't believe someone with such a lovely place didn't have that many friends. He had the opposite problem. Who not to pick? He had had such a busy social life during his college days, pre-Covid, that he found himself listing off ten people in less than 30 seconds. "Anthony. Steve. Allen. Rick, maybe? J.J. John. Other John. Jon without the h. Have to invite Barry. He's soooo much fun."

"We get it; you're popular," Christian said sarcastically with the slightest hint of jealousy.

"Well, you asked," retorted Sebastián.

"Fair," Christian smirked.

"We should do it," Sebastián said. "The Covid bubble, I mean. What do you think?" he inquired, pretending like he was throwing the question up in the air, even though both of them knew it was anything but an ill-conceived line of thought. Sebastián knew that they both wanted this. It was the only way to return that brilliant spark they had felt during the first month of their relationship, and it had to work.

"Yeah," Christian replied. "I think we should."

When they returned to Christian's apartment, they started brainstorming ideas for who they should invite into their bubble. Sebastián put on an episode of *Little Rascals* titled "Forming your Squad." It was one he had listened to before, where Dr. Angela King went over some 'dos and don'ts' for selecting people that will reduce your risk for infection. He watched Christian listen to this *Lit-*

*tle Rascals* episode, taking particular pleasure in seeing his partner react to jokes he knew were coming.

"We all have that one friend," King chuckled dryly through Christian's MacBook Air speaker, "Let's call her Sarah. Sarah is a blast. But she's not the most reliable. She is always showing up late to brunches and parties. Don't invite a Sarah into your bubble. How can she be trusted not to catch Covid if she can't even show up to brunch?"

Sebastián borrowed an old notepad from Christian and began scribbling down people he considered 'Sarahs.'

"Ugh, I love Allen," Sebastián said, finding it pleasurable to judge his friends in comfort. "But that bitch cannot show up to do something to save her life. Such a Sarah." Sebastián scribbled down half of his friend group—all of them too flakey or too judgmental to be a part of this new circle of trust. It didn't help that he hadn't talked to them in months.

Christian wrote a name down too. Samantha, a woman who he claimed he worked with at the base. He didn't know her well, but something about her seemed to rub him the wrong way.

"What makes her a Sarah, then?" Sebastián asked.

Christian seemed to catch himself because he quickly added, "I've never really had any reason to dislike her. She gets all her work done, and she isn't mean. It's just that she fucking acts like she's better than you all the time," Christian sighed.

"Yeah, that sounds like a Sarah to me," Sebastián said.

"If you were in my shoes, Sebastián, you would want to cut this bitch out of your life too." Christian paused, contemplating the words he had spoken carefully. "Does that make sense?"

Sebastián nodded his head. "Yep, it makes sense, Christian."

He honestly thought his complaint sounded a little sexist but nodded anyway. Things were already so shaky, and he just wanted this to work.

The two of them whittled the names down to a list of acceptable people who fit King's criteria—three committed and thoughtful friends. The only problem was that none of them were currently in the city: John was staying with his parents in the suburbs, "Other" John had moved with his partner to their condo in the Rockies, and Barry had taken a flight to Mexico the moment the lockdowns started. The only person in his friend group who was still around was Rick.

"He's your friend, right?" inquired Christian.

"Yeah, I guess so. Rick's more of a group friend, though. He sort of hangs on there, and no one likes him, but he's been around so long everyone feels obligated."

"I do," said Christian.

Based on their conversation so far, Sebastián was getting the nagging feeling that Christian might be many people's group friend.

With no one else to name, they scrolled through Grindr profiles. The day turned into a giddy exploration of torsos and buttcheeks. They would pass phones back and forth, informally interviewing people without their knowledge.

"Do you think he's a Sarah?" Sebastián asked, showing the profile of a man with the username *Fuck My Hole*.

"Yeah, a total Sarah… How about this one?" said Christian, lowering his phone so Sebastián could see the profile. It was of a user called *Covid, right?*, who had a simple but snarky profile that got a good chuckle from both of them. He was a tall, dark-skinned man with a small fro and an undercut.

"Very hot. And smart. Add him to the list."

They ended up settling on three King-approved profiles, all within a 5000-foot radius: *Covid, right?*, or Emmett; a Texas import called *Whiskey please,* whom they would come to know as James; and *No Worries* or Jon, the young man who Sebastián learned Christian had slept with that one time he had bailed on their date. Sebastián was feeling more and more confident about this. They were assembling a team, like one of those sports movies he had never watched or the acapella girls in *Pitch Perfect*.

"I guess we message them," said Sebastián.

"Yeah."

**Christian**



All of them said yes.

# Chapter 13

*Christian*

Christian found the first time they all got together to be very awkward. The five of them sat around his large, L-shaped couch, passing around bland small talk. They were each spaced apart from one another. This distance was not out of an obligation to social distance (they weren't wearing masks) but because no one seemed quite comfortable in each other's presence. None of them knew each other well, except for Christian and Sebastián, and even that relationship was weaker than Christian would like to publicly admit.

To Christian, no one seemed very eager to start being intimate. The looming potential of that uneasiness was bringing everyone down. They talked about the weather and traffic, and after a few tense minutes, they didn't have much to say. Several moments of silence followed as they looked at each other, taking in this feeling of uncertainty. The room was still enough that Christian could listen to everyone's breathing, exhaling in and out. It was enough to form a slow rhythm of anticipation, and as Christian looked at all of them, he could see the expecting look in all of their eyes.

"Do y'all have anything to drink?" asked James, who at this point they only knew as *Whiskey please*, breaking the silence. He was a bulky yet fit white man who wore red flannel and faded blue jeans. James had a posture that was both confident and disinterested at the same time. He slumped in his seat with a devilish smirk as if he knew something the others weren't yet aware of, and in a way, he was correct. They would all be fucking soon. Christian knew this. They all seemed to know this in the back of their minds, but most pretended that the sexual tension wasn't there.

"Of course. Does anyone else want a glass?" inquired Christian as he made his way to his cabinets. Liquid courage. Why hadn't he thought about that? He opened the white-varnished doors, continuing to stare out at the new bubble as he rummaged for glasses. His kitchen was designed to be open so that it bled into the surrounding living room—the only delineation being the floor changing from carpet to wooden panels. He counted the number of raised hands as he walked back into the kitchen. Everyone wanted a drink except for Jon.

"Modest. How charming," complimented Sebastián.

"It's not… I don't really drink ever," Jon answered when everyone looked at him expectantly. He was by far the youngest in the group and also the leanest. He had come in shorts and wore a t-shirt with the words 'This hipster can get it,' which contrasted nicely against his pale skin. Although Jon looked nervous, he seemed to be trying to bury that feeling, so it didn't show to the group, making it even more apparent. He sat up straight in his seat, fighting the slouch that Christian wagered he had developed from years of looking down at a phone. "Dad's an alcoholic, so I've decided not to chance it," he added.

"Well, none of us are going to pressure you," Sebastián reassured him, though Christian didn't know enough about everyone's preferences to tell if that promise could be kept. They all barely knew each other. Everything was moving incredibly fast.

"Not with alcohol anyway," James joked. Christian laughed out of politeness, and everyone else nervously did as well.

Emmett had not spoken much yet. He had come in a pink polo and khakis. He was sitting the farthest away from everyone else on the couch, up against one of the arms. His ebony skin popped against the ivory leather. His joints were tight, pressing themselves into one another. It was like he was willing himself to disappear. Christian wagered that Emmett's muscles were so tight that if you placed a quarter on his shoulder, it would not roll off.

"How are you all holding up?" Emmett asked nervously.

"Honestly," said Jon, "I'm losing my mind."

"Right?" smirked James.

"I think I have watched all of Netflix at this point," Jon joked.

"I'm anxious at the best of times," Emmett interjected. "This has not been great for that."

"Me too, I think," said Sebastián, "Though I've never done therapy or anything like that."

"Oh, do you not have insurance?" Emmett asked.

"It's not that. I've never been comfortable with that sort of thing, you know?"

Christian returned from the kitchen, "Here you go," he interrupted, handing a glass of whiskey to Emmett. If there was one thing he didn't want to discuss, it was all their emotions.

"Thanks," Emmett mumbled.

*Coward*, the voice said, clawing back from the recesses of his mind.

He just had to ignore it. It wasn't healthy to dwell on the negative.

Christian passed out the other drinks and sat back on the couch, sitting between James and Emmett. He plopped into the seat cushion, which caused the two of them to re-adjust their positions, so they didn't fall into him.

"Oops," Christian said.

"It's all good," James responded heartily, placing a hand on Christian's shoulder.

Things progressed quickly from there. Within moments, Christian and James were kissing. It had not been planned, at least not actively. It was more of a gnawing thought that clung at the back of his mind. He had wanted those wet lips since this gathering had been planned. When his tongue pressed against James', frantically writhing, he thought his existence could cease here and now, and he would be happy. He spent so much time being unhappy, but this right here was good.

Later, Christian would tell Sebastián that James had kissed him first. They needed to talk after everyone left. Fucking their bubble had not been outwardly discussed, but the implication wasn't a stretch. It had created some jealousy in Sebastián, whose anxiety had him reverberating with a need to break down every detail of that moment.

"Had you wanted this?… Who kissed who?… Do you like him?… Do you want to date him?… Do you want to break up?"

"I want you, baby," Christian assured him, and this felt true enough. He did want him. He just wanted these other men, too. "And I didn't kiss him," Christian gaslit. "He kissed me."

Yet this was not true. Christian had not been drunk. He knew what he wanted. Deep down, Christian knew he was being shitty here but didn't care. Christian wanted to kiss James and feel the bliss that it brought to his mind.

So, he had done precisely that. He lunged for James, which caused everyone else to react. Jon turned to Sebastián and tilted his chin upwards, beckoning him forward—an action that quickly turned into intense foreplay. Emmett started playing with himself, voyeuristically watching as everyone else made out. It was an average-sized dick, about five inches, which surprised Christian. He had expected it to be much bigger.

*Racist*, the voice lectured.

Without turning his attention away from James, Christian grabbed it and pulled Emmett closer to them. The three of them kissed, circling the tips of each other's tongues. They then proceeded to rub against one another. Christian slowly peeled Emmett's foreskin back, revealing the creamy head underneath. It was lighter than Christian would have thought. Emmett's eyes widened when Christian licked the tip of his foreskin, his tongue dancing around it.

He was focused on the task at hand, but he had not phased everyone out either. From the other side of the couch, he could hear Sebastián speak loudly into Jon's ears. "Should we take this to the bedroom?" he asked Jon—their two heads only inches apart.

"Um, yes, please… " said Jon before pausing and giving Sebastián a perplexed look. "Wait, aren't you also a top?"

"Oh shit, yeah. You're right… Hey, sweetie," Sebastián called out to Christian.

"What?" he asked, removing his mouth from Emmett's lower region. He was somewhat distracted by James, who was also nibbling firmly on his neck.

"Are you the only, you know…?" he said, forming a circle with his fingers and pulling his thumb in and out of it.

"Ahhhhh, maybe?" He stared directly into James. "Oh shit, maybe?" he repeated.

"I'm a straight top, darling," James smirked.

"I'm vers," Emmett joined in. Christian was still grabbing Emmett's cock, and he could feel it grow as he said this. He wanted to be fucked by the group very badly.

"Well then," Sebastián said as he and Jon walked over to Emmett, looking up and down at this slender Black body in a way that seemed filled with desire and objectification simultaneously. "Someone is about to get a lot of attention." Sebastián lifted Emmett's legs into the air, so each one sat on his shoulders. He leaned in close to Emmett's face and whispered, "Would you like that?"

Emmett nodded.

Christian, who had enjoyed watching these events unfold, still held onto Emmett, more instinctually than anything else. He wanted something to grip onto as James removed his pants and teased his butt cheeks. Fuck, it felt good. He could feel Emmett's excitement as Sebastián consumed him—this stranger, neither of them knew that well—and yet it didn't feel strange. It felt fucking fantastic. How could this be anything but right?

Later, after they had all finished, and Christian was nuzzled in the base of James' armpits, as this hunk of a man lazily pulled off the condom and tossed it to the floor, it occurred to him that he didn't know everyone's names yet.

"What's your name, by the way?" James asked as if reading his mind.

Christian replied with his, and then everyone else swapped theirs as well. The realization that they had only exchanged names after fucking caused everyone to laugh awkwardly.

"Well, nice to meet you, Christian," James said as he straddled between Christian's legs. "How does round two sound?"

Christian nodded, licking his lips nervously as James entered him.

*Holy fuck*, he thought, keeping his eyes locked on James, who was already deep inside him. He gasped, and Christian's eyes rolled to the back of his head in pleasure.

He could get used to this.

# CHAPTER 14

The Gang™

The first two weeks together were filled with utter bliss. They created a group chat on Grindr called *The Gang™* because it sounded funny and unserious, precisely the kind of energy they all told themselves they wanted. They would all end each day exhausted and happy, cuddling in each other's arms on Christian's massive king-sized bed. It didn't matter what they did because you could always tell that everybody liked one another, or at least, no one complained much about each other's faults, which felt like the same thing.

Every night, they had dinner together. They would sit around Christian's large circular dinner table, usually after ordering takeout, and would tell each other little details about themselves. Their histories would bleed out suddenly and painfully, all desperate to share the thoughts they had held in for months. The ever-shy Emmett disclosed his bipolar disorder, which he tried to keep a secret from almost everyone in his life. Jon revealed that he ran over a dog while drunk driving, which was part of why he had become sober. James had participated in a homophobic hate crime in Texas when he was closeted. Sebastián had been having a miserable time at work. And Christian, well, he was depressed, something that predated Covid. Tears streamed down their faces as *The Gang*$^{TM}$ unburdened themselves with these secrets.

Each was desperate for validation, though some needed it more than others. Christian was particularly in need of distraction because focusing on someone else drowned out the voice in his head, but he was not alone there. Emmett heard them too, and so did Jon, and really, the lot of them. All of them preferred to be in the arms of another then focus on the darkness brewing in their minds. This intimacy made *The Gang*$^{TM}$ feel safer. They would hold each other's hands as they told these secrets, which would lead to rubbing and caressing and eventually fucking each other's brains out.

Yet, it wasn't all confessions and fucking inside Christian's apartment. Sometimes, they would head to the park for a picnic or stay up late and watch a movie. Their lives had become a string of idyllic dates that gave them an oasis of refuge against the world. Just as Christian and Sebastián had spent their early days exploring the nooks and crannies of the city, so too did *The Gang*$^{TM}$. They walked through old neighborhoods and new alike, sharing the locations of mosaics and popup exhibits like they were pieces of currency.

"The museum is giving away free pins."

"There's a cool rock in the woods. It looks like an owl."

"A coffee shop has a nice outdoor patio overlooking the river."

The prizes at the end of all their trips were never the point. It was merely the act of exploration that they enjoyed. The chance for *The Gang*$^{TM}$ to be in and experience the world together. They would end every adventure, tired and fulfilled, inside Christian's apartment, which would always lead to fucking. They would fuck for thirty minutes or so and then, almost immediately after cumming would collapse into Christian's sheets, close together, in a deep and sustained state of sated bliss.

And just as quickly, it would begin again, as one arm found its way on another one of their cocks. It was like Christian's apartment had transformed into their new playground—a place that had become less a home and more of a blend of moans, laughs, and cute small talk.

**Whiskey please (James)**

what movie should we watch tonight.

**Christian**

Captain America WS!!!!

**NoWorries (Jon)**

Another Marvel movie?

**Looking (Sebastián)**

is that snark I detect?

### Whiskey please (James)

someone's going to get it.

### NoWorries (Jon)

Cute banter like this had become a staple of all their interactions, especially when it came to teasing Jon. He had always been the most opinionated in the group. He would regurgitate whatever hot take he had seen on social media that day—a fact that drove other people in *The Gang$^{TM}$*, particularly James, nuts.

And so, to sidestep this tension, they all played a game where if Jon ever became too 'talkative,' they would shut him up by making him suck one of their dicks. He had a growing submissive side he was only starting to explore, though it was not as passive as Christian's. He was far more bratty in his sexual games, purposefully annoying the others so they would 'punish' him. However, they were all new to this dynamic, so sometimes they confused his actual opinions as peacocking, making him feel insecure, as he dissociated from the ridicule, totally unseen.

### NoWorries (Jon)

I don't talk that much. Do I?

Jon's insecurity was a refreshing surprise to Christian, who also struggled with self-confidence. He had seemed so confident during their first encounter, and Christian thought it was nice to know that even sure people could be insecure when you got to know them a little bit—when your opinions mattered to them.

*The Gang$^{TM}$* pressed its influence onto all of them. Christian found himself more assertive now that most of their interactions happened inside his apartment, somewhere he felt like he controlled. Sebastián was far less assertive emotionally now that Christian directed more of his life. Where he had been loud and domineering earlier, his voice had softened in recent weeks. His classic move of storming away during difficult moments had transmuted into a more demure hug. Emmett was as assertive as he had ever been emotionally, but sexually, his entire world had flipped. He had been more of a top in his past encounters but was a bottom now with *The Gang*$^{TM}$ and grappled with this new position.

One night, as they were all watching yet another Marvel movie, Jon found himself between the thighs of Sebastián for making one too many comments about Captain America's imperialism within the MCU. They were right before that stage where gentle foreplay turned into full-blown fucking. Jon was looking at his phone, uninterested in the movie and not quite ready to suck Sebastián off.

"Whose George Floyd?" he asked the group as he reacted to various tweets on his timeline. "It looks like he just died or something."

# Chapter 15

## Black Lives Matter

The world shifted after George Floyd's death. Sure, he had experienced racism before. His white friends had always expected him to have the hookup at the best Mexican joints, and he constantly had to navigate people assuming that he worked in lawn care or was a janitor. There were the occasional sideways glances full of scorn and disgust whenever he started to speak Spanish out in public. But in the past, he had clung to his white-passing identity as much as possible, rarely speaking Spanish unless around family, and even then, it depended on the eyes around him.

Conversations about race that he had once ignored like the plague exploded into mountains of urgency and complexity. Ashamed as he was to admit it, he had never really been awake to these injustices. Emmett Till, Malcolm X, Angela Davis. These names had never come up before, but he knew them now. He changed his profile name to *Black Lives Matter*. It was the right thing to do, after all. It wasn't enough to be a bystander, not in a moment like this.

He started posting more regularly on Facebook and Instagram. 'Black Lives Matter,' 'Say His Name,' 'Take a knee.' He spread these messages like the black flags of revolutions past. Sebastián felt, more than anything, that the world could and should be a better place and that he could make it happen. He even got his sister Elena to start sharing some of his posts on Facebook, which was a big ask given that where she lived was pretty conservative.

The only ruffle in this new direction was Emmett, who had not communicated with *The Gang*$^{TM}$ for several days after that evening when they learned the news. He changed his profile name to *No Justice! No Peace!* and stopped responding to their messages. Sebastián was puzzled by Emmett's absence at this moment. Surely a Black man like him would want to be involved. He didn't understand why Emmett wouldn't trust him. Sebastián considered himself a progressive and felt somewhat offended by the silence. He tried reaching out to him with no luck.

**Black Lives Matter (Sebastián)**

you okay?

Six hours later.

**Black Lives Matter (Sebastián)**
hey

Twelve hours later.

**Black Lives Matter (Sebastián)**
listen, I don't want to overwhelm you. We just haven't heard from you in a few days. Let me know if you need anything, but no pressure.

Sebastián had sent him these messages privately so as not to make other people in *The Gang*$^{TM}$ uncomfortable, particularly James, who seemed triggered by the uprising. Sebastián wanted to get through to Emmett to see if there was anything he could do to help, but then he read an article telling white people not to bother their Black friends at this moment and immediately apologized.

**Black Lives Matter (Sebastián)**
hey, sorry about that. Don't worry about it.

Sebastián started to read even more articles from Black writers complaining about the deluge of comments from their white peers. Every white person in their life was asking the question, 'how they were doing.' One writer on Medium even received random messages from someone he had not spoken to since high school, 'just wanting to know if he was okay.' Sebastián thought that these people sounded like the worst. They were pretending to help, but really, they wanted to assuage their guilt, hoping that this outreach would make centuries of oppression blink out of existence.

**Black Lives Matter (Sebastián)**

hey, just so you know, this
is a safe space.

**No Justice! No Peace! (Emmett)**

Thank you for reaching out. I have been
feeling bad. So sorry to scare you.

**Black Lives Matter (Sebastián)**

sorry to hear that. Anything I can do?

**No Justice! No Peace! (Emmett)**

No, I'm good. Jon is going to a protest. You
should come with.

Jon had seemed to embrace this shift in public opinion. He had changed his name to *Dismantle white Supremacy* and had started going to protests mere hours after the news broke. He Instagrammed every rally and posted forthright opinions on Facebook. His feed was awash with stern selfies in front of a sea of signs. Jon had been a lot to deal with before the police shooting and even more now. But if it meant being there for Emmett, it was a sacrifice Sebastián was willing to make.

**Black Lives Matter (Sebastián)**

sure, I'll go.

The moment Sebastián clicked send on that message, his anxiety spiked. A part of him felt nervous about being outside amongst all those people. His heart pounded with dread. He had only been outside in large crowds a few times since Covid, and he was always hyper-aware of every action people were making and could not wait to be back inside. Still, his friend had asked him to join him during this moment of crisis. And he told himself that being a good ally was more important than his guilt.

Christian didn't want him to go either, and they got into a huge fight. They went back and forth, hammering on the same points repeatedly. Christian thought it was a stupid risk, and Sebastián accused Christian of not being there for their friend. They shouted so loudly that the neighbors must have thought something was up. Christian came at him with the most absurd things. There was so much anger in him.

"If you don't care about Covid, then go," Christian said condescendingly.

"You don't even care about Covid," Sebastián corrected.

"I do, too."

Sebastián realized that this was their first real fight. He had been trying not to be too difficult for weeks now, but this was too much. He considered himself stubborn by nature, and there was only so much nonsense he could take. The man was wrong, and Sebastián was done with being tolerant. He would not listen to what Christian was saying, and instead, he used that time to formulate his perfect counterarguments.

But Christian was passive-aggressive and even mean at times. He would likewise not listen and take every opportunity to make a remark that hurt.

"You don't care about my opinions," Christian stated matter-of-factly.

"Everyone going is masked and outside, so the risk is low, but clearly, you don't care about the data," Sebastián continued.

"As if you even care about that. We are fucking three strangers we met online, but figures the healthcare lobbyist would twist the data," Christian cut.

"You are so… argh."

Sebastián was so frustrated he couldn't even finish his thought. He stormed into the other room and closed the door. Of course, he cared. Just because they had a Covid bubble didn't mean he thought they should ignore all precautions. He was tired of having to argue with Christian. They were close, had been close, but for the past week, they were both acting as if they didn't know each other at all. Was Christian this uncomfortable about a stupid protest? It didn't make any sense at all. Had he always been this prickly when it came to race? Sebastián would have known if he was dating a racist, right?

He made up his mind. Sebastián was going. He sent Jon a message, and they agreed to meet an hour later in the same park where he once drank coffee with Christian every morning. If it turned out to be a wash, at least the protest would have a pretty view.

The park wasn't far from the apartment, so he spent twenty minutes deciding how to dress for the occasion to kill time. He knew that business attire would be frowned upon, but was he supposed to just go in shorts and a t-shirt? It felt too impersonal. He rotated through every article of clothing he had brought to Christian's place, throwing one after another onto the bed. He left them there, spitefully knowing it would annoy Christian.

When he arrived fifty minutes later at the park, he did so in khakis and a polo—clothing Sebastián immediately regretted when he looked at the far less polished protestors. He couldn't find Jon or Emmett. The park and the surrounding streets were packed with people. There was a carnivalesque atmosphere to it all. Some groups paraded in the streets with massive puppets. Others had colorful shirts with revolutionary slogans. People were constantly moving, walking up and down the streets. They high-fived each other, yelling, holding up signs, and shouting well-worn chants in unison that started and died on a whim. Some were even dancing to music blasting from their phones. The song *Fuck the Police* was quite popular, as well as generic pop songs like Katy Perry's *Roar*.

The people there were protesting a variety of injustices. There were signs with the names of people killed by the police, many of whom Sebastián did not recognize: victims like Breonna Taylor, Atatiana Jefferson, Philando Castille, and many more. The phrase 'Black Lives Matter' was everywhere, as well as derivative phrases such as 'Black Trans Lives Matter' and 'Black Dreams Matter.' These sentences were on signs, shirts, and bamboo tote bags—people snapping pictures of their favorites to post to social media later.

"Sebastián," a familiar voice shouted.

Sebastián turned to see Rick, the hangeron in his previous friend group. The man that would always bring down the vibe of whatever group he was in by never being able to take a hint. He was dressed in a light pink tee and appeared to have dyed his hair a pale blue. Rick held a handmade sign that read 'Justice for Tony McDade,' a name Sebastián didn't recognize.

"How are you?" continued Rick. "It's been a minute."

"Heeeyyyyyy Rick," Sebastián replied. "Yeah, sorry. I've been totally turtling. I'm good. What's up with you?"

"A whole lot of bad, to be honest." Rick sighed.

"Same."

There was a moment of silence as Sebastián didn't know what to say. God, why was Rick so awkward? Sebastián tried to remember when he had first started to dislike Rick so much. It was an opinion that seemed to have emerged from the collective disgust of his friends, and he had mirrored them—an assessment Rick seemed to confirm at every available opportunity by being so fucking awkward.

"There you are!" shouted Jon. "I was beginning to think I lost you."

Jon was in his standard shorts and tee. The mask he was wearing had the phrase 'fuck the system.' He held a plastic spoon in one hand and coffee in the other, and it looked like he hadn't slept in a while.

"There's a lot of people here, aren't there?… Jon. Rick. Rick. Jon." Sebastián said, introducing the two.

They both said hi, and then Sebastián quickly made an excuse to leave Rick behind. "We have to go find our friends," Sebastián lied. "But it was nice seeing you. See you around?"

"See you around," Rick repeated.

Sebastián and Jon pushed their way further into the crowd.

"How did you get here so quickly?" asked Sebastián.

"I was at a bodega right next to that spoon café."

"*The Silver Spoon?*"

"Yeah, that's the one. I came from another protest and needed my fix." Jon laughed, gesturing to the coffee.

They hugged each other deeply, not seeing the point in social distancing when they were in each other's bubble. No one seemed to respect it in the crowd anyway—though most everyone was masked and avoiding contact.

"Is Emmett coming?" Sebastián asked Jon.

"Oh, I didn't ask him to come. I figured that would be a bit much, you know?"

"Totally," Sebastián responded meekly.

Sebastián thought back to their chat and realized that Emmett never said he was coming. He felt slightly hurt by Emmett not wanting to spend time with him but decided to shrug it off. He had read an article telling him not to make this moment about him, so Sebastián set this thought aside for now. There was plenty of time to message Emmett later.

Sebastián and Jon joined the crowd in chanting, funnily enough, 'No Justice, No Peace.' This went on for an uncounted amount of time as they became part of the sea of people, swaying to the rhythm of the crowd. It felt good to chant and speak loudly while also being so peaceful and unified. He felt like he was in the crowd waiting to hear Eva Perón in *Evita*.

A woman with a microphone could be heard somewhere ahead of them. She talked about George Floyd and the inhumanity of the police system. She started chanting 'Defund the Police' and even 'Abolish the Police,' neither of which Sebastián felt comfortable saying, but he moved his lips all the same and lost himself in the words after a few seconds.

"And just like that unfair system, this statue has been here for seventy years. Seventy years highlighting, reinforcing, embracing the racist idea that Black and Brown people should be subordinated to white people."

There was applause at this. A round of whoos and shouts filled in the gap. "Say it louder," screamed a listener.

The woman continued. "They wanted us to be thankful for the crumbs, and we are not going to take it anymore. Tear it down. Tear this racist symbol of oppression down."

The crowd pushed forward. Sebastián wasn't sure what was happening at first. He and Jon were trying to keep their space from everyone, but their curiosity to see what was happening trumped this initial concern. They went closer to see that a rope had been hung around the statue's neck, and a line of people was tugging at it. Moments later, it came tumbling down.

A few more moments passed, and now the crowd was in a dense circle. People were gazing down at the rubble: some cursing at it, some crying, some jumping up and down with joy. News cameras were flashing everywhere. The police, for once, had seemed to be calm and had not directly intervened in the demolition. Everyone was allowed to participate in this moment of the statue's destruction, an approved symbol of resistance, and it felt nice to be with them—for his actions to mean something.

Jon posed in front of it and snapped a picture. He stood tall, with his head looking slightly down at the camera, poised like a man who could take on the world. This was intentional: a pose he had bragged about using in the past.

"This is going to get so many likes," Jon said happily.

# Chapter 16

*Christian*

Christian felt like he was losing his boyfriend, and more than that he felt himself being frozen out by *The Gang*TM, his only real social outlet at the moment. They treated him like you would a pustule on your body. He was a part to be neglected and ignored, but still there, hanging on underneath layers of history and guilt. In the beginning, they liked him because he was there, and now, he thought, they hated him for the same reason.

Just because he was not in support of these protests, he had suddenly become the villain of the week. The only person who stood by his side was James, who seemed to be put off by *The Gang*TM's new wokeness. They would share a look of disbelief whenever Jon would go off on one of his Twitter-based rants. The type of look that read, 'These people don't know what the fuck they are talking about.'

They had fucked once alone, away from the rest of *The Gang*<sup>TM</sup>. James had come over to his apartment simply to come.

"It's great not to be around those people all the time," James said, taking a glass of whiskey from Christian.

"Yeah, Jon and Emmett, in particular, are getting on my nerves," Christian said.

He was standing over James, looking down at his bulging frame. James had worn tight blue pants and a thin white crew neck that was almost translucent, allowing the man's hard pecks to peek out from underneath.

"Not your boyfriend?" James asked. "Sebastián's got a nice ass and all, but sometimes that boy can be a lot," he chuckled.

"Yeah, him too. And he's not my boyfriend," Christian corrected. "We are just dating."

"Well, let's not talk about them right now. Let's focus on us," James hushed, standing up to face Christian.

The two of them were so close that he could feel James's hot breath hit his face. The scent of expensive whiskey filled his nostrils. Christian kissed him, and the two pressed against one another like two collapsing stars. James wrapped his arms tightly around Christian, sucking in as much air as possible from his throat.

James started taking off his clothes, and Christian followed. It took only seconds for their pants and shirts to hit the floor, and then James lifted him off the ground and carried him to the bed. Christian was thrown onto the covers. He closed his eyes and felt pricks of pleasure as James's firm hands worked the various crevices of his body, massaging them, kneading them.

"Condom?" James asked.

Christian gestured to a shelf hanging over the bed. He heard the sound of rifling, the tearing of a wrapper, and then the sound of it crinkling as it made contact with his body. It felt cold and firm.

Christian wanted every day to be like that one. He wanted to feel this load in him every fucking day, but James had a demanding job as a day trader. Now that cryptocurrencies had become such a thing, he could only meet sometimes during the evening. Christian would send James messages, and the man would respond a day or two later.

Christian

are you seeing these
riots everywhere?

Whiskey please (James)

Sorry, I have been out of it. I didn't know that. That's horrible!

Christian

No problem. Talk to you soon.

Yet 'soon' was an increasingly farther and farther away occurrence. Christian spent most of his time alone, staring at one screen or another. He had become obsessed with binging Dr. King's podcast and YouTube series. She at least was not telling him to feel bad for not participating in the stupid protests. She was at least there.

"Know your boundaries," she lectured during one episode. "You should never feel bad for expressing yourself."

She made him feel so utterly complete. Christian would spend evenings with a beer, watching her comfortably from the couch, eating a side of day-old French fries. Every word enraptured him.

*This was what good friends sounded like*, he thought to himself.

All sorts of friends came on to her show. Doctors. Lawyers. Activists. Professionals who laughed and smiled at her jokes about subjects they had mastered rather than half-assed to sound intelligent on social media. Many of them were skeptical about Covid. They brought up some valid points about herd immunity and the narrow specificity of the disease. They maintained a cordial tone, making these ideas sound reasonable to Christian. If Dr. King had brought them on her show, and they had degrees in medicine, how could anything they were saying be wrong?

The algorithm suggested all sorts of people these days: Ben Shapiro, Dan Bongino, InfoWars! People like Jon told him to be wary of these sources, but many soldiers on base loved them. He didn't agree with everything they said, but some of their claims made sense. They all seemed to have the same underlying skepticism and political agenda. Despite their very different backgrounds and areas of expertise, their opinions mirrored each other, making Christian feel like part of a community.

He was going to be all right. He wasn't alone.

## Black Lives Still Matter

Over the next few weeks, Sebastián found himself falling into organizing. It was so fulfilling to do something that mattered. He often posted online, resharing quotes from anti-racist educators like Robin DiAngelo, trying to instill in his friends and family the urgency of this moment. People were starting to forget, to go back to normal, and he couldn't let that happen.

"Black Lives *Still* Matter," he posted on Facebook.

He drafted an email to his boss, demanding they set up a committee to increase diversity at his company. "We need more representation now," he typed in the subject line.

Sebastián found himself more invigorated by the fall-out of George Floyd's death than he had in months or even years. It was okay to go outside and hang out with friends again! As long as they were masked and protesting police brutality, he didn't feel nervous or judged for being outside anymore. He would never do something as extreme as blocking traffic at intersections, but he felt giddy going to the more peaceful protests. He was like a young Erin Brockovich fighting an oppressive society.

He even made up with Emmett. Admittedly, Emmett was angry with him at first. "You have been a lot," he said the first time they saw each other in person after George Floyd's death.

"Sorry," Sebastián apologized. "I've been an ass. I made everything about me. And I'm the worst."

Emmett simply stared at him.

"I'm doing it again, aren't I?" Sebastián laughed, "Look, can we, like, start over?"

"Sure. You weren't being too terrible. Besides, I was going out of my mind with boredom. It's just been my cat and me for weeks."

The two hugged, and like that, everything returned to normal, or as normal as Covid could get anyway.

Sebastián would meet up with Jon and Emmett at a protest, spending hours shouting into the void at the concept of injustice. The police occasionally got a little handsy, but Sebastián and company quickly left whenever things got too rough.

After every protest, they would head to Sebastián's studio and fuck. Since Emmett was the only bottom in the group, the two of them would usually end up Eiffel-towering him. One of them would pound his voluptuous ass repeatedly from behind. Sebastián and Jon would kiss deeply over Emmett's tender body, laughing and giggling with excitement.

"He's very good at taking dick, isn't he?" Sebastián told Jon one day. "Aren't you?" Sebastián said again, slapping Emmett's ass.

Emmett nodded as he choked on Jon's cock.

Sebastián imagined that Emmett loved to be objectified. He would moan deeply whenever the two of them fixated on him. Emmett clearly loved being the center of attention—loved that these two basic twinks were worshiping him, pressing themselves into his Black body. He could hear Emmett gasping with pleasure as he hit his prostate, touching himself so he didn't release before the others. They didn't stop until all of them had finished. Sebastián made sure of it because he was such a good fucking ally.

Christian arrived in a huff as all of them were wiping off and putting their clothes back on. He had been texting them to see if they wanted to play, and Sebastián hadn't replied.

"Did you not see my texts?" he asked.

"Sorry, babe, we were a little busy."

This was a half-truth. Sebastián had been the first one to finish, and had snuck a peak at his phone. He'd seen six notifications from Christian pop up on his feed, but he didn't open a single one. Instead, he had rolled his eyes at them, annoyed by what he perceived as Christian's clinginess, and dove back into Emmett's hole.

"Not a problem," Christian responded coolly.

They had been fighting like this, if you could call it fighting, a lot recently. Christian had made it clear to Sebastián that he didn't like that they were going to the protests. He disagreed with 'this whole thing,' as he called the Black Lives Matter movement. Christian called Sebastián a hypocrite for demanding the bubble mask and social distance when that wasn't happening at the protests. Sebastián mentioned that news reporting didn't think the demonstrations had spread Covid, but the argument had become intractable. Christian would merely scoff and ask Sebastián if he trusted the mainstream media. What did that even fucking mean?

As a result, Sebastián spent less and less time in Christian's apartment. He hadn't officially moved in there anyway, but it felt like things had been going in that direction before this situation. It would have been nice to still spend his mornings on that patio, staring at the schmucks scurrying below. Now, the two of them had sputtered backward into the unknown. It felt worse than an end. It was an interminable growth choking out everything else so that no other relationship could thrive. He often counted the minutes until Christian left, and they could all hang out without him.

Christian sat down on the couch and waited for them to get ready. They had planned to watch a movie, but the energy for it was no longer there. "Is James coming?" Christian asked.

"He's on a business trip, remember?" Sebastián reminded him in a tone that sounded like an accusation.

"Sorry, I can't do a movie. I got to bounce," said Emmett. The look in his eyes made it seem like he wanted to be anywhere but there. He kissed Sebastián and Jon goodbye.

He did not kiss Christian. He didn't even give him an awkward hug. They had not had an official falling out, but Sebastián knew Emmett was mad at Christian for not understanding the importance of the uprising. The three would talk about his stubbornness often, and it was hard not to absorb some of Sebastián's bitterness over their deteriorating relationship. He waved goodbye, and then there were three.

"I can do a show," chimed in Jon, firmly implying that a movie was not an option for him either but that he could stay longer.

Sebastián knew that at the moment Jon was not into Christian as much as he was the rest of *The Gang*$^{TM}$. Proned to gossip, he had told Sebastián as much during one of their many fuck sessions. Jon leaned more into his bratty personality when interacting with Christian. While this made for some amazing sex, it also made him a bit of a chore to interact with, as he always seemed to be stirring up tensions.

At Jon's suggestion, they put on an episode of *The Office*. He selected an episode from the first season, which was unfortunate because it was when Michael was the most insufferable. They watched it sitting close together, but not too close, not yet comfortable enough to fondle each other. It was an emotionally charged episode. One of the characters on the show was monologuing about how he was a failure. The tension hung over Sebastián as he thought about how he no longer liked Christian very much. Christian's refusal to embrace or accept the reality of what America was becoming, or maybe had always been, tinged every word with bitterness until all there was between them was silence. The naked pain of people grieving their lost sons and daughters was in plain view, and Sebastián couldn't look away. He could feel his face burning from the mere thought of Christian's stubbornness.

Jon was in the middle of them. His legs sprawled out. He was probably hoping to get a good hate fuck out of it, which was a dire misreading of the current situation. Christian and Sebastián had not fucked in weeks. The episode was almost over, and nothing had happened.

Getting the hint, finally, Jon had stopped paying much attention to the show. Instead, he was looking at Instagram on his phone.

"Oh my Goooddddd," he gasped.

"What?" Sebastián asked.

Jon tilted his phone to reveal it to Sebastián and Christian. It was a picture of James, shirtless, standing next to a bald man with glasses, whose arms were wrapped around his shoulder. They were on a beach with palm trees in the background, surrounded by maskless people. The location for the picture was tagged San Clemente.

"That's in California." chimed in Christian.

"That sneaky motherfucker. I wondered why that bitch was not answering my texts?" shouted Sebastián.

They had not seen James over the past six days. He had claimed he was on a business trip. Before heading out, he had taken a Covid test and emailed them the results. James had promised to keep exposure at a minimum and quarantine before re-entering their bubble.

Sebastián was furious, and as far as he could tell, the rest of *The Gang*<sup>TM</sup> was as well. This was a betrayal. Within moments, they had dialed into a conference call with Emmett, filling him in on the situation.

"Does that look like minimum exposure to you?" asked Jon.

"It fucking does not," responded Emmett.

They collectively decided to add James to the call. He answered, not quite knowing what he was in for. It quickly became a shouting match as they bombarded him with questions, directing all their pent-up rage onto an easy target.

"Is this your first time?"

"How long have you been seeing other people?"

"How could you?"

James became defensive almost immediately. He claimed to be growing apart from them for a while and blamed them for not seeing it. "Ever since y'all got involved with this social justice warrior nonsense, it has made me uncomfortable. I've been feeling right alienated from the group."

"Okay, I'm out," said Emmett. "You guys decide how you want to deal with the racist." He disconnected from the call.

"See, that is the language I'm talking about," irritatingly interjected James.

Jon looked at Christian and Sebastián from offscreen. He mouthed, 'W-T-F,' and they both shrugged. "Yeah, this isn't going to work," said Jon, positioning himself back in the frame. He hung up the call, leaving him alone again with Christian and Sebastián.

They were still angry but no longer at each other. They laughed at how ridiculous James was being, and after one or two 'accidental' brushes, they started to kiss.

# CHAPTER

## 18



Christian was feeling ecstatic. *The Gang*™ was getting back together with less deadweight under the group name *The New Gang*™. He felt guilty for dumping James like that, but he couldn't argue with the results. No one hated him anymore. *The New Gang*™ had gone through a honeymoon phase after dumping James, who retrospectively became the source of all their problems and a convenient reason for Christian to get back into their good graces.

Christian and Sebastián started hanging out again, gossiping about other *New Gang*™ members late into the evenings. They would go out onto the balcony and split a sleeve of Oreos—a break in the diet they had both started after watching one of Dr. Angela King's TikToks. They would munch on the cheat Oreos and giggle happily from the high that came with sugar and judging others.

"Look at me. I totally care about Black people now that it's popular, selfie!!!" Sebastián said, mocking Jon's high-pitched voice.

"I never talked about racism until literally a month ago," Christian said in Emmett's standard monotone.

The two of them laughed and laughed into the night. Christian felt so happy to have found someone who understood him—someone who cared about him as much as he cared about them. It felt so much better than being alone, braving the truth of the world by yourself.

"I don't think I've ever laughed this much," he said.

"Me neither," Sebastián said with a carefree smile.

A buzz came from Christian's phone. He looked at it.

**Whiskey please (James)**

> traitor. I was there for you when every1 abandoned you, and u did this????

The arrogance of that man. Christian muted his phone. He would not let James ruin what he was building with Sebastián. Their lives were merging, and once again, everything was happening quickly. Random possessions of Sebastián started to find their way into Christian's penthouse. Half his clothes were there (although they would often wear each other's clothing interchangeably, so it was hard to tell what was whose anymore). Christian started wearing their hoodies and black jeans, and Sebastián his button-downs. Christian had been so unsure of his feelings for Sebastián before. However, this settling into one another felt like how a relationship should be.

Christian and Sebastián were talking all the time, including more often about day-to-day practicalities. It was not uncommon for Sebastián to ask how much he needed to Venmo Christian for his half of the weekly grocery bill or if he needed to run over to the CVS to pick something up at the last minute. All that was left was to have a conversation about moving in together. It was the next logical step; however, Christian could never find the time to bring it up. He didn't want to lose his chance. He didn't want to be the one to push Sebastián away, and yet he felt so afraid of being rejected.

*Unable to commit. What a stereotype*, the voice lectured.

He had to push for what he wanted, and soon, or their Covid bubble, *The New Gang*$^{TM}$, would drown this moment out with their constant presence. This possession creep was happening for Jon and Emmett, too. Emmett had left behind several shirts and underwear, which had been neatly folded and placed into a drawer that was unofficially 'his.' Jon had permanently left a backpack stocked with a pair of clothes and an iPhone charger. He had stashed it behind the couch, out of the way, but known by everybody there.

They were like an infestation creeping in. Christian's home was beginning to feel like all their homes, and he was unsure if he wanted that. He contemplated being passive-aggressive, freezing the two out bit by bit until they eventually got the hint, but that would make Sebastián angry, too, and then he might lose everything. He needed to keep this status quo with them in his penthouse. At least here, Christian could control the situation. There was no way to make them leave, not without being 'the asshole.'

A consequence of being nicer meant that he had stopped arguing about the protests. He still didn't agree with them. However, he no longer wanted to fight about it, and more importantly, he didn't want to be compared to James, who everyone in the group agreed was racist. Christian had been raised to believe that racists were buffoons who always revealed their racism when prompted. Christian told himself that he was definitely not that, but tensions were high, and he worried he might get lumped in with the real racists.

And so, he decided he would go to one of the solidarity marches with the others in the nicer part of town. They agreed that they wouldn't stay too long and would leave before sunset to avoid the more rowdy elements of the protest. There would be no problems, Sebastián assured him. Everything would be fine.

Christian found the experience difficult. He winced when the protestors used more extreme language, such as calling to defund the police or labeling all cops bastards. They were being so unreasonable. Didn't they know no sane person would join them if they were saying all of this? It was a path toward failure.

Nonetheless, he found it cathartic to be out and about surrounded by hundreds of people. It was freeing, and the music was good. It was like being in a wave of humanity with all these other protestors and police officers. The chanting was fun once he set aside that he didn't believe in any of it. It was like acting on a massive stage. He got lost in one chant after the next, waiting for his turn in the order. "No Justice. No Peace. No Justice. No Peace. No Justice," the chant died down.

People were shouting, and not too far away, he heard a whack. He turned and saw that someone had been pushed to the ground by what looked like a police officer. People around him were screaming at the officer, telling them that the person he had shoved was a journalist. Sure enough, there was a man sprawled out on the ground wearing a lanyard with the word journalist on it. An expensive camera lay shattered on the pavement next to him. Christian couldn't quite process the information and simply repeated what he saw.

"That cop pushed a journalist. Oh my god, that was a journalist." Christian looked around to see if anyone else had seen it.

"Pigs, right?" said a fellow protestor.

Christian now realized that he had gotten separated from the rest of *The New Gang*$^{TM}$. His phone was dead, and he had no idea what time it was. It was getting dark. The cops appeared to be pressing forward into the crowd. He saw some officers with helmets and body armor as they pushed through protestors, not letting anyone else through.

"They are kettling," the protestor said, a word Christian didn't understand.

He started looking for a way out, but every direction was cut off by the police, who were holding riot shields and dressed in military-grade armor. A series of canisters whizzed into the crowd. Plums of white smoke soared upwards from the black concrete. Christian started to cough. He stumbled away from the smoke against the only section not blocked off by police—a stretch of closed shops with windows boarded up by plywood. He saw people pushing up against the doors, but they were barred shut.

"Christian," shouted a familiar voice. It was Sebastián. His forehead had a red gash, and his knees were scraped. He had never seen them look more beaten. "Christian, we have to go."

Christian hugged him.

"Ow," Sebastián cried.

"You alright? What happened to you?" Christian asked.

"We darted when the cops came, but I saw you weren't with us, so I came back. I was pushed to the ground. I don't know by who. It happened too fast."

"I love you," said Christian.

There was a pause.

"I love you too," repeated Sebastián, his voice cracking.

The two of them kissed. Christian was terrified; all he wanted to do was be anywhere else. They waited for the police to move closer and closer. Officers started to pluck people out of the crowd and drag them away. Some were handcuffed and moved into the backs of police vehicles. Others were pushed further into the crowd (or worse) if the cops perceived them as moving too close to an ever-moving, imaginary line. Some officers had clubs, beating people with them over the head.

One of the people shoved to the ground was a Black teenager who could not have been any older than 16. He had a shaved head and a look of profound terror on his face. Five or six cops were working to detain him, taking turns snapping his elbows together and dragging his arms behind his back. He started to cry. Two cops pressed his face down into the pavement as they tied his hands together with zip-ties and then dragged him away.

Christian and Sebastián waited for their turn to be handcuffed, but it never came. They were pulled out of the kettle, one by one, and then told by a cop to leave.

"Go home," a cop said sternly.

*You are in the way*, the voice stated.

*That's right*, Christian thought. Christian was. He had prevented the cops from doing their jobs and, worse, created more difficulties for them by making it hard for them to find the real criminals. They had known he wasn't like these other protestors, and now they were asking him to do the one thing he should have done in the first place: leave.

And so the two of them did. They walked quickly away from the scene, past fellow white protestors asking for bail money to get the others out, and then, when far enough away from the scene, darted home. They ran instinctually, taking the routes they had spent months mapping, not stopping until they were outside the doors of Christian's apartment building.

Sebastián's route was faster, after all.

Christian felt relief when he closed his apartment door and something more—a feeling that sunk into the pit of his stomach that he couldn't quite identify.

# CHAPTER 19

## Some Schmuck

*Black Lives Matter. Feelin' Lucky. Sebastián.* He didn't know what to call himself anymore. He felt shell-shocked by his experience with the police. He was afraid and angry at them. Why would they do that? Why would the police just assault innocent bystanders? A journalist and a kid. This brutality didn't make any sense. Why did so many just stand there and watch? Why did he? He felt guilty for leaving that park. He also paradoxically felt ashamed for protesting in the first place, feeling like he wasn't strong enough to do that work.

*I will never call myself an activist ever again,* he thought.

He opened his app and deleted his username. He couldn't call himself *Black Lives Matter* anymore. He didn't know why he thought that name was ever appropriate. He tried to think of what to replace it with, but words escaped him. He wasn't an activist. He certainly wasn't a hero. He was just *Some Schmuck*. Some pathetic Latino Jew from New Jersey who thought he could change the world and realized he didn't fit into it.

Sebastián tried not to talk to Christian about that night because it would always devolve into the same conversation. The same argument. Christian felt validated by his earlier opinion that the protests were unsafe, though he did not examine the source of that unsafety. He instead became more supportive of the police, that idiot, as if the decision to back them up would undo the fear he felt after that night. He talked glowingly of their ability to preserve 'law and order.' He pointed out that the police had a right to defend themselves.

"They were only doing their jobs," Christian would say to Sebastián later that night.

Sebastián was too tired to argue. He thought Christian was ridiculous, yet all he could do was sigh. He let the silence linger as he rested his head on his pillow and drifted off to sleep. He had nightmares of broken glass and officers screaming at him in a demonic, otherworldly tongue. Sebastián dreamt of his head being pushed into the pavement by oversized gophers in dark hoods. Their green-glowing eyes stared into his frightened, squinting ones. Their tiny hands clawed into his skin. He awoke screaming several times in the night to an already alert

Christian. The two of them would hold each other softly and say nothing as they went back to sleep.

He tried to get back to normal. The following weekend, everyone attempted to resume their routines as if nothing had changed. Jon and Emmett came over to Christian's apartment for a quick fuck. Sebastián stripped naked like the rest of them, but after a couple of weak kisses, he couldn't bring himself to engage. He decided to opt-out, indifferently watching everyone next to him on the bed as they kissed and moaned in pleasure.

His fear fell into benign indifference. His gaze settled on the floor, where he noticed a crack running along several tiles. He hopped off the bed, well, fell really on account of being very unobservant, and he reached out to touch the crack, slowly feeling his way across its jagged outline. He rubbed his fingers across it in a wide-ranging manner and thought again of the gophers clawing into his skin.

"I think I heard that boy's skull crack," he said absentmindedly as he caressed the crack from the floor, the words pushing out of him.

"You say something?" Christian moaned, too busy being fucked above him.

"No, nothing," he said. Sebastián stood up. "Nothing at all."

After everyone finished, they cleaned up. They packed up all the empty glasses and condom wrappers in trash bags and started putting their clothes back on. Sebastián picked up his towel, which he had forgotten in the bathroom, and wrapped it around his waist. As he walked back into the living room, he saw that *The New Gang*$^{TM}$ was splitting a joint. Emmett handed him the non-burnt end, and they talked about the dumb things you do when high.

"Do you think that crack was a sign?" Sebastián asked.

"What are you on about?" Jon chuckled.

Sebastián tried to explain, but his words made no sense. He broke out into laughter. "I'm not even sure what I'm laughing about," he told them.

Soon, they were all laughing at nothing, interspersing their cackling with random non-sequiturs. It took a while for Sebastián to adjust to the flow of this conversation, as he constantly found himself spacing out. He realized that someone had been trying to have a conversation with him that he had missed entirely.

"What?" he asked.

"I said we are going to another protest tonight to stick it to the cops if you want to come?" Jon asked eagerly.

"I think we'll sit this one out," Christian replied for both of them.

Sebastián wanted to say something to defend himself. He tried to apologize for being a coward, yet when he opened his mouth, nothing came out except for a vague 'ah' that trailed off into nothingness.

"Understandable," said Emmett to Christian. "You got a taste of what Black people deal with constantly. Rest up. Just don't stay out too long. And text us if you need anything." He said, placing a peck on both Christian and Sebastián's lips before heading out the door. Christian and Sebastián lingered for a moment after he had gone, staring at each other with uncomfortable, hungry looks.

As the weeks passed, Sebastián opted out of going to protests altogether. He was afraid, and he rationalized that fear with an increasing nihilism. "*None of the activities I have engaged in have made any difference,*" Sebastián would tell himself angrily inside his head. The representatives he had written to had responded with generic form letters. The local initiatives he had pushed for had all failed to pass. His boss had responded to his 1,000-word email calling for more diversity initiatives with one word: "NO."

He had worked so hard, and nothing had happened. It all seemed so pointless and, worse than that, draining. Activism involved a lot more logistical work than he first thought. The paperwork and hours of legwork were all arduous, and in the end, he felt utterly useless and dispirited. He hadn't been able to make a real difference after all. This experience had left him bored and hollow. He thought that if someone opened his body up right now, they would find nothing but a black, cavernous shell.

Sebastián needed to get out of this apartment: to get out of his head, and stop thinking about how he was a failure. He started to Google parties happening in his local area. There was a lot more going on than he first thought. The posters for the parties all had hunky muscle men in tight underwear doing cool or sexy poses. The signs had themes like 'After Dark' and 'Masks Off.' The locations were all listed as TBD or 'Text for more details.' These were largely underground events. He looked at some of the Facebook event pages for the parties, but they were all dead, and the same for their Instagram and Twitter profiles.

There was only a phone number posted several comments down in a months old post. *If* he wanted to go to a party, he would have to contact someone directly. The thought of calling someone instantly triggered his anxiety. What if this was something he wasn't cool enough to do? What if he didn't know the right people? What if this were a trap from the cops? He decided to text the organizers instead of calling them, and to his relief, this was all he needed to do. It took only several texts and a Venmo payment to get the address. The organizer sent this information three hours before the event, most likely to reduce the chance of it getting raided. They were happy to charge an extra $100 for that privilege.

He spent 15 minutes staring at the rusted-over metal doors where the party was taking place. He felt like Sandra Bullock on a stakeout in *Miss Congeniality.* The building looked like it had endured a good decade of wear and tear. The doors were attached to an old warehouse, the thumping music from inside clearly audible from where Sebastián stood. He looked around the neighborhood. It was a run-down industrial area, with some buildings crumbling and a few boarded up.

Well-dressed gay men approached the door. They looked to be in their 20s or 30s. Some of them had Latino names, but they were mainly white. Most of them gave off a clean, wholesome vibe. They looked like they were auditioning for a weird combination of a reality dating show and a gym membership commercial. Some looked like they might be drunk already, while others were so giddy they might have been high. But they were all filled with an almost childlike excitement.

A bouncer dressed in a black suit and tie checked people's tickets on their phones. Sebastián walked up to him. He looked to be in his late thirties or early forties. He was a little on the tall side and bald. The bouncer looked him up and down, taking in the sight of his pink polo shirt and recently shaven beard, and then gestured for him to go inside. Sebastián took a deep breath and followed.

There were so many people packed in there. It was dark inside and musty, but the walls and ceilings were covered in swirling colored lights. The music was loud, and a large crowd gathered around the center of a giant, wooden dance floor. Sebastián entered the fray and pushed through until he found a spot in the middle of the action. He danced his heart out as people made out, and clothes were ripped off and tossed indiscriminately on the floor. He navigated around the room, snagging free drinks off random people and winking at pretty guys as he went.

At some point, the music cut off to the sound of groans. A man named Frank Miller boomed over the speakers. He was the event organizer who owned several gay bars downtown. His voice sounded hoarse and old. He was breathless. "Thank you so much for coming. It's been a long couple of months," he paused here for the laughter that inevitably followed. "I'm so happy to see our community coming back together again. There has been much hatred toward our community these past few years. Republican Senators being homophobic. Hate mobs trying to attack men, trying to attack what gender even means."

There were shouts of shame at these fictitious straw men. Sebastián joined in.

"We survived those attacks, and we've come back strong," said Frank Miller. "We are here to tell the world that homophobia and hate are not welcome in our neighborhood!" The crowd cheered. "Thank you for coming, and enjoy."

Sebastián drank more and more and a few drinks more still. He felt the world spinning around him and liked it that way.

"Sebastián," called out a friendly voice.

In front of him was a hunky man in his late thirties. He had short hair, plenty of muscles, and nothing on but a shimmering golden jockstrap. He had known this person for years. It was Barry. His best friend. A man that he hadn't spoken to in months.

"Barry, omg, I miss you bitchhhhhh," Sebastián slurred, hugging him. "Where have you been?"

"Where haven't I been?" he laughed. "What's this I've been hearing about you dating some man?"

"Christian, yeah, it's sort of new?"

"You met during coronavirus? Scandalous," Barry gasped. "Okay, so now we definitely need to talk."

A man half his age grabbed Barry's ass. Barry gave the man a kissing motion and turned back to face Sebastián.

"Listen, I'd love to catch up, but I have some business to attend to," he said, gesturing over to the twink. "I'm free tomorrow. Let's do lunch."

"Let's do brunch," Sebastián added excitedly.

"Omg, yes bitch. We will do brunch. Tomorrow."

"Tomorrow."

"Okay, I got to go." The young 20-something Barry was hanging out with grabbed his hand and escorted him to the stairs.

Sebastián then sat down for a breather, flirting with anyone he could get his hands on. There, indeed, were many options to choose from, all their maskless faces beaming back at him. He left the party at 2 am, doing exactly what you would expect him to do. He brought a stranger back home with him, a fit man with a snake tattoo whose username was *Bye Felicia*, though Sebastián would later learn was named Ronald.

"Perfect," he thought.

When the two of them reached what Sebastián thought was his front door, he realized too late that he was at Christian's place. He had been so used to going there every night that he had walked there half-drunk on autopilot with a fling.

# Chapter 20

*Christian*

Christian opened the door and immediately knew that Sebastián and whoever he was with were drunk, and he was furious, but he remained calm. This was not the time to make a scene. He considered an outright confrontation in front of a stranger rude, and if there was one virtue that had been drilled into him above all else, it was politeness. He held the door open and stifled a sigh of frustration, gathering every ounce of willpower to force a smile.

"Um, who is this?" he asked, not needing an answer. He knew exactly who this fuckboy was. He was a flirtatious twink who couldn't handle his liquor, whom Sebastián had selected over Christian for some reason. He understood things hadn't been great between them these past few weeks but had they devolved into this? To having sex outside the bubble? To cheating? To openly flaunting their problems with a stranger?

*Does he even like you anymore?* The voice mocked. *Now that he doesn't have to be trapped with you?*

Christian's cheeks flushed red as he tried not to cry. He felt ill as his belly knotted. If he were not sober, he'd think he was about to hurl from a hangover. This was it, was't it? The beginning of the end. The moment their relationship would splinter into nothing more than a drunken night of sex followed by drunken assholery in the morning.

"Do you want to have sex with us?" Sebastián asked, not trying to obscure what was happening now that he was already in so deep.

Christian wanted to say "no." To say, "Please don't do this. We can fix this." He should have. He should have at least told Sebastián to go fuck himself. He was so angry with him, yet he wasn't at the same time. He was relieved that they didn't have to deal with the pretense of masks and death numbers. He had long since stopped caring about Covid. No one at the base took it seriously anymore.

"The media is brainwashing the public on this thing," the Admiral had remarked as an aside at a recent meeting, regurgitating a Facebook post he had shared to the family's Whatsapp group earlier that morning. "The virus isn't that lethal. It's manageable, and the base might be switching back to a full work week soon."

As Christian thought about it, he was a little relieved that Sebastián seemed to be changing his position on

Covid. It made their relationship feel like it might not fall apart if they could somehow move past tonight's stupidity. 'If' tonight didn't explode in their faces. But having sex right now was still an idiotic idea. Things weren't that great between them, and he wished Sebastián hadn't put him in this position at 2:30 in the fucking morning.

They shouldn't have sex.

And yet, he wanted to get fucked. He could feel his cock twitch in his pants. The blood rushed to his groin at the thought of being fucked by Sebastián and this stranger. "No, no," Christian tried to say, but the words escaped him. Sebastián looked down at him to observe the obvious tenting in his pants.

He laughed, still looking down at Christian's sweatpants. "Oh, you really want this, don't you slut? This is going to be so much fun," he promised.

Christian's eyes flared in anger, but then his cock twitched twice as hard. "Fuck it," Christian said.

He let the two of them inside. He buried his annoyance over Sebastián's betrayal, weirdly happy that he had brought the hookup here rather than hiding his indiscretion, and then decided to make the most of it. He could make this work. Stronger relationships had been built on worse. They had been having sex with other people in the bubble. Was this any different? Christian downed several shots of whiskey at the minibar to feel less awkward about being the only sober one in the room and then took off his shirt.

"What's your name?" Christian asked the mystery man.

"Ronald," the man slurred.

Christian looked the skinny twink up and down. His white skin was smooth and taut with muscle. He was broad and sinewy. The man's most attractive feature were his piercing green eyes, which he directed right at Christian, not looking away, even as he stumbled and couldn't speak straight.

"Are you, like, alright to do this, Ronald?"

"You betcha."

As Ronald said this, he tripped, hitting his foot on the leg of the couch. He yelled, "Ouch," hopping around for a moment before setting his leg back down.

"I think I'm bleeding," Ronald said, staring at the blood dripping down from his leg onto the carpet.

"Shit, this is a nice rug," Christian yelled. He lifted Ronald into the air and placed him down several feet away from the carpet. "Can you get a napkin and like a rug cleaner?" He asked Sebastián, an edge of annoyance in his voice. Of course, this is what happened when he let his guard down for one fucking minute.

"On it." Sebastián moved into the next room, undoubtedly trying to remember where the cleaning supplies were while drunk—that idiot.

"I feel a little woozy. I think I might lie down," Ronald said. He then plopped back onto the couch, immediately passing out.

Christian tried to move him again. "Jesus, he's heavy. A little help?"

Sebastián came back from the other room holding a plunger and some Windex. Christian cursed himself for sending the drunk person to get the supplies. Sebastián set the supplies down and helped him move Ronald to the floor. They hastily put a bandaid on Ronald's cut and tossed a blanket over him.

A tense twenty minutes of frantic cleaning followed as they tried to get the blood out of the carpet. Christian was icy silent as they cleaned, only to communicate critiques of how Sebastián was cleaning. He would not give him any camaraderie at this moment. He would periodically scoff and sigh whenever he looked in Sebastián's direction. They were mostly successful at cleaning, though a small brown dot remained on the couch.

"I'd like to talk about this," Christian said when they finished. He yawned, "But I'm tired. Let's go to bed."

And so, they did. Sebastián fell asleep immediately. He coughed and reeked of cheap booze, saliva dripping onto the pillow they shared. He woke up only once to make Christian promise that they would hang out with his friend Barry tomorrow.

"Promise me," Sebastián slurred loudly, half asleep. "Promise me we will not MISS BRUNCH WITH BARRY."

"I promise, okay."

But Sebastián didn't hear him. He was already asleep. His drunken ass snored so loudly Christian had to turn him over. For this reason, Christian found it more challenging to go to bed. He tossed and turned all throughout the night. His anxiety rippled through his body, shooting out the tips of his toes, which caused them to jerk. He did not shut his eyes until the sun rose. The sound of birds clawed at his senses, making going to sleep a desperate effort.

"I think that this was a stupid idea," he murmured sleepily.

Christian didn't know when he had fallen asleep, but he must have because he woke up in the early afternoon, still tired. Ronald was gone. Sebastián was asleep. He figured he should skip brunch plans with Barry. He didn't even know who the man was, but Barry had somehow found him on Grindr—his handle was *Hung AF*.

**Hung AF (Barry)**

Hey, Im Barry. Sebastián's friend. I don't think we've met, but Sebastián and I made brunch plans today, and I figured his drunk ass wasn't up yet, so I'm pinging you. Sorry for the stalker vibes.

**Christian**

No problem. Nice to meet you. Sorry I don't think that is going to happen. He's out cold.

**Hung AF (Barry)**

boooooo.

**Hung AF (Barry)**

Well, we were going to talk about you anyway. Come. I'd love to meet my bestie's new beau.

**Christian**

Sure, why not.

Christian couldn't get his partner to wake up. He poked and prodded at him to no avail, so he met Barry alone at *The Silver Spoon* for a quick coffee. They sat around one of the tiny tables in the outside patio area. The bare wooden chairs were old and slippery, and Christian could not use the high bar stools for fear of slipping. It had just rained, and all the surfaces were wet, but it couldn't be helped. Restaurants were allowed to have patrons again as long as they were outside and spaced six feet apart, and this was the best that could be done.

Barry was in his late 30s. He was a gym bunny with his hair dyed blond, meant to conceal several gray hairs he joked openly about 'refusing to admit to himself.' He seemed uncomfortable in his mask, having to constantly readjust it when it slipped past his nose. He had glasses, which looked more suited to some porn star attempting to be a librarian. Barry had a mostly clean-shaven face, though he did have some unruly dark stubble along his cheeks. He wore tight black pants and a bright white button-up shirt. His shoes were pristine, as was his watch.

The two of them chatted about life, which was awkward because they didn't know each other. Christian apologized for Sebastián's absence, and Barry took it in stride, acting like he was interested in learning about Christian all along—some stranger he had only just met.

*This man could make dung beetles feel important*, the voice barked. *Get a hold of yourself.*

But it didn't feel like Barry was humoring him. He was interested in many of the same things Christian was, like Marvel movies and video games. It was strange to talk with someone you had only known for a few hours and feel like you were already good friends. Barry laid his life bare on the table, revealing every little detail: the men he had slept with, how he had gotten into bread making and yoga. He mentioned several parties he had gone to recently. Barry was even planning a romp to the Bahamas with an actor friend, and Christian realized that maybe nothing had changed for him during this pandemic after all.

"There is another party this weekend. You should come," Barry encouraged.

"That sounds wonderful. Will it be safe?" He asked this question reflexively, even though he realized he didn't give two fucks about 'alleged' safety.

"No safer than this," Barry countered, gesturing to the surrounding tables.

"Good to know. I'll think about it," Christian responded.

He didn't quite think Barry's reasoning was valid, but at the same time, he didn't care. This whole Covid nonsense was overblown anyway, and the idea of mingling with a crowd of ripped gay men like his partner had undoubtedly done last night sounded like the perfect decision to him. Why should everyone else get to have fun but him?

The next few days were rigorously devoted to debating whether *The New Gang*<sup>TM</sup> should attend this party.

**No Justice! No Peace! (Emmett)**

Absolutely not. This is precisely what we dropped James for.

**Dismantle white Supremacy (Jon)**

well, that and the lying.

Christian

if everyone at the party is masked.
How's it different from the protests?

No Justice! No Peace! (Emmett)

cuz the protests matter more
than some new dick

Dismantle white
Supremacy (Jon)

Some Schmuck (Sebastián)

well I think the same logic applies. If
people wear masks, then it shouldn't
matter. I say we go.

While this conversation was heating up, Sebastián sent Christian a direct message to chat about his indiscretion.

Some Schmuck (Sebastián)

I'm fine going, but we still have to talk about
last night. And maybe tell the others???

Christian

Do we have to? You got drunk and
slipped up. I forgive you. Why worry
the others about a spat between us?

Some Schmuck (Sebastián)

I guess. I was being dumb last night. But we
still need to have a conversation. And, like,
be responsible and stuff.

Christian

Do we tho? Let's just have some fun,
& not worry about it.

### Some Schmuck (Sebastián)

okay, if you're sure

**Christian**

it'll be our little secret ☺

They then switched back to the group message.

**Christian**

I vote yes too.

Only Emmett voted no, and he reluctantly came anyway because, Christian assumed, he did not want to be left out. *Everyone had principles until they had to do something about it*, he thought to himself.

The party was in a large rowhouse on top of a hill in the heart of a Hispanic neighborhood that was rapidly being pushed to the suburbs. It overlooked a gigantic park built at the turn of the eighteenth century by the wife of a diplomat who had wanted America to rival the sophistication of their European counterparts. The park may not have lived up to the grandeur of Old Europe, but it was home to some of the city's most important and beautiful houses.

They ended up in the backyard patio of the house. It was walled in with brilliant red terracotta tiles. The couple who owned it were white power gays who worked for Deloitte. They had been inspired by the Dorne scenes from *Game of Thrones*. The doors and windows were painted a pure white, with golden frames around the opening. Each wall held either a mural of an old white man's face or a vertical display of various florals. It looked like a scene out of a movie, which seemed appropriate, considering the money that must have been used to renovate it to its current state.

Sebastián appeared to be in love with it all. "It's simply perfect," he said.

Several people were playing beer pong underneath the transparent roof of the patio. One of the balls flew into the cup, and a man pulled off his mask to take a sip. He did not put it back on.

Emmett saw this and pulled Christian aside. "We need to go," he stated, tilting his head toward the maskless person.

"Come on," Christian responded. "We are outside."

Emmett scoffed at this, but it appeared to shut him up.

"Hey, sexy. I didn't know you would be here. How are you?" It was Ronald, their failed hookup. He was wearing the same ripped tee from yesterday and oblivious to the fact that Christian and Emmett were fighting.

"Who's this?" Emmett asked.

"Oh, we hooked up last night," Ronald slurred. "At least, I think we did."

"Seriously?" Emmett said, annoyed.

"Hey, don't slut shame," Ronald shot back.

Emmett gave Christian a look transcending anger and annoyance and read merely as unadulterated disappointment. "Fine, whatever," He said curtly, walking off.

He left the group chat seconds later. *The New Gang*$^{TM}$ was no more.

# CHAPTER 21



Every headline Sebastián skimmed told him that Trump would win again. Every time there was a ping on his phone, it filled him with a sense of dread. Ping! An update on how the post office was being tampered with by Poster Master General Louis DeJoy. Ping! Republican legislatures were passing ID laws and other voter restrictions. Ping! An article was profiling why a former Hillary voter would vote for Trump. Ping! Trump Latino voters in Florida were surging. Ping! Ping! Ping!

It also didn't help that Elena was trying to get him to commit to seeing his family in New Jersey for Thanksgiving, Christmas, or both, which he did not want to do. He was already excited at the possibility of going to Christian's cabin for the holidays, dining on caviar and champagne.

"My kids picked out you and Christian stocking stuffers," she guilted.

Sebastián replied with a Santa Claus emoji, wanting to not think about seeing his family during the holidays. The idea of bringing Christian back to his abuela's cheap house for Christmas made him shudder.

He would try to bury these feelings with last-minute donations to the Biden-Harris campaign. $5 here. $20 there. It became something he would do drunk while taking a break from the dance floor of an underground house party or club. He had never donated before and took an almost visceral pleasure in receiving a 'Thank you for your donation' email. It made him feel important, like he was doing something. He even changed his username to *Just Vote* with the hope that it would reach someone, anyone.

"Do you have those drinks yet?" shouted Jon, who was now going by the username *Bite me*. He had come over to check in on Sebastián at the bar. The music was thumping loudly from the club speakers, forcing them to shout into each other's ears. Jon was wearing cat ears with painted-on whiskers as a last-minute Halloween costume. It was a gimmick the entire group was doing. Sebastián and Christian had gone as puppies with cheap plastic dog ears and leather collars.

"Almost," replied Sebastián.

Jon looked down at Sebastián's phone. "Are you on Grindr?"

"No, ActBlue," Sebastián replied, showing the donation portal on his phone.

"Are you still subscribing to the fallacy of the two-party system?" Jon scoffed.

He had recently become enamored with the Green Party, whose memes he was sharing constantly on Facebook and Instagram. The entire group had fractured politically. Christian had secretly confessed to wanting to submit a ballot for Jo Jorgensen, the Libertarian candidate. Jon said he was voting for Green Party contender Howie Hawkins. Only Sebastián and Emmett planned to vote for Biden, though they hadn't talked since the house party in September. He only knew this by creeping on Emmett's Facebook page.

"Yup, you caught me. A big ole Democrat." he joked.

Jon tugged on Sebastián's collar and planted a wet kiss on his cheek. "Bad puppy," he said in a sultry whisper. He then slapped Sebastián's ass and gestured to the dance floor. "Come on, let's get back in there. They're playing *Thriller* again!"

Sebastián's phone vibrated. He glanced at it, dreading another terrible headline. It was a message from Emmett in the group chat.

**No Justice! No Peace! (Emmett)**

Really????

**No Justice! No Peace! (Emmett)**

I can't believe you went to another party.

**No Justice! No Peace! (Emmett)**

They are not even wearing masks.

"How did he… " Sebastián stopped himself as he saw Jon take a selfie and post it to Instagram.

"Valencia just works for me," Jon said out loud about his Instagram filter, humming to the tune of *Thriller* as he edited the photo, spilling his glass of water onto the floor.

**No Justice! No Peace! (Emmett)**

Y'all know that Christian and Sebastián are fucking around with others, right?

Sebástián did not try to explain away Emmett's comment. There was no point. Jon and Barry didn't care that he and Christian were fucking others outside the bubble: they all were now. Emmett was just being petty at this point, and Sebastián didn't see the point in engaging with him.

Sebastián slipped his phone into his pocket and joined the dance floor with drinks in hand. The club had gone all in for this Halloween weekend. Cobwebs and fake Styrofoam tombstones hung from the ceiling, shrouded in blue strobe lights and mist. Blow-up spiders and white and black penises were scattered everywhere, tossed around by the dancing crowd. The loud thumping music meant there was no real opportunity to talk, only dancing and grinding up against strangers and friends alike.

Some people wore masks. Technically, it was something everyone was supposed to do. The signage on the walls read "Mask Must Be Worn At All Times" in big red letters, but in reality, it wasn't a practice being enforced. Many were maskless and making out with their peers on the dance floor. It was a super spreader event in more ways than one.

This was another Frank Miller party—a real estate magnate who apparently owned most of the gay bars in the city. Miller was a major donor to the national Democratic Party and was frequently pictured around town at the various gay nightclubs and bars he owned. He had made another one of his grand speeches about protecting the gay community and maleness from attacks. He was becoming quite the fixture; some even joked about him running for office.

"Kamala and Miller. 2024," one twink shouted from the crowd.

Everyone laughed.

They stayed there for another hour before heading back to Christian's apartment. Barry joined them. He had gone to the party in full drag as Cruella DeVille, holding leashes attached to Christian and Sebastián's collars. They remained on, even as they lay on the couch, chatting about the night.

"Emmett is being so petty," Jon growled. "We all voted on this. You can't complain just because you were outvoted."

"I thought you didn't believe in voting," Barry joked.

Jon rolled his eyes. "Bite me," he retorted.

"He's so angry all the time," interjected Christian, moving the subject back to Emmett. "I get that he has a lot going on. We all do, but why is he so angry?"

"Forget about that square, darling," Barry stated in his best Cruella DeVille impression, which was admittedly very good. "Why worry about that downer when you can go to the beach?" Barry elegantly revealed five tickets from inside his fur coat. He started fanning himself with them, presumably waiting to play this reveal all night.

"You got them?" Sebastián asked in disbelief.

"Of course, darling," Barry said dramatically. "Everything was confirmed this afternoon. We will have to take two plane transfers and a boat ride to avoid certain regulations, but we are headed to the Bahamas to party with an actor friend I know."

"Shut up," said Jon excitedly.

"I believe that's what you'll be doing soon enough, little kitty cat, but first," he said, tugging Sebastián's collar. "I believe that someone has been a naughty dog."

Sex came very quickly after that. The bubble fucked raw. Sebastián was happy at this because Christian had never been a fan of barebacking. He contemplated checking in with everyone about this sudden development but decided not to press it. He really wanted to go to that secluded island. Sebastián wanted to have the life Barry and Christian were born into and not just be a passenger forever hearing their stories. He figured that being a busybody would not make him popular with the group, so he held his tongue.

He thought of the ocean as he entered Barry—the waves crashing against the shore. People on boats and jet skis riding on the blue water. Giant dolphins swimming above the surface. He pictured himself laid out on a towel, looking out into the sea like in a movie, and his anxiety lessened. He wanted this.

Barry seemed to be having the time of his life. "Yes, darling," he said, breathing heavily as he came.

Sebastián spasmed as he released into Barry several seconds later.

Next to him, Christian was bottoming for Jon. Sebastián reached his hand out to hold Christian's. The two touched weakly, Jon and Barry's bodies preventing them from fully clasping each other's hands. *It's going to be okay*, Sebastián thought. *Everything is going to be okay.*

The next day was a frantic scramble to arrange all their logistics. Christian's apartment became the headquarters for the group to coordinate travel time. Christian had to request time off from the base last minute, promising to cover someone's double shift the following week. From what Sebastián could tell, this was more of a formality, as his boss did not seem to care. On his end, things were a tad harder. Sebastián had surprisingly managed to book the time off, but he still had to take one conference call while there, which no one else in the group would have to do. Jon was already transitioning out of his internship, one he had only received because he was blowing the communications director of a nonprofit. He talked incessantly about how he would have to apply for jobs soon. And Barry, well, Sebastián was still unsure what he did for work.

These plans were all made naked, which prompted Jon and Christian to almost fuck again.

"We don't have time, you naughty dogs," Barry said, lightly smacking them over the head with a rolled-up newspaper. "Our flight's in less than two hours."

"Ugh, Rick somehow learned about the trip," Barry said, looking up from his phone. "I was trying to keep it a secret from him."

"Well, we don't have an extra slot, right? So tell him that," chimed in Christian.

"Like technically, we do have a slot, but do we want 'Rick the Lame' to drag us down?"

"Nah," Sebastián replied.

They crammed everything into two oversized suitcases split among the four of them. They chaotically threw in a pile of underwear, socks, and of course, iPhone chargers. Jon had no extra clothes at Christian's apartment, but they all promised he could borrow some of theirs.

"Besides," quipped Barry. "You being naked wouldn't be the worst thing in the world."

They grabbed a redeye down to Chicago and then Miami. Miami! Sebastián felt like Carmen Sandiego with all this travel. They landed at Miami International Airport, and Sebastián was immediately in awe of the tropical climate. He loved how the palm trees swayed in the wind, reminding him of every picture he had seen of the tropics. There was even an iguana sunbathing on top of one of the airport signs—a creature that Sebastián had never seen in person before. It was big with vibrant grass-green scales. It simply sat there, perfectly still as they walked by, as if everything were normal, which, of course, it was.

Sebastián had to dial back his excitement, as no one else seemed particularly fascinated with the wildlife or vista. They hailed a taxi to the Miami harbor. Their route took them through the 836 highway—a concrete river sandwiched on either side by houses and lush green trees. There was a fun, chaotic energy to the bustling industrial area that Sebastián felt he could quickly get used to.

"I think Miami is the only city I've seen that seems alive," Sebastián said in awe.

Christian, in contrast, was not impressed. "Miami reminds me of everywhere else I've been," he said, his voice a monotone. "It's a concrete desert, plus a couple of palm trees."

Sebastián could see skyscrapers all around them, which eventually gave way to a thin strip of land surrounded on both sides by the brilliant blue waters of the bay. The wide roads disappeared into the water, with little fishing boats gliding lazily by. The pristine blue was contrasted with colorful splashes of life – sunbathers, mothers feeding their children, joggers, motorcycles, and even tropical birds that Sebastián had never seen. He thought it was a beautiful landscape, and he tried to imagine how he would spend his days there. He had never traveled this far South before.

They almost missed their boat ride. They rushed onto the deck of the ferry three minutes before it departed. It was crowded. There were no more seats outside looking out into the water, so they had to settle for inside on a cramped bench on the second level by the bathroom. Most of the tourists were headed to other places in the Bahamas. The bubble's stop was technically not an official destination, but Barry had pulled a favor with the gay couple who owned the ferry company. It took three and a half hours to finally reach their destination, spent awkwardly clutching their luggage, trying to stop it from moving too much with the crashing waves.

When they landed on the island, shirtless men were everywhere, primarily engaged in drinking, light foreplay, or often both. Before Sebastián knew what was happening, he was herded underneath a roof made of dried palm tree leaves with the rest of the half-naked men. The Hollywood actor they were all there to party with had just arrived via a private ferry. They were all going to take a picture.

Exhausted, Sebastián smiled meekly beside a group of men he barely knew.

"Say cheese," said one of the native tour guides.

"Cheese," they all said in unison.

A stranger next to him squeezed his ass and called him cute. They started kissing shortly after that. It was perfect, a dream come true.

# CHAPTER

## 22



"The island life," as Christian called it, suited him well. He loved strolling along the water's edge with nothing but a jockstrap and a hefty amount of water-proof sunscreen lotion.

Low tide was his favorite time of the day. He watched the water recede, revealing sandy ripples that stretched out into the distance. Christian's feet would sink into the mushy sand. He took a visceral pleasure in lifting them in and out of the muck. Large hermit crabs would flee from his feet, scurrying towards the retreating tide. They were an army of brilliant shells scuttling back into the water.

It reminded him of summers in Connecticut. His grandfather had lived on the banks of Compo Beach, and the two spent summers kayaking along the shoreline. These were the summer days he looked forward to most as a child. His grandfather would instruct him on how to navigate the waves. It was Samuel's way of passing on his skills to Christian, but it was also a test of will against nature itself.

"If you can keep the kayak afloat for a couple of hours without going under, you are a capable navigator," his grandfather would say. "It's a test of our manhood."

Christian had never had a day pass where he didn't feel tested. Even now, he was still proving himself. Not only to be the sole administrator of his trust, but to prove that he wasn't an embarrassment to the family, that being gay was more than a liability.

He made his way down the beach, with the tide creeping ever further into the jungle. The beach was a long way from Connecticut, and the people here were nothing like the posh socialites of Westport that he was supposed to end up with. He would bump into the actor's entourage everywhere on the tiny island, and they were engaged in the sort of hedonistic pleasures his grandfather would scoff at—pleasures he had avoided 'openly' to stay in that man's good graces.

He came across a group of models making out. All of them were ripped with well-defined abs and pale, flawless skin. He envied their ability to breeze through the sexual maelstrom with nary a moment of pause or doubt.

*Do you really deserve to be here*, the voice whispered.

"I've earned this," he reassured himself, returning his gaze to the waves he had once conquered before returning to the mound of men.

He gave one of them a look—a blond dude, already naked, whose body glistened in the sun—and that was all it took to pull Christian towards him. His feet moved forward as if enchanted. He dropped his jockstrap to the ground and began stroking himself. He was going to fuck the blond, or more accurately, he would be fucked by him.

They kissed— a deep kiss from someone who knew what they were doing. The blond grabbed Christian's hand and positioned him standing doggy style over a towel. The beach's white sands caked his toes and the palms of his hands as the blond gyrated his hips and ground his pelvis against Christian's hole.

"You're fucking hot," the blond said to him.

"Fuck," Christian shouted in relief. "You too."

A model found him hot. He was being fucked by a model on a beach in the Bahamas. It didn't feel real. This man was built like a Greek God; his body was chiseled as if from stone. His muscles were taut, and his skin glistened with moisture from the ocean. The type of face slapped on posters, streamed in adverts, and fucking other flawless people in porn. A model thought he was pretty, and Christian thought that maybe he was doing things right; that he wasn't an embarassment.

*He's probably high, sweetie,* said the voice.

But Christian ignored it, blood rushing in his ears from excitement.

Other models arrived. They spread out around the towel and started unbuttoning their tops. Christian decided that he would conquer them all like the waves of his youth. One of the models next to him said something in French. He didn't understand the words, but within moments the French man shoved his dick inside Christian's throat.

*Ah, that was what he meant*, Christian thought.

There were so many people around them kissing and fucking, that it took him a moment to realize that his partner, Sebastián was there too. He was being fucked by a man Christian recognized, the actor, the reason why they were all there. The actor's dick was deep inside Sebastián's throat. His partner's eyes went almost completely blank as he concentrated on the actor's thrusts. His face was red, and tears dripped from his eyes. Christian thought they were the results of gagging on the actor's dick, but from a certain angle, it looked like Sebastián was crying.

It must be a really big dick.

# Chapter 23

## Eager Slut

Sebastián realized rather quickly that the models on the island didn't give a fuck about voting. He didn't think his Grindr handle would matter here because they were on a deserted island after all, but with dozens of gays in such a small area, many not knowing each other very well, it quickly became the default platform for communication. His feed was awash with rippling torsos and stunning smiles, but the few people he reached out to claimed he was too serious, too political.

It made him angry. He spent the first hour on the island alone, staring out into the bay as he tried to ignore the self-loathing. He watched the seagulls and cracked jokes about how the birds represented the gay men around him—always flighty. He wanted to scream at how vapid and stupid these men were being. It wasn't supposed to be like this. Rich people were supposed to be sophisticated and charming, and yet, these were the vainest people he had ever met, and Sebastián's friends weren't exactly competing in decathlons.

More than anything, though, he wanted to get fucked, and he was angry at himself for wanting it. He wanted to bend a chiseled model over and plow his hole. So he swallowed his pride and changed his name to *Eager Slut*, the most straight-to-the-point handle he could think of. It worked perfectly. Like a well-made net, it immediately brought in catches. Men sent him message after message.

**The 1 tru dong**

hey there, sexy cute pic.

**Eager Slut (Sebastián)**

right back at you.

**The 1 tru dong**

a few of us are meeting on the west end beach. You should cum :).

**Eager Slut (Sebastián)**

I'll see you there.

Sebastián was on the east end of the beach. He wasn't sure how far away the west end was from him, but knowing how quickly things could develop, his instinct told him to run. His feet sank into the wet muck as he jogged along the sands. It was hot. The sun had burnt through the cloud cover, and took the breeze with it. Beads of sweat formed on his forehead as he pushed forward. His face was beet red. His breaths were sharp and hard as he went, but he didn't care. He didn't care about anything but getting that sweet release.

When he finally got to the west side beach, he looked around at the crowd there. All those hot, shirtless guys in the midst of fornicating. How lucky can a man get? It was perfect. It was so much sexier than any porn he had ever seen. He was twitching with anticipation as he decided what to do. There were so many possibilities. He could just get in line and watch them all fuck each other or walk up to a random guy and take him to one of the canopies. He considered both possibilities, but the idea of approaching a random stranger he hadn't even talked to made him nervous. He opened up Grindr and saw that **The 1 tru dong** had messaged him.

### The 1 tru dong

I'm with the group

Sebastián looked over and saw a hunky model staring over in his direction. The man's muscles were rippling in the sunlight. His body was awash with a swirl of black ink. Sebastián walked over to him, smiling, and lowered to his knees so that he could blow him. His feet sunk slightly in the wet sand, firmly rooted there as the model had his way with his mouth. The pressure was intense. The man shoved about 7 inches all in. Sebastián briefly withdrew his mouth from the shaft to breathe.

He hadn't noticed until now that others had surrounded him. Multiple men were hitting his face with their dicks. Many more were watching from the side, jerking off. How had he so quickly become the center of attention? Someone lifted him into the air and rubbed his dick against Sebastián's hole. Sebastián felt himself immediately tensing up. He had wanted to have sex, yes, but this was too much.

"Take him into the water," someone said. "Like in one of your films."

Sebastián suddenly realized that they were talking to the actor who was the reason they all were there. He had been too overwhelmed to notice him until then. The actor had a toned body, wavy black hair, and long lashes that melted into his face. His eyes were a deep brown. His body was lean and beautiful. Sebastián had just watched one of his movies the other day, the one where he performed his own stunts as a rescue pilot in California. His character was funny and confident, with plenty of one-liners.

Now, though, he said nothing. Sebastián felt nervous. He wanted to collect his thoughts for a moment, only a moment. For the actor to ask him if he wanted to make love in a witty piece of dialogue that made his heart flutter. For Sebastián to say yes in an equally entertaining way, and then for the two of them to laugh and for the camera to fade to black. But the question never came, and he couldn't say no. Countless different hands were restricting him: they covered his mouth and held him down. He tried to resist, and the mass of digits held on even tighter.

"No," his muffled voice said.

"Stop."

"Please stop."

But no one heard him, or maybe more accurately, they chose not to. Either way, he stopped fighting. He was just a pathetic, worthless schmuck afterall. The loser the world was supposed to walk over. Sebastián went limp as many hands brought him into the sparkling water. His backside partially submerged as he looked into the actor's stunning blue eyes. He was so pretty and perfect and entered without uttering a word. The actor thrust into him, then moved back and forward. Sebastián could feel the actor's cock pushing against his prostate and was aroused and terrified all at the same time.

Sebastián looked away into the sky and watched the clouds roll by until everything was over. The actor pulled his dick out, not caring to be gentle, and swam away—never speaking to him. The entourage went back to the hut to eat. One of the models asked if he was coming, but Sebastián refused. He wasn't in the mood to socialize. This life was not for him. It had never been.

He sat on the beach, wet and tired, with parts of sand rubbing uncomfortably up against his thighs. Sebastián sat with this irritation for a while, not wanting to move from that spot. Not even the tide eking forward caused him to move. He considered letting the tide take him, for his body to drift to some nameless shore, but the thought of moving anywhere, even a fun place, exhausted him.

Sebastián's boss tried to call him. This was the time when he said he would be available for a meeting, but he didn't take it. His boss would probably be mad at him for some asinine reason, even if he did take the call. Sebastián was a schmuck, after all. So why bother? Why be berated and mistreated by yet another person? He watched as the notifications from his angry boss ticked upwards, immobilized by indifference.

When he finally did rise to his feet, it was nighttime. The insects chirped, and animals croaked all around him. It sounded much like the jungle theme on his Google Home, except deeper and less rhythmic. Animals would rustle in trees, and the ocean breeze behaved far more erratically than the melodic sounds he had grown accustomed to. Sebastián could hear generic pop music blasting nearby. The bright light of a large bonfire could be seen on the beach, radiating an ember orange from miles away. He walked towards it, talking himself into being okay. He could hear the sounds of laughter, and he imagined others making fun of him for being a bad lay, for being weird, for being weak, for being imperfect.

It was not until he was on top of the noise that he realized that these were his friends huddled in an oversized hammock, not concerned about him at all. They were talking about all the men they had slept with on this trip, engaging in light foreplay as they stared at the stars.

"Hey, we thought you were dead," Barry said after realizing it was him standing there in the darkness. "Where have you been?"

"Around," Sebastián replied brusquely. His friends were the last people he had wanted to see.

"Get in here," Christian said, beckoning him to hop into the hammock with them.

Sebastián complied, and all of them had to hold on tightly so as not to fall out when the force of his hopping in caused them to sway back and forth above the sands. Sebastián hugged Christian tightly as he did his best to stay present within that moment, but he was failing miserably. He kept thinking about his last sexual encounter.

It should have been a dream come true, yet this entire experience felt wrong… was wrong.

"They still haven't called the election yet," said Jon, not looking up from his phone.

"Hey, I don't want to hear anything about that election shit," Barry interjected. "Why don't you make those lips useful?"

Jon, who lay on top of Barry's crotch, dropped the subject and started pulling out Barry's cock from his swimsuit.

"I didn't vote," Sebastián admitted guiltily. "I didn't vote, and now Trump might win again." He was crying. His damp tears dripped onto Christian's shoulder.

"Hey, baby. It's going to be okay," reassured Christian.

"I didn't vote either," admitted Barry, unbothered. "This is America. Most people don't vote. Not when they have so much living to do. How about you, Mr. Social Media?" Barry asked Jon. "Did you vote for Howdie Hawkeyes or whatever?"

"Howie Hawkins," Jon corrected.

"Yeah, him," Barry said, annoyed. "You vote for him?"

"No. I forgot." Jon sheepishly admitted.

They laughed and then looked at Christian expectantly. There was a moment of silence.

"Yes," Christian stated simply.

Barry lightly punched Christian in the shoulder. "For who, you ass."

"Jo Jorgensen."

There was a collective groan. "The libertarian," Jon scoffed.

"At least I voted," Christian quipped.

They laughed and laughed, and for the first time in hours, Sebastián felt not so terrible, and then he remembered what had just happened to him. Sebastián once again was sick to his stomach. He bent over, his hands dropping to his knees, and proceeded to hurl onto the sands of the beach.

Everyone assumed he was merely drunk.

# CHAPTER 24

*Christian*

Christian only got several hours of sleep. Sebastián had been a terror that night, screaming and thrashing about in their bed. Only Sebastián would turn literal paradise into a nightmare, Christian mused.

"Wanna talk about it?" Christian asked.

"I'm fine," Sebastián had remarked, clearly lying.

The two of them didn't say much after that, but Sebastián struggled to sleep, so Christian's equilibrium for the night was thrown off. He had grown so accustomed to Sebastián's warm embrace that his absence felt almost painful.

It took them forever that morning to head to the wooden docks to leave the island. There was a gaggle of gays there waiting for the boat. Christian started swapping information with them, particularly those he had slept with. He exchanged Instagram and TikTok handles with other 'It' models and influencers, which prompted their followers to follow him until he had hundreds of more in seconds. He wasn't used to this level of social media usage, but he found it fun all the same. The models all made dozens of short videos and pictures of the moment, bragging about the new friends they had met and, unstated, would most likely never see again.

"Best vacation ever," a model said, beaming into his phone as Christian stood in the background, one degree of separation away from millions.

Christian was sad to be leaving. He had traveled plenty in his life but hadn't gone on a trip like this since before the pandemic. He found that Barry was cheery as always and was already planning another trip: a party they were invited to in Mexico for New Year's Eve.

"Tickets are selling out fast, so you better buy them soon," he ordered.

Jon was ecstatic as well. He had managed to snag a Social Media Manager position from one of the models. The job was back in LA and he was going to stay with the model for a bit more time on the island to 'learn about the job' before heading out.

"I guess I'm moving," he told Christian, hugging him faintly on the docks.

Minus Jon, they boarded the boat. It was crowded, filled with exhausted tourists returning home from packed vacations all over the Bahamas. Christian had bought a small bottle of cheap champagne from the boat's bar, and they toasted to a successful voyage. Sebastián avoided a glass. It didn't seem like he had much drink left in him. Given how much he threw up last night, he must be thoroughly hungover. Christian ignored his partner's sad state, engaging in small talk with Barry instead.

"Life is, like, so random, isn't it?" asked Barry.

"It's like this water. Always changing," Christian mused.

The boat zipped over the water, occasionally hitting a choppy wave, causing the boat to jolt—an action that upset the stomachs of some of the more hungover passengers. Though strangely not Sebastián, who was holding his own on the deck. People were rushing to and from the boat's single bathroom, one person not making it and having to hurl over the side.

"There goes another one," Barry joked.

Two flights later, they landed back in their city at noon, and immediately, something in the airport felt off. People were screaming with joy. One woman was weeping. The crowd in front of them waved, wolf-whistled, clapped, cheered, and laughed.

"He's won," shouted one happy woman.

The televisions hanging everywhere in the airport all said the same thing—Joe Biden had been officially declared President. There was jubilation in the air.

Christian was horrified. He had been following the election. Even if he had preferred Hawkins, he had been certain Trump would win over Biden. How could that deranged man have snagged this unlikely result? It didn't seem possible. He had been so happy only hours before-hand, and now he almost wanted to cry but was holding it inside, not wanting to offend his more liberal colleagues.

The three taxied into the city, but Barry urged them to stop early to revel in the crowds dancing in the streets. Several were even on top of cars, shaking their bodies to the rhythm of the music. Miley Cyrus's *Party In The USA* was blasting from someone's cell phone. Christian didn't want to seem like a downer, so he started to dance along-side Barry and Sebastián, who appeared to be in a bet-ter mood.

"Isn't this great?" Barry said, who Christian thought was happier about the party atmosphere than the actual election results.

"I guess there was nothing to worry about after all," Sebastián said tearfully.

Christian said nothing.

# CHAPTER 25

## F@ck You

Sebastián was still having nightmares about the beach. He would toss and turn so much that he eventually would get up from the bed around 2 or 3 AM every night to make his way to the couch, just to scroll through his phone aimlessly without waking up Christian. He had considered telling Christian about the—you know—but just thinking about that day made him feel sick and unclean. And besides, he had wanted to be there: he had been the stupid one for letting this imperfect thing happen to him.

Around 6 AM, Sebastián would often take a shower to scrub away the feeling of uncleanness that washed over him after a night of running through dark thoughts. He would let the hot water wash over him, standing there as he lost track of time. Christian sometimes slipped into the shower an hour later as he got ready for work, wrapping his arms around Sebastián's naked body.

"Another bad dream?" he asked.

"Yeah, another one," Sebastián sighed listlessly.

He had trouble keeping motivated with anything. Not after he had lost control like that. Sebastián ignored Jon and Barry. He even ignored his mother and sister, neglecting to make plans to see them for the holidays: something he previously would have booked well in advance at this point. Sebastián retreated to the comfort of movies: rewatching romances like *Sleepless in Seattle* and *When Harry Met Sally*. He had historically loved watching grand confessions of love, sometimes watching compilations of monologues on YouTube rather than the movies themselves.

These movies didn't make him feel happier, though, like they once had, but angry. He wanted to punch someone in the face. On Grindr, he changed his name to *F@ck You*, and while watching rom-coms, he would scroll through his feed and angrily call out men for being shitty.

F@ck You (Sebastián)

How you doing, racist?

Sebastián commented to someone saying their preference was for white people only.

F@ck You (Sebastián)

Fatphobic, much?

He wrote to someone who said thick people should look elsewhere or go to the gym.

F@ck You (Sebastián)
Just say you are ableist and
get it over with.

He commented to someone who requested 'no crazies' in their bio.

It took no time for his account to get suspended. *It seemed like skinny white men really didn't like being criticized*, he thought to himself. And then he was back to staring at one screen rather than two.

About a week into his self-loathing, Sebastián received a message from his sister, Elena, whom, like everyone else, he had ignored. He ignored it again, only to get another and another, until finally, she started to call him.

He answered: "Hello?"

"I'm outside." Elena said brusquely.

Sebastián was confused. "What?"

Elena continued like this was the most normal thing in the world. "I'm outside your place. It's by the Chinese place, right?"

It took Sebastián a moment to click that she was at his studio apartment over by Ninth Street. He hadn't been there in weeks, not even to get new clothes. "I'm not there?" he said sheepishly. "I'm at my boyfriend's place."

They decided to meet at a Panera a block and a half away. Elena was wearing bike shorts and an oversized tee, pushing a black stroller around with her youngest kid, Jacob, sleeping inside. She was on the muscular side of stocky. An obsessive Zumba fanatic, her arms looked like they could bench the stroller with ease.

She kissed Sebastián on both sides of his cheeks, hugged him, and immediately got into the meat of the conversation. "Hermano, what is going on? Are you ignoring me, Sebas?"

"I'm… not, El. I mean, I'm not just ignoring you."

"Funny." She laughed and then shifted her focus to the gray disc in her hand. "Oh, my food's ready," she said as the buzzer hummed loudly. "Watch your nephew," she commanded, pushing the stroller toward Sebastián.

She returned later with a sandwich and soup combo with a side of mac and cheese. "So what's this I hear about you not coming to Thanksgiving or Christmas?"

"It is a pandemic," Sebastián said defensively.

"Then quarantine and rent a car like the rest of us. Either that, or give me a shovel so I can dig your grave after abu kills you."

"Is that why you came—to yell at me?" Sebastián huffed.

Her face lightened somewhat. "No, I came because I have barely spoken to you in seven months and wanted to know why."

Sebastián realized that she wasn't angry with him as much as worried. "I'm a little depressed." He admitted.

"Don't big shots like you go see therapists when you are depressed?" She joked, and yet a part of her seemed serious.

"I don't think just lobbyists can see a therapist," he deflected.

"Well, remind me of that when my next water bill is due. Listen, are you coming to Thanksgiving or not?"

"I'll think about it."

Elena frowned but bit her tongue, probably realizing that the tough love approach wasn't working. "I'm worried about you, that's all. Promise me you'll take care of yourself, Sebas."

"Only because you said so."

She smiled. "Good. Now help me eat some of this mac and cheese. You look like you are starving."

# Chapter 26

*Christian*

The drive to the cabin had been disappointing. Christian had been looking forward to the trip to see his family for Thanksgiving. He had wanted to show Sebastián all the stops he loved to make on his pilgrimage to the cabin: the beauty of the red maple and black birch trees swaying in the wind, almost bare after shedding their brilliant leaves; a statue of a cannon in a nearby park; this one sandwich shop owned by an elderly couple that knew his name because he had just been going there for so long.

He loved driving along this quaint, aging highway that had started to fade into obscurity since the construction of the Interstate so many decades ago, but Sebastián hadn't seemed 'into' this trip. Christian had assumed it was because he was on probation at work for missing a call during their vacation to the Bahamas, but he didn't quite understand why. Sebastián didn't seem to like his job very much, but it had put him in such a funk. He hadn't paid attention to the trees and had hardly taken a bite out of his sandwich. Sebastián had sat in the passenger seat, forlorn, sighing deeply about nothing in particular.

"You okay?" Christian asked.

"It's nothing," Sebastián replied, sighing yet again.

"It doesn't seem like nothing." Christian was so annoyed by this woe-is-me routine.

"I'm just nervous about visiting your parents."

"They are going to love you," Christian reassured.

"Do you really think I belong there?" Sebastián said this like it was more than an offhand joke, but he couldn't understand why. He had nothing to worry about.

"Of course, baby. Of course. Just make sure to get on my grandfather's good side, and don't insult my mom's cooking, and you'll be in the clear."

Christian laughed at this joke to signal to Sebastián that it was okay to lighten up, but no laughter came. Sebastián grimaced awkwardly, and they returned to saying nothing. They listened to a Top 50 playlist on Spotify, humming Ariana Grande in silence, as Christian fumed. Why was Sebastián already ruining this for him?

They pulled into the cabin at around 6 PM. The sun was starting to set, but there was still enough light to see that the driveway was packed with over a dozen cars from the Muller clan, so they had to park around back in Gary's lot.

"He's the groundskeeper. Lives here full time," Christian added, pointing to the one-level house that was a short walk from the main one, obscured by darkness.

Sebastián nodded, not saying anything.

"And not to add any pressure."

"Wouldn't want that," Sebastián joked.

"But," Christian plowed on, "You are the first, you know," Christian gestured to Sebastián's person, "that I have ever brought home."

"You haven't brought what home? A guy? A Latino? A Jew?"

"Woah, I was not bringing race into this," Christian said defensively. "I was talking about a guy."

"And you are telling me this now?"

"Well, it just hasn't ever come up before," Christian said, squeezing Sebastián's hands for added emphasis. "So, if you could, you know, pretend to have a good time. That would mean a lot."

Sebastián put on a big, gregarious smile. "Like this?" he smirked, every pearly white in his mouth beaming with sardonic displeasure.

"Perfect," Christian said, giving Sebastián a small peck.

They made their way to the front of the house. His mother had decorated for Christmas early this year and overdone it as usual. Twinkle lights had been strung up outside all along the cabin's many trees, ablaze with warm whites and oranges.

He could see his family members waiting by the door. They had heard their car pull in and waved at Christian and Sebastián from behind the glass. His excitable nieces and nephews were jumping up and down. Christian waved back.

"Hello, Mother," he said as they approached. She had opened the door. The brisk autumn wind rippled through her long dress. It was patterned with leaves and adorably cute pumpkins with faces on them. She looked older than when he had last seen her, as if the world had pressed into her creases and pores, exploding into wrinkles everywhere.

"Decorated for Christmas early this year," Christian snarked.

"It's Thanksgiving. That's the holidays," she stated calmly. "Besides, I only did the lights."

"You must be Mrs. Muller," Sebastián said warmly, extending a hand to Christian's mother.

"Mom, this is my boyfriend, Sebastián," he said firmly. Boyfriend? Christian realized that might have been the first time he had publicly used that word to describe their relationship.

"You are even lovelier than how Christian described you," Sebastián added.

Mrs. Muller blushed. "Stop, you are going to make me blush. Call me Ashley. Nice to meet you, Sebastián," she said, accepting Sebastián's hand. "Christian has told us so much about you."

"All good things, I hope," he laughed heartily. Louder than he had seemed to be in over a month.

"Wonderful things," she beamed, then looked down at his bag. "I'll get Gary to bring your things to the room."

"Oh, I don't mind carrying them," Sebastián said, tightly holding to his red carry-on bag.

"Nonsense, he has hardly anything to do now that the snow has covered his beautiful garden. Gary," Ashley said, turning to an elderly Black man hunched over in a chair in the corner. "Can you bring their bags down to Christian's room?"

"Right away, Mrs. Muller," Gary said with a muted expression. He grabbed their bags and ferried them out of sight.

"Hi, Father," Christian said to his dad, a lean man who had stood silently several feet away.

"Hello, son. Nice to meet you, Sebastián," he stated simply. He continued to stand there, but his eyes seemed to glaze over, as usual, checked out. Christian watched as Sebastián tried to dole out the same amount of flattery that he did his mother, but his father simply nodded, unmoved.

With pleasantries exchanged, Christian found his attention being pulled in a thousand different directions. He fielded comments from his mom, his brothers and sisters, and their spouses. He turned around and saw that his nieces and nephews were pulling Sebastián's hand into the next room so he could play a game with them. Sebastián gave him a terrified 'please don't leave me with these children' look.

"You'll be fine," Christian whispered as he was dragged away by his sleeves.

Christian ended up in a circle with the 'men'—his brother Sammie, his sisters' husbands, his uncle, the Admiral, and his grandfather Samuel, who was leading the pack. The only man who wasn't there was his father, who was off by the bar, making everyone his signature rosemary gin and tonic. Christian could smell the pungent, almost charred wood-like smell of the herb from here, permeating the room, bringing back memories of Thanksgiving's past.

"And do you have to wear masks?" his brother Sammie asked.

"Sorry, what?"

"I was asking," Christian's grandfather Samuel chimed in, repeating something Christian had obviously missed, "has the base made you wear a mask? Your brother's firm is demanding it starting Monday."

"Oh no. They stopped all of that."

"Now, why would you even ask him that?" Admiral Thomas said indignantly. "You know I wouldn't subject him to that."

"I was merely making sure, Thomas. Contractors can be different. Now see, Sammie," Grandfather Samuel said, continuing some conversation Christian wasn't following. "You can't brainwash military men."

"Isn't that exactly what you do in the army? Get brainwashed?" cut in Doris, Samuel's second wife and the only person he let speak back to him. She was younger than Samuel by about thirty years, wearing a white dress adorned with shimmering rhinestones or real gems for all Christian knew. She stood adjacent to the men but not quite included. She was by herself, having refused to help the women in the kitchen like always.

"Nonsense," Grandfather Samuel said defiantly. "No one thinks harder than men of service. When I went to West Point, we read…"

"You read what? The books they told you to?" she interrupted.

"Someone's being sassy," Sammie mocked.

Doris rolled her eyes and crossed her arms, causing her dress to ripple like an iridescent flame. Christian had always known that the two of them didn't love each other, not like how Samuel had loved his first wife Mildred, but the quarantine seemed to be getting to them.

Then, Sebastián walked in, giving all of them a welcomed distraction. He moved next to Christian, giving him a peck on the cheek.

"Where have you been?" Christian asked.

"I was helping Gary bring some chairs up for dinner."

"Why?" Christian asked, confused.

"Oh, he looked like he needed help. And Ashley asked… Problem?"

"No, no problem," Christian said, sipping from his drink.

"See, initiative. I like him," Grandfather Samuel said. "You seem like a smart young boy. What are your thoughts on mask mandates?"

"I think I might need a drink first before delving into politics," Sebastián joked.

"You boys are going to have to wait till after dinner to discuss that," Ashley said, coming in from the dining room. "Because dinner is served. And if there's one rule in this house, it's that we don't do politics during dinner."

"Just one rule," mumbled Doris passive-aggressively.

No one heard Doris, or if they did, they ignored her comment and made their way to the dining room. It was as beautiful as Christian remembered: the oak wooden paneling, the large bay windows, the countless little Christmas ornaments hanging from the chandelier. Sebastián sat by his side, which was the most natural thing in the world. He was gay, and his family didn't care, not even his grandfather Samuel. Full access to his trust seemed closer by the minute.

He looked over at his brother Sammie, who was giving him a mean look as he clutched his wife Rebecca's hand, undoubtedly seething that Christian was living the life he had denied himself.

*Eat it, prick*, Christian thought happily. *I don't have to be repressed to get what I want.*

"Let us pray," the Admiral said. Everyone joined hands and repeated the words to *Our Father*.

"So, how did you two meet?" His mother, Ashley, asked after they had finished with the prayer.

The two of them looked at each other awkwardly. He couldn't let his family or his grandfather know that they met through Grindr. It would be the ultimate embarrassment, and it would lead to yet another hushed, one-on-one as Samuel pulled Christian aside to lecture him on how he could be cut out in an instant.

"At a park," Sebastián lied.

Christian had to stop himself from releasing a very audible sigh of relief, squeezing Sebastián's hand instead. "It was a beautiful day," he added. "And I was sitting at a waterfall overlooking the city."

The lie cascaded from there, and soon, the two of them convinced his family that they had had a romantic meet-cute that blossomed into a beautiful, monogamous relationship. Samuel nodded at the details. This was the life he wanted him to have. If he was going to be gay, Christian could at least not make a scene about it. He could at least be normal.

His grandfather would pull him aside later that evening, thoroughly drunk. He was, for a brief moment, worried it would be one of those talks, but Christian's worry melted the moment he saw Samuel's pearly white smile. "So far, so good," he said, gesturing to Sebastián in the kitchen. "28 is not too far off. You might earn your trust yet," he cheered, patting Christian on the back before transitioning into a long-winded monologue about how taxation was theft.

# CHAPTER

## 27



### *Jingle Balls*

Sebastián had opened up Grindr the moment Christian had abandoned him to his nieces and nephews—who were a lot. They all wanted to play a different game, and none of them could agree, so he would sneak a peek at the app whenever he could. He knew he should probably call his family and wish them a happy Thanksgiving, but he kept putting it off. Besides, Grindr was a lot less stressful.

Surprisingly, there were many gay men in the area for being in 'the middle of the woods.' He changed his name to *Jingle Balls*, thinking it would get a laugh out of the repressed conservative men out here.

"Play hide and seek with us," said one of the kids whose name Sebastián had already forgotten.

"One second, I just need to check something on my phone."

He scanned Grindr. It was a lot of faceless torsos and pictures of scenery, but he recognized one face.

"Wait, Sammie's gay?" Sebastián mumbled to himself, looking at a '5 feet away' blurred profile of one of Christian's brothers. His crooked nose and shit-eating grin clearly came from the man he had met upstairs.

"What does gay mean?" asked one of the kids, confused.

"It means Sammie likes butts," the oldest one joked.

"Gross."

"Come on, let's play hide-and-seek," another one said, bored by this secret they did not understand.

"Uncle Sabashchin," one of the girls said. "Won't you play with us?"

*Dammit, kids really know how to be cute.*

"Fine," Sebastián sighed.

And so, Sebastián ran through the basement floor of the mansion, which was definitely not a cabin, finding the kids in their poorly thought-out hiding spots. He found them by the curtains of the home movie theater, inside an unfilled jacuzzi, and underneath a giant, reclining chair made of leather. Each spot they sat in revealed to Sebastián precisely how rich the Muller Clan appeared to be. They were loaded, like the spoiled brats a movie protagonist would scoff at.

"You have another exercise room?" Sebastián said in disbelief.

"I watch *Coco* here from my iPad," a kid giggled.

Sebastián kept getting pings from his sister Elena to call her. "Why aren't you answering?" she wrote.

He sighed, realizing that he couldn't put it off much longer. He managed to hide away in the hallway and began to dial Elena, but he was rudely interrupted.

"Oh, there you are," said Ashley. She looked like she was on a mission, holding a netted bag of fingerling potatoes. "I wondered where these kids carried you off to. Listen, I hate to be a bother, but whenever you get a chance, would you mind helping Gary bring the chairs up? His back is not what it was."

Sebastián felt like this was a strange ask. Would she have requested this if Christian had brought someone along like Jon or James? Yet he didn't want to make a scene about it, and besides, it gave him an excuse not to call Elena, so he relented.

"No problem Mrs. Muller." He said, defaulting into service mode.

"Ashley, remember."

"Of course, Ashley."

"He's down the hallway," she said, pointing across the length of an average-sized house to a small closet.

Much to their disappointment, Sebastián left the children, but Ashley threatened to take away their Thanksgiving presents if they didn't cooperate. Who gets Thanksgiving presents? But it appeared to work, so Sebastián didn't say anything.

He met Gary at the end of the hall. He was struggling with a foldable plastic chair. He couldn't get it to close quite right, and it was too big in its present form to pull out of the closet.

"Here, let me help you," Sebastián said, moving in to grab the chair.

"Thanks," Gary said simply. A moment of silence followed, and then. "So you're the boyfriend."

"That's me," Sebastián responded, unsure what to say.

"Very good."

The two of them worked silently to carry the chairs up the stairs to the first level. Ashley followed this by asking him to take the trash out, and then asked if he wouldn't mind chopping some carrots with the other women in the kitchen. Sebastián was beginning to think this conservative family had filed him away as 'one of the women,' which he didn't know to perceive as an insult or a compliment.

"You are putting him to work," said Rebecca, Sammie's wife, who was stirring something in a pot. Rebecca was bulky and fit. Her hair was cut short. If Sebastián was being honest with himself, she looked very masculine.

"Nonsense. Am I treating you too hard, Sebastián?"

"No, Ashley. These carrots would have to be a whole lot thicker for this to seem like work." All the girls laughed at this, though Sebastián didn't think it was that good of a joke. In the distance, he saw Christian laughing with the other men and one woman Sebastián was told was Doris. It looked like they were having fun.

"That Doris is the worst," said Ashley.

"Ashley," gasped Rebecca. "You are terrible," though Rebecca was laughing at this remark too.

Sebastián could hear his phone abuzz with texts, so he muted it to focus on prep work. It took a while to make dinner. There were a lot of moving pieces: more vegetables had to be chopped, spice rubs made, meat defrosted, and dishes cleaned. Ashley kicked him out of the kitchen to hang with the men, something he was thankful to do, but less than five minutes later, they were all sitting down for dinner.

The food was good and Sebastián was hungry from all the work. He let the smell of creamy mashed potatoes, turkey, and succulent string beans wash over him, savoring every bite. It was a good thing the food was so good because the conversation was as dull as an uncooked potato.

"The weather has been wonderful," Ashley gabbed to a bunch of listless nods. "So, how did you two meet?"

Sebastián found himself weaving an elaborate lie. He certainly couldn't tell the truth that they had met on Grindr. This family wanted a perfect partner, and being a little slut wasn't perfect. He waxed poetically about their meeting that day on the waterfall and fibbed from there. Thankfully, Christian was more than willing to play along.

"How lovely," Ashley remarked.

"That reminds me of how your father and I met," Ashley continued. "It was very romantic. We were in Provence, and we decided to make a last-minute…"

"No one wants to hear about you going to Paris, Ashley," interrupted the Admiral. "Like… we love you. But come on. We want to hear about the new couple. Sebastián, if you aren't already preparing to run for the hills, what are your thoughts on family?"

"Thomas, we said no politics," Ashley cut in nervously.

"I resent that classification," the Admiral quipped.

"Well, big fan. Ah." *Shit*, Sebastián thought desperately. *What do you even say to that?* He could feel the weight of all their eyes on him. "I grew up with my mother and my abuela. My father, unfortunately, passed away when I was young, so strong women have always been around."

"I'll drink to that," said Doris.

"Umm, but also a lot of brothers, so they had their hands full," Sebastián joked meekly.

"Upwayla?" the Admiral said, confused. "I thought Christian said you were Jewish."

"Thomas," Ashley said.

"What? I can't ask a question?"

"No, it's totally fine," Sebastián interjected. "I'm both. My mother is Jewish. My father was Mexican."

"Well, ain't that something," Admiral Thomas smiled.

There was a clearing of a throat from Samuel. The daggers cast from his eyes, causing Thomas to go silent. "I think this calls for a toast," Samuel interjected. He held up his glass, and everyone did the same. "To family. Both old and new."

"To family," everyone clinked.

Everyone started breaking out into smaller conversations. Christian leaned into Sebastián's ear, whispering: "That went well."

"Thank you," Sebastián smiled. "Hey, you didn't tell me your brother Sammie was on our team."

Christian made a hard gulp. "Wait, he told you? Listen, I didn't steal his first boyfriend if that's what this is about"

"Ummm, no, you are going to tell me more about that later... I saw him on our favorite app."

"Ah," said Christian. "He's, well. It's complicated." However, Christian refused to say anything more than that.

It was after dinner when everyone was really drunk that things got a bit saucy. Holding his third or fourth rosemary gin and tonic, Admiral Thomas started to rant about the deficit and how people needed to care more about it.

"And soon," he slurred, "or this entire country is headed for one nasty retirement."

"That's right. That's right," applauded Sammie, "This is why I think you should run for office, sir. You'll teach those leeches in Washington how to run this country like a proper business."

"Uh oh, the men are talking about politics," Ashley said, though she didn't do anything to stop the conversation. Instead, opting to go into the kitchen and start cleaning up.

Sebastián decided to join her, realizing that that had to be better than listening to this old Boomer rant about politics. He positioned himself next to Rebecca, drying the dishes she washed with an old washcloth.

"So, how are you enjoying our crazy family?" Rebecca asked giddily, happy to have someone new to gab with.

"It's been fun. Different from mine. But fun."

Sebastián heard a loud groan in response. Doris had made her way into the kitchen to grab another glass.

"Mine broke," Doris said nonchalantly.

"What's your problem, Doris?" Rebecca scoffed.

"Well, besides not having a drink in my hand," she slurred. "I thought I could marry my way into a life that wasn't mine, and now I'm bitter. What's your excuse? Is that queer still not sleeping with you?"

It took Sebastián a moment to realize Doris was talking about Sammie.

Rebecca's face looked like it was going to cry. "Fuck you, Doris," she said before storming off.

"How about you, kid?" Doris asked. "You think you can live this life?"

Sebastián didn't know what to say, so he laughed and continued cleaning.

"See, you are learning already," Doris hiccuped, sashaying away to the living room, undoubtedly to harangue her husband.

Sebastián got another message: "Abu is asleep. Don't bother calling."

# Chapter 28



Christian could not stop looking at the news. He had turned on notifications for several apps on his phone and would take quick micro-breaks throughout the day to skim the headlines of the latest insanity. Biden was claiming to have won the election. It was madness. He may have voted for Jo Jorgensen, but he was starting to have regrets. His favorite YouTubers claimed the election was stolen, and Christian was assessing the merits of their claims. He was reading about voter fraud and its definition when he heard a throat clearing. He looked up and saw an impatient Sebastián staring daggers at him.

"I thought we went over this when we visited your parents. No phone while we are together," Sebastián chastised.

Sebastián was holding a string of tinsel. They were in the middle of decorating a Christmas tree in Christian's apartment. A fake one he had purchased three years ago and had left inside a cardboard box in his closet until now. Christian huffily put down his phone and positioned himself behind the tree so he could grab the other end of the tinsel and wrap it around.

"Better?" Christian asked as he snaked the tinsel back to Sebastián.

"Much." Sebastián smiled. He was wearing an ugly Christmas sweater with a grumpy cat meme itself wearing a Santa hat. It was hideous, and he was forcing himself to put up with it.

There truthfully wasn't too much more to hang up. They had received decorations from Amazon that morning as last-minute touches for their party. The two of them had flown back from his parents' lakeside cabin in Connecticut two days ago. Sebastián had, again, been a hit with Christian's family. He had been charming and polite without being so effacing that he was burdensome. Everyone had been impressed, even the Admiral, who was a notoriously hard man to please. Most importantly, his grandfather had been pleased.

"You have yourself a keeper," he had said approvingly, with a bemused smile.

Sebastián had been careful not to share his opinions during their trip. He had been very guarded. The only thing Christian could gather was that Sebastián had seemed vaguely happy and that the decorations had blown him away. He had insisted that they order supplies for their own last-minute holiday party. The earliest date they could get them was today, several hours before their guests arrived. The morning had been a mad rush to set everything up on time, and it still didn't quite live up to their experience at the cabin.

As opposed to this mad rush to the finishline, the trip to the cabin had been stress-free. They arrived a couple of days before Christmas, helping Christian's mother hang up glass and porcelain decorations, some purchased in designer catalogs and others passed down the generations. His parent's cabin had a large, green pine tree shipped to them from a Maine forest. It spanned twelve feet into the air, tall enough that a ladder was needed to place many decorations on it. The tree itself was decorated with white lights, a myriad of ornaments, and green garlands. And, of course, all the other touches had been set up before their arrival: the meticulously curated Christmas village, with intricately painted ceramic houses and piles upon piles of white tuffs, meant to symbolize snow; bulky stockings hanging above the fireplace; green garland wrapping around the winding staircase.

Yes the holiday had met his expectations. And more to the point it had seemed to satisfy his family's high expectations as well. Everyone was quite pleased, except for Sammie, who Christian suspected wanted him to fail at every possible opportunity.

Sebastián had obviously wanted to emulate that experience, not knowing that such Christmases in the Muller household took months of planning. And so their efforts had of course fallen flat. They had set up this stingy plastic tree that totaled a height of about seven feet. The tree was sparsely decorated as they had under-ordered the supplies, leaving significant gaps that did not give it that stereotypical abundance you associate with Christmas trees. The Christmas Village they had ordered came with only four houses—each tinier than their online pictures had suggested. The nails that came with the stockings fell out of the wall the moment they were hammered in, so the stockings were lying on the ground right underneath the fireplace.

Sebastián had wanted Christian to go to the hardware store to get new ones, but then a knock came at the door, followed by another more aggressive one. Rick was the first to arrive—precisely at 7:30 PM, as the Facebook invite had listed. He wore a sweater with a picture of a gerbil, who was wearing a pink and light blue sweater of his own. It was cute, if not a bit tacky. Rick also brought an $11 bottle of wine he claimed was 'authentic.'

"Am I too early?" he asked.

"No," Christian lied.

Rick awkwardly stood around them, engaging in small talk as Christian and Sebastián prepared the cheese board and chips.

"Are you sure I can't help?" he asked.

"No, we are good," Christian said, stressing out that they hadn't purchased enough mini hotdogs for the other guests. He tried not to glare at Rick as the man simultaneously shoved two or three in his mouth. "You sit down. Relax." He assuaged him.

He thoroughly disliked this man, a feeling he had learned to hold from Sebastián, though he was not quite sure why. As far as he could tell, no one liked him, yet somehow, he got a begrudging invite to every large gathering. He was so weird and awkward: always hanging around longer than he should and never seeming to quite get a clue. He would have to ask Sebastián later why they continued to accept this person they all clearly hated.

"Oh, I got you a gift," Rick said, handing them a poorly wrapped box—the J.C. Penny tags for whatever rag he had purchased stuck through the wrapping.

"Thank you so much." Christian smiled, taking the undoubtedly cheap gift and tossing it on a nearby table. Rick was something else if he thought this was enough to get into the bubble's good graces.

J.J., one of Sebastián's friends that Christian had never met, arrived shortly after that with a giant cooler of cheap beers. His ugly sweater was a shirtless Santa, with ripped abs and a bright red speedo. J.J. insisted on putting on Mariah Carey's Christmas album, specifically her song *All I Want For Christmas Is You*, which they, of course, started singing to the words.

"All I want for Christmas is yooooooooUUUUUUUuuuuu." Christian sang poorly, shrieking with joy.

Barry and Jon arrived as the song ended, insisting that everyone put it on again. They were now apparently dating and made for one obnoxious couple. Christian complied, though he wasn't happy about it. He sang the words again quietly, not quite as mirthful as the first time.

"Make it stop, please," he whispered sarcastically in Sebastián's ear.

"You'll be fine," Sebastián replied, handing him a beer.

"So this is a thing?" Sebastián asked Jon, pointing to Barry and Jon as they nuzzled each other with red plastic noses they had worn to match their Rudolf-the-red-nosed-reindeer sweaters. The cheap plastic antlers kept falling off, and they had to push them back on their heads every now and then.

"Un-huh," Barry replied before giving Jon a kiss. "Now get me a drink," he told Jon, slapping him on the ass and sending him along to the fridge.

"You're so bad," Jon replied as he walked off toward the kitchen.

Barry turned back to Christian and Sebastián. The bags underneath his eyes were more pronounced, the weight of having to entertain someone much younger than him visible.

"Where were we?" he asked, distracted by the fading sight of his boyfriend's behind.

"You were going to tell us when you started dating?" Christian asked, somewhat annoyed.

"A month now. Well, we are seeing each other, not dating."

"What's the difference?" Christian asked.

Barry shrugged.

"So how did this start," Sebastián continued.

"We met up in LA. Chad, the model Jon was working for," Barry said, placing air quotes around the word working. "Had just fired him for creative differences. Jon was a little bit of a mess, so I agreed to take him out for a consolatory coffee, and well, here we are."

"What's he doing for work, then?" Christian interjected. He was worried about how Jon seemed to be squandering his working years away—how would he be able to get a proper job at this rate?

"Oh, I hired him," Barry smirked, "He's actually a perfect assistant. Well, when he's not fucking up, that is."

"Aren't you a lobbyist for Juul? Doesn't Mr. Green party have issues with that?" Sebastián asked wryly.

"Oh, he does. That brat complains constantly, but he also likes when I take control," he said, pausing to admire their relationship. "It's like a game we play."

"One drink. Extra strong like you like it," remarked Jon, budding into their circle with a red solo cup.

"Thanks, slut," remarked Barry. Jon blushed, and the two started to bicker about the ethics of consent.

More guests trickled in over the next hour. All of them brought with them mid-priced alcohol and little else. They wore ironic ugly sweaters to meet the theme, most of which the guests had purchased from Amazon. The party was a swirl of Ruth Bader Ginsburgs, calls to 'Resist,' and funny Internet memes.

The only person who had worn a genuine Christmas sweater was James, now going by the handle *Right on!*, who was wearing one knitted for him by his grandmother. James was back in their good graces because the reason they had ostracized him was no longer relevant. Social distancing and masking were no longer something they were doing, thank God.

"We overreacted," Christian told him when they had a private moment together. "Sorry."

"Don't sweat it," he responded calmly. "Here, I brought you some real whiskey." He handed Christian a bottle of Texas Straight Cowboy Bourbon. Christian smiled and made a mental note to proposition James later.

The last person to arrive was Emmett. They had not expected him to come. He had responded to their Facebook invite by saying that he would only go if everyone took a Covid test, which Christian hadn't agreed to. Emmett looked disheveled. His hair was unkempt, as if he hadn't received a haircut in months, and his beard was likewise much longer than before. He looked angrier somehow to Christian. Emmett's sweater didn't help matters. It was the 'this is fine' dog—the yellow cartoon dog surrounded by fire and everything.

Jon greeted him, and their main group followed suit.

"How have you been, Em?" Jon asked, giving Emmett a hug he initially hesitated to take before melting into him.

"Not the best, honestly. It's just been me and Mittens." He looked on the verge of tears. His whole face was twisted in pain. He was obviously conflicted, Christian noted. He didn't want to be here but was desperately alone.

"Whose Mittens?" asked Jon.

"My cat." Emmett cried.

"You got a cat?" Jon continued.

"I've always had a cat."

"It's been a rough couple of months." Jon deflected.

"Well, you are here now," consoled Sebastián, patting him on the shoulder.

Christian wanted to approach him, but he wavered. It had been so long, and he had said so many hurtful things behind Emmett's back, some of which he was sure had filtered its way through group chats. Christian still stood behind his initial decision. People were overreacting to Covid, but the hurt on Emmett's face made him briefly reconsider how he had gone about it. You can be right and petty simultaneously, and Christian felt ashamed of that.

"Sorry," he told Emmett as he approached. "Sorry I made you feel this way, Emmett." That apology may not have sounded sincere, but he meant it. Just because Emmett was wrong didn't mean he wasn't hurting.

"It's okay, man," said Emmett, very obviously crying. "I'm okay."

They all sat down for dinner almost immediately after Emmett arrived. They crowded around the long plastic table Christian had borrowed from an army buddy on base—an elegant white tablecloth draped over it, obscuring the cheapness underneath. Christian would have to buy a new table soon—something that wouldn't read as so pedestrian.

The meal had technically been advertised as a potluck, but people didn't bring much food: a few store-bought desserts and chips. Most of the cooking had been done by Christian, who tried to replicate his mother's recipes with mixed results. The mashed potatoes were buttery and succulent, but the ham wasn't cooked all the way through, and he had to, shamefully, in his eyes, put it back in the oven to bake. It came out slightly dry, and most everyone had to douse their slices in cranberry sauce or gravy.

The conversation was light and overly flirtatious. They avoided politics. They no longer agreed with each other in that regard and probably never did. They could only agree on taking a picture, which Rick volunteered to do, going off to capture everyone's smiling faces as they turned to him.

"Say cheese," he instructed.

The electronic sound of his phone shuttered, followed by a flash.

The picture was filled with twenty people huddled around a table with plastic smiles. It was a nice picture, but nothing compared to the atmosphere that had permeated the room in the heat of the moment.

When they finished eating, the party moved back to people standing around in various huddles and drinking. Some took this time to say their adieus, but as the night progressed, especially after undesirables like Rick had left, people started to get more frisky. Many of them had met through Grindr, so they were no strangers to each other's bodies.

The original *Gang*$^{TM}$ of Emmett, Sebastián, Christian, Jon, and James found themselves on Christian's white couch, right where they had started, kissing. Emmett had removed Christian's pants and started playing with his cock. His grip felt amazing—a wonderful gift for the holidays.

# CHAPTER

## 29



Elena still hadn't forgiven him for skipping Christmas. She had stopped texting him altogether. Sebastián would be lying if he claimed that that withdrawal didn't sting just a little. She was being beyond petty. Being in Christian's family would set him up for life, and yet she was complaining about him not going to their rundown home in Jersey. Didn't she know he had to do everything he could to hold onto this perfect life? To make his sacrifices worth it?

Besides, Sebastián had big plans in January, so much so that he had changed his name back to *Eager Slut* and added an exclamation point. *The Gang*™ had been reborn since the holiday party and purchased tickets for another tropical trip, this time in Puerto Vallarta, Mexico. The plan was to spend New Year's Eve dancing the night away with sixty sweaty strangers on a fleet of boats that would set anchors on the blue waters of the 'Bahia de Banderas' or, in English, the 'Bay of Flags.'

It was going to be perfect. The only problem was that Sebastián still had nightmares, specifically about waves. His body was lying on the sands, but he was unable to move. He'd watch the tide come in, horrified that he'd be dragged below the depths, waking up as the icy cold water splashed his face, screaming. Christian had tried to talk about it once or twice, but Sebastián didn't want to ruin the fun. They had a trip planned! This life was still possible. Sebastián didn't have to throw this dream away because he was having a nightmare or two.

Christian and him were packing silently, placing piece after piece of clothing into their suitcase. Sebastián moved on autopilot, neatly folding underwear into a small pile, unconscious of his surroundings. They were no longer fighting. Sebastián felt like he had settled into a nice place with Christian, like a groove worn down into place. They just fit. They had to.

"Are you sure you want to go?" Christian asked Sebastián in a rare moment of introspection.

"Of course."

"It's just… you've folded way too many clothes than can fit in this suitcase. You seem off recently."

"Umm, I'm good." What was there to say? That he didn't want to go. That the thought of another tropical vacation sent shivers down his spine. No, that seemed absurd. Who would turn down a weekend on the water? "Just nervous with cases spiking," he added, thinking this was a plausible enough excuse,

Christian scoffed. "It'll be fine," he condescended.

Sebastián wanted to scream at Christian for telling him to share his feelings, only to shut them down. "Why even ask?" He wanted to shout. He had every right to be nervous. Cases had skyrocketed, and hundreds of thousands of Americans had died. These facts and figures sat at the back of his mind, ready to come out at the start of any argument, but he held them back this time.

*He was fine*, he thought to himself. They were headed to literal paradise. Why would he be nervous about going on a tropical vacation? They would have to take Covid tests to be eligible for the trip—something Christian had not been happy with but agreed to because the venue demanded an uploaded document before landing. The chance of infection, in his mind, was next to zero.

And yet still… he was afraid to go. A shudder traveled up his spine whenever Christian excitedly mentioned all the guys they would sleep with. His mind raced back to the image of being suspended above the water. His legs were strapped around a star. He imagined them burning in the sun as his body bobbed back and forth, caught in its deadly gravity.

He wasn't very talkative during their walk to the CVS for their Covid tests. Sebastián listened to his partner excitedly gossip about future attendees he had already swapped handles with on Instagram. He nodded along to brags about how hot they were or how hung their dicks seemed. Sebastián found little solace in Christian's small talk, constantly feeling that his partner was oblivious.

They put their masks on to enter the store, skillfully ignoring an unhoused person begging near the sliding doors. Sebastián watched Christian enter the nurse physician's office. He came out several seconds later with a frown on his face.

"Wrong location. It's in the trailer out back."

They swung around to a gray trailer beside the main store. It was windowless and depressing. Christian put on his mask and entered. He came out several minutes later with a reassuring nod.

"It was a piece of cake," Christian smiled.

Sebastián walked in after him—the two of them had booked back-to-back appointments. He sat in a blue, plastic chair against the wall, listening to the nurse lecture him about the process. She had him blow into a tissue and then crane his neck upwards to insert a swab into both nostrils. She pushed them both firmly in, and he had to stop himself from squirming from the discomfort.

"You should get your results back soon. Do you want them by text or email?"

"Email," Sebastián responded with a happy smile. He had this in the bag.

Afterward, they began their walk back home. It was an uncomfortable walk, with the frigid breeze making it challenging to find a comfortable pace. The afternoon sun was high above them, and few people were outside because of the brisk day. The city was as quiet as a city could be. A few cars could be heard in the distance, but that was about it.

Christian's phone pinged, and the two of them stopped walking so that he could read them. His test had come back positive.

Several minutes later, Sebastián's did as well. The world seemed to fade from his view. His mouth felt dry and strange. His eyelids were heavy. His hands were shaking. Sebastián wasn't sure how this could be happening. It couldn't be. He had been so careful. The bubble was supposed to have worked, to have kept them safe.

He was soon back at Christian's apartment, though he did not remember how they had gotten there. Sebastián must have gone on autopilot again. He wondered if this was what the Sunken Place felt like from *Get Out*. He was sweating profusely. His heartbeat had sped up again. Had he run there, or was it the stress? He didn't know. Christian was ranting about the test. He must have been doing so for some time, though Sebastián hadn't registered his words until now.

"This is such bullshit," Christian shouted, "I can't believe you talked me into taking this test. Now I have to cancel the trip and tell the base. This is a nightmare."

Christian was blaming him? Him? For a virus, he had no control over? He just stood there, too stunned to react. He felt nauseous again. He leaned forward and vomited on the floor. Fuck, was this Covid? Was nausea a symptom? He didn't know.

"Seriously?" Christian exclaimed.

Sebastián used his hand to wipe the vomit clinging to his lips. "You are so fucking selfish," he said, almost in a whisper. Sebastián wasn't sure if he should be this honest, yet he had to. Christian was being such a shit that he couldn't bear it right now.

"Excuse me," said Christian.

"So what were you going to do," Sebastián scoffed. "If you could go, I mean. Ignore that you have the virus. Get people infected?"

"It's not even a big deal. We have it, and we didn't even notice."

"And some people die from it. It doesn't… Fuck. Are you really doing this right now? I didn't make you take the test. You agreed to it."

"I need air," Christian said, grabbing his keys.

"We have to quarantine." Sebastián corrected.

"Fuck quarantine," Christian rebuked, slamming the door behind him.

He would not return till later that night, crawling into bed, alcohol on his breath. "Sorry," he whispered, his voice raspy and tearful. "I'm so sorry."

Sebastián did not say anything. He was exhausted, and it was completely dark outside. He was curled up in a ball, his head resting on his arms. He thought now might be an appropriate moment to cry, to show Christian that he cared, but no tears ran down his face. He wasn't sure that he did care anymore.

They had to cancel their trip, which was just the start of the mess that followed. The following morning, Christian was already up. His mom, Ashley, had called him. His grandmother Doris had been rushed into the hospital due to complications with Covid and was currently plugged into a ventilator. Details were scarce. Sebastián pictured a dying woman coughing in a hospital gown and trying to tell an orderly something terribly sarcastic but gasping for air instead.

"Is it our fault?" Christian asked. He had been Googling for hours—some sources Sebastián had tried to get him to read before, only for him to scoff. "I don't even like Doris, but I don't want her to die." He started to cry again.

Sebastián didn't even know what to say to that. "We were there during Christmas and Thanksgiving. We've done a bunch of risky stuff. The timeline fits. But we can't know. We never will." Sebastián answered truthfully.

Both of them were asymptomatic, but the email instructed them to enter immediate quarantine. They made arrangements at work and started notifying friends from the Christmas party. Some people ignored him. A few reacted with rage. Others were indifferent.

### Hung AF (Barry)

Well, I don't have it. I tested negative.

### Eager Slut! (Sebastián)

We just saw each other.

### Hung AF (Barry)

And I got tested this morning

### Eager Slut! (Sebastián)

Just because you tested negative
then doesn't mean it won't develop
over the next few days.

### Eager Slut! (Sebastián)

you really should get tested.

Barry stopped responding after that. He went silent, and Sebastián assumed he had ignored them and left for Mexico without saying a word.

Sebastián felt like his life was ending when more bad news arrived. The party they had planned to go to on the waters of Bahia de Banderas had ended in disaster. Sebastián watched in horror as people he knew were being rescued on sinking boats. He saw Barry clinging to a ring buoy and treading water. A boat was sinking behind him, lost to the blue waters, which had seemed to represent fun and adventure only days ago.

Suddenly, Jon tried to call him for some reason, but he ignored it. He didn't have time for that man's social justice shenanigans. Sebastián had more stuff to worry about. He was worried about his friend. Sebastián tried texting Barry, hoping to reach him. He even sent an email through his work, only to get a bland form letter in response. Finally, he reached out via Grindr.

**Eager Slut! (Sebastián)**

I saw the news. Are you okay?

**Eager Slut! (Sebastián)**

hey call me back when you get this.

**Eager Slut! (Sebastián)**

hey, a little worried.

**Hung AF (Barry)**

hey, still processing. Can't talk right now.

Processing? What the hell did that mean? Did that mean he was safe? He was at least alive, though he might as well be dead, according to many people online. People were gleefully tearing Barry apart on social media, calling him a clueless, white gay who jeopardized a Browner community. They were being so extreme. Sebastián was angry that people were dragging his friends online during one of the most traumatic moments of his life. He made post after post defending them.

"These are decent people, who just made a mistake," he tweeted.

Leftists with anime avatars and roses in their bios dragged his comments online. They called him a 'libtard,' 'blue MAGA,' a 'rad lib.' Many people hated him online, but many other liberals loved him. A model from the Bahamas trip retweeted one of his posts, and his follower count grew into the thousands, as he spent hours going back and forth with disgruntled leftists. He would try to respond, but the barrage of posts made him frustrated, which caused him to double down, which led to even more frustrating comments.

"Stop being so cruel. I voted for Biden. We are on the same side," he tweeted after one day of reading insensitive comments. It was technically a lie but true in spirit. He would have voted for Biden now.

"We aren't on the same side, lib. We never were."

He was obsessed with Twitter and started to hyper-focus on it, ignoring texts and calls from friends. People were so mean to him, and he just wanted to set the record straight: to make things perfect. The day didn't feel like it could get any worse, and then his timeline started to morph. In between threads of clapbacks and pedantic corrections were disturbing images of men and women storming the US capital. "Insurrection at the capitol," went one headline he skimmed. He saw videos of people dressed in tactical gear as well as ordinary winter clothes, waving blue and red Trump signs. They scaled ledges and hopped over barricades until they were inside the building.

"Where are you, Nancy?" he heard from one particularly unsettling Instagram video directed at Speaker of the House Nancy Pelosi.

He posted his frustration online, almost instinctively, dumping his emotions onto the world. He wrote the first words that came into his head. He called the insurrectionists 'terrorists,' 'hicks,' 'uncultured brutes,' and more, which prompted angry posters to hop onto his feed.

"We r coming for traitors like you," tweeted MIKE-FROMNEVADA.

Sebastián was incensed. He sent reply after reply against all of these haters. He mixed up a post about the boat crash with the coup and called a leftist dragging him a terrorist by accident. "Go back to your side of the country," he tweeted angrily in response to someone he thought had just called him a 'reactionary faggot,' but really, the poster was just frustrated by his continued defense of Barry in Puerto Vallarta, Mexico. Sebastián deleted the post the moment he realized the mistake, but people screenshotted it, and pretty soon, more were talking about him in new subtweets than they had ever done on the original post. Thousands of notifications flooded his inbox. He felt like his life was ending.

"Stop tagging me. I apologized for this a thousand times over. I said I was sorry."

"Whatever, traitor," typed PRESIDENTTRUMP4LIFE87.

"He's such a snowflake," responded ANTIFA&BLACKLIVESMATTER.

He didn't think anything could get worse, but somewhere between the shuffle, he got another notification from Jon.

Bite me (Jon)

Do you ever answer your damn phone. :(

Eager Slut! (Christian)

sorry, I have been busy.

Bite me (Jon)

Emmett is in the hospital, you asshole. He might die. I have been calling for days.

The news shot through him like he was slapped all over his body. Dying? It didn't seem possible. He had been at their party only two weeks ago, smiling. His mouth was opened wide, happily taking them all in. He felt strange that his last image of Emmett was of his mouth wrapped around his cock. He pictured his semen dripping down Emmett's chiseled cheeks.

He quickly logged into Facebook. His old inbox was flooded with texts, mainly from Jon asking, "Why the fuck are you not answering me?" He perused Emmett's timeline. It was filled with people sending their love and worry. Emmett had started to get sick a week ago. Sebastián's heart sank as he ran the mental calculus in his head. Their party. It had to be where they all got sick. Over 20 people had gone to that holiday party, talking, laughing, breathing, and pressing into one another.

And now, one of them was dying, possibly even dead. He couldn't help but feel responsible. He scrolled through the last message he had ever received from Emmett. It was before the party. "Hey, I'm super nervous to go. Do you promise it will be safe?"

"I can't promise that," Sebastián had written. "But some risks are worth it?"

What a load of shit. Had he believed that? He wanted to take it all back. To tell Emmett to stay far away from him, but that wasn't possible now. He saw that his family was hosting a prayer circle for Emmett to be held online, over Zoom, but Sebastián didn't know the code for it. He had not been invited. He emailed the cousin organizing it, but Sebastián got no response from his first message or even the next six. He then tried Facebook Messenger, Instagram, Pinterest, and finally, Linkedin.

"Why won't you answer me?" he asked.

Three dots formed in the chat, indicating that his cousin was typing. The dots disappeared and reappeared again until a message finally beeped into existence.

"Because you people probably killed him."

# CHAPTER 30

*Christian*

Emmett was in the hospital, dying. He possibly was dead even now. Died? Deceased. Expired. Departed. Passed on. Six feet under. Pushing up daisies. With God. At peace. Perished. No more. Lost. Gone. Killed?

He might die from Covid. Covid might kill him. Christian might have killed him.

Bad people kill people.

Christian was not a bad person.

This was not his fault.

*Denial,* the voice said.

Christian ran up to the roof of his apartment building. He needed to be somewhere, alone, where he could scream. He needed to release the anger building in him from every direction. He screamed so viscerally he could feel his throat vibrating like it could shake the Earth itself. With each explosion of sound, Christian felt his pulse jump and his breath speed up. He didn't know how long it went on for or how long he cried, but he eventually ran out of air and collapsed to his knees, exhausted and panting.

He sat down and looked up at the twinkling sky— as twinkling as the satellites and planes flying above him could be anyway. The sky was primarily black, lit up by the lights below. He felt so alone, not even connected to the universe, just drifting into blackness.

He then stared at his roof's ledge.

*Cowards like you don't jump*, the voice mocked. It sounded like his grandfather's voice. Maybe it always had been.

For a moment, he thought about jumping. He thought about falling into nothingness and the bliss that would descend as he faded away from this realm, his life. He imagined for a moment that he would experience so many emotions he had not been allowed to feel. Happiness. Joy. Tranquility. Emotions that were lost to him, trained out by those who claimed to love him.

*But men don't complain about their problems. They conquer.*

"You're right." Christian laughed. "For once in my life, you're right."

He snapped back to reality as a familiar coldness settled into the bottom of his chest. He didn't want to die. As much as he hated himself, he knew he couldn't end it. His grandfather had always told him that suicide was the coward's way out, and he felt this to be true in his very bones, resigned to it even.

Fuck Emmett. He didn't understand why he had to feel guilty just because something terrible had happened to someone else. Emmett had been an adult. He had made his choices, and now he had suffered the consequences. People were solely responsible for their decisions. That was the lesson his grandfather had always tried to teach him, and it was about time he listened.

Christian stood up, brushing the dirt off his knees. Only then did he realize that Sebastián was also there, standing on the roof, looking out over the edge, much closer to it than he was now.

# Chapter 31

*Sebastián*

He had followed Christian up here, after telling him the news that Emmett was in the hospital. Christian's eyes had become glassy, and he had walked out of the room, unresponsive to Sebastián's calls to stay. He had watched Christian walk toward the ledge, scream, and then back away just as quickly, and that's when the idea to jump had occurred to Sebastián. He could end it here, if he wanted. He had made his way to the ledge, a step away from nothingness.

"Please don't tell me you are going to jump?" Christian pleaded to Sebastián.

Sebastián didn't say anything because he had planned to do precisely that, or at least, he wanted to think about it, to stew in the moment. He had been so sad since their trip—since that man had, he couldn't even say it. And now, this business with Emmett in the hospital—it was too much to bear.

Sebastián wanted to disappear. He wanted to jump off the roof and fly headfirst into the ground, burying himself within the Earth, never to see the sun again. Like Virginia Woolf in *The Hours* or Virginia Wolf in real fucking life. Not everything had to be a reference to a movie all the damn time. He could want to kill himself like a normal sad person. That was what was going through his mind when his boyfriend called out to him.

"You are not responsible for this," Christian said. "None of us are. Sometimes bad things just happen."

Sebastián scoffed at this. Really? Even now? It was too much. He had been burying all of his opinions in a desperate attempt to cling to Christian's life, to his wealth, to this world that felt so close and yet so far away. And in the process, he had lost that cocky guy who always said what was on his mind. "I'm not sure I like myself very much," Sebastián admitted. "I'm not sure I like you very much either. Did you know that that actor raped me during our trip to the Bahamas?" Sebastián finally found some relief in saying the word he had ignored all these months.

Christian went silent at this, so Sebastián continued. "You didn't, did you? You are so involved in your own shit that you haven't even realized how much I have been hurting. You know… even though it wasn't you, I still blame you. I blame you because you are the person I'm supposed to be able to share this stuff with. That's what love is."

Christian reached out to touch him, only for Sebastián to immediately slap his hand out of the way. "I don't want you to touch me. I don't want you to touch me ever." Sebastián paused and then sighed deeply. "But I'm exhausted… I can't make any more decisions today."

And with that, he walked back down the stairs to Christian's apartment.

# CHAPTER

## 32

*Christian*

"**A**nother one from Jon," Sebastián complained to Christian.

They sat on their outdoor patio, sharing a cigarette over gourmet coffee and scones. They had just recently taken up smoking. It helped Christian think, or rather, it kept the thoughts at bay as he processed the fall-out after Emmett's hospitalization. The endless if-then statements about right and wrong. Christian took in a deep drag. He let it wash over his throat. The raspberry flavoring of the tobacco with the after-taste of scone in his mouth made him feel like he was tasting a tart. He exhaled the smoke, pushing it out like he was opening up for another bite.

The two of them had retreated into the apartment, refusing to think about the consequences. Christian felt like everything was on the verge of crumbling. Sebastián had said he didn't like him. Even if that had been said during a moment of intense grief, Christian had known it to be true. He had tried to mend the grief by being there for Sebastián, ordering ridiculous amounts of take-out, and trying to nest in his apartment—as if spending enough time there would lessen the rift between them.

"What does he want us to do? Turn back time?" Christian said hesitantly, handing the cigarette to Sebastián.

"It's ridiculous," Sebastián agreed.

It had been weeks like this from Jon. Every day came with a new thing they should or should not have done. The parties they shouldn't have thrown. The cautions they should have adhered to. The places they shouldn't have gone. It was a never-ending parade of guilt, as if Jon hadn't been there every step of the way, encouraging them in the fun. He was so angry at all the liberal hypocrites in his life.

"And did you see this happening with the vaccine? They are letting obese people get it before essential workers. It's ridiculous." Sebastián commented, verbally processing some argument he was having on Twitter.

Christian nodded but didn't say anything. Being open about how he thought would be the end of everything. He had learned weeks ago that getting in between Sebastián and whatever argument he was having with the world was pointless. He watched his partner type feverishly on his phone, only interrupting to get another drag from the cigarette.

Besides, he was still skeptical about the vaccine. Christian had been reading about all sorts of side effects. Dr. King had recently done an entire episode on adults who had taken the vaccine only to end up with heart attacks. One elderly grandmother named Mrs. Green died a mere hour after receiving her second dose. Although Green was nothing like Christian's grandmother, Doris, he still couldn't help but think about her. Doris had survived her bout with Covid after a short stay at a private hospital. It had hardly been worth worrying about, but when it came to the vaccine clearly, not everyone was so lucky. Dr. King had provided a picture of Mrs. Green in the show notes on her website, and Christian had saved it to his phone. She may have been larger than Doris, with white hair instead of a dyed brown, but she had the same discerning look as his grandmother. In the picture, she was pulling out a tray of chocolate chip cookies, maybe baking them for her grandchildren. Well, Doris wasn't a baker, but still, the point was the same—Green was now dead, and these vaccines were dangerous.

"I wonder when we will be eligible for it?" Sebastián asked absentmindedly, pulling Christian out of his thought spiral. "I want to get the vaccine so badly."

"You'll have to figure that out." Christian deflected, trying not to sound too judgy.

Sebastián sighed. "Seriously, still." He chastised.

*This is it*, the voice mused. *When he leaves you.*

Christian watched Sebastián set his phone down and give him his undivided attention. Sebastián peered into him like a vulture appraising the meat of a carcass in the desert. Christian didn't want to say anything, but Sebastián didn't pull his stern gaze away.

"I just," Christian stumbled. "Sorry, I'm not trying to judge you at all. I just… Dr. King says."

"She's not even a real doctor. She never finished her degree, did you know that?" Sebastián asked.

"Let's not talk about this. You're right. I was being stupid." Christian said, hoping that his deference would allow this conversation to stop. He wanted nothing more than for them to continue like they were, awkwardly together but not unmoored.

"No," Sebastián pushed, "I want to hear from you why a hack's opinion is more important than the voices of the greater scientific community."

"That doesn't mean the points she says are invalid. She…"

"Like not getting a life-saving vaccine. That's valid to you?" Sebastián chimed in before he had a chance to formulate his thoughts.

"Will you let me finish? Fuck," Christian shouted. He had lost track of the cigarette between his fingers, and the end had burned down to his hand. He dropped it to the floor, stomping it forcefully with his shoe. "Sorry, that wasn't at you."

This whole conversation was pointless. He wasn't going to reach through to him. Sebastián was too stubborn to understand his perspective. Christian was trying to value life: to save those he cared about. Why couldn't Sebastián see that? How was he dating someone this selfish?

"I said I don't want to talk about this," Christian said at last.

"Fine." Sebastián huffed.

"What was Jon even complaining about anyway?" Christian asked, changing the subject.

"Oh," Sebastián reached back for his phone, scanning the message. Christian got the sneaking suspicion that he hadn't read it. They were both so annoyed by Jon that he could see how the mere ping from that liberal poser might have been read as an imposition.

"He wants us to give to Emmett's Hospital Fund," Sebastián continued. "Oh, that's, like, reasonable. We did, you know…" Sebastián's voice trailed off, unable to acknowledge what had been on his mind for over a month now—that he believed they had somehow contributed to Emmett's approaching death. He was still fighting for his life in the hospital, even now, but things weren't looking good.

Of course, this was a ridiculous thought. If Christian's grandma had survived Covid, there's no way it would kill someone as young and healthy as Emmett.

"I don't know," Christian said, realizing a second too late that it was a stupid thing to say if he wanted to keep the relationship.

*You've done it now.* The voice taunted.

"You know. That we… That we contributed to this, maybe, possibly," Sebastián said clinically.

"We have no way of knowing that."

"No, but come on. We flaunted restrictions and threw a party. We facilitated it, even if we weren't the carriers," he carried on in that same condescendingly clinical tone.

His voice was croaking, the strain of trying to distance himself from this reality taking its toll. "You know that," he added as if trying to make the insult final and irreproachable.

They hadn't talked about Emmett's hospitalization a lot, even though it was almost always on their minds. Christian still didn't understand why he felt so bad about it. It wasn't his fault. He hadn't caused Emmett to come to the party, to inhale others' germs, or to suck on his dick. He didn't give Emmett Covid, assuming Covid was even the real cause of his hospitalization.

"You know what," Christian replied, standing up dramatically. "I need some air."

"Really? Fine. I need space anyway."

Fuck.

*It's over*—the voice cut.

"I will see you later," Christian whispered as he bent down to kiss Sebastián. Sebastián refused to kiss him on the lips. Instead, turning so all Christian was able to peck was his cheek.

"Bye," Sebastián whispered back.

Christian tried not to show his anger and disappointment as he stormed off in a huff. He was angry that Sebastián got to say whatever he wanted in this relationship while he had to stay silent. A world of opinions was buried within him that he'd kept hidden for so long. He wanted to let them out, and feel something other than numb and angry.

In his anger, he had not taken anything with him, which he immediately regretted since it was pretty chilly that afternoon, but he refused to go back up 'there.' He paced around the block, doing his best to stay warm. He considered going into a bar, but everywhere had a tyrannical mask requirement, and he didn't have a mask either. He had stupidly left his hanging on the doorknob of his apartment.

"This is ridiculous," he said to no one in particular.

Angry, he decided then and there that he would fight this injustice. Sebastián's not the only one who can go to protests. He whipped out his phone and searched Twitter for anti-mask protests. He luckily found one close enough to him—God bless the Internet.

He sprinted over there. When he arrived, he found they were a group of no more than twenty people. These men and women held up signs like 'my body, my choice' and 'end mandates now.' These signs were simple and crude but still spoke to what these people believed and what he thought, and for that, Christian felt a connection with them. These protestors certainly looked like him— tired, frustrated, and unable to move on. Their white faces all beamed with indignant rage.

"Join us," shouted someone in the crowd, and soon they were all saying 'join us' over and over again.

Christian hesitated for a second before taking the plunge and entering the throng of people. "Screw masks," he shouted. "Screw them all."

They cheered.

"Right on, brother," one of the protestors said.

As he moved through them, he realized that the protestors weren't just angry but looked happy, too. When they weren't screaming, they all had smiles on their faces. It was exciting to be with them and making a statement.

Maybe, in a small way, they could push back against this insanity. Christian felt, weirdly, like he was at home: a feeling that did not often come to him.

"My body, my choice," someone in the crowd started to chant, and pretty soon, they all were saying the same. Christian repeated the words, unable to tell where their voices ended, and he began.

# CHAPTER 33

*Sebastián*

Sebastián learned about the protest within moments. He got a ping from Jon, who now just went by his first name on Grindr. It was a TikTok video where Christian was attending an anti-mask rally, amongst men, women, and children—children—chanting outside *The Silver Spoon*, whose owners had been particularly strict with requiring masks for anyone who wanted to go inside: The building was still open, even as it was surrounded by a group of fifteen or so protestors. One patron, a lanky man in a winter jacket, tried to sneak away from the protestors, only for them to focus their ire directly on him.

"How can you call yourself an American?" one of the protestors shouted, unmasked, spit flying directly in the patron's face.

Sebastián was horrified. He saw that Christian was near him. He was lifting his fist in the air, screaming, 'No more masks,' and the cringiest of all, 'I can't breathe.' He looked strangely more driven than he had in weeks. Christian must have been freezing in his t-shirt and jeans, but he didn't appear to care. This had to be what he wanted—his voice, his movement.

Sebastián did not remember what he did immediately after watching the video. He had blacked out. All he wanted to do was scream at Christian, to punch him in his condescending, hypocritical face. He looked down at his hands. They were shaking. He had shredded apart a book in rage, and now bits of paper were strung about on the floor. His hands stung from fresh paper cuts, and he had to suck one of his fingers to stop it from bleeding.

Fuck that man! Had this relationship ever been a good idea? Sebastián decided he had only ever been in love with the idea of Christian, which was now ruined by this. How could he have been so stupid to move in with someone he had only known for less than two months? Stupid, stupid, stupid. He had compromised everything about himself for a man who didn't care about him, not if he was doing this.

"Single at 29 during the middle of a pandemic. But better than continuing one more day in this relationship," he tweeted before packing his things, tears running down his cheeks. He got 36 likes in minutes. He used to judge Jon so harshly for being online all the time, but he finally got it—the thrill of dumping all your thoughts and feelings somewhere. Seeing how a few simple clicks could impact other people was exhilarating, and his followers seemed to appreciate his honesty.

He hurriedly packed all his things into a suitcase, tossing crumpled socks, t-shirts, and short shorts, tweeting as he went. "He's never going to see these again," he wrote, posting a picture of a jockstrap to the world.

He crammed his entire life into that unwieldy black suitcase, pushing so hard that it bulged at the seams. Too much to fit, and yet hardly much of anything when all was said and done. Over a year of a relationship, and after all that, it was contained inside a single box. It was pathetic. He had devoted so much of his time to a man he was pretty sure didn't love him.

And so he left.

He thought he would be devastated, but he felt nothing. He was numb to his partner's bullshit. Their relationship had died weeks ago when Emmett went to the hospital, and he was now processing the cindered ashes.

As the weeks progressed, Sebastián distanced himself from the bubble. He wasn't talking to Christian, obviously, or James, who had become even more dogmatically anti-vaccine in the intervening months. Jon still hated him, lashing out online about how he had hurt Emmett.

Jon

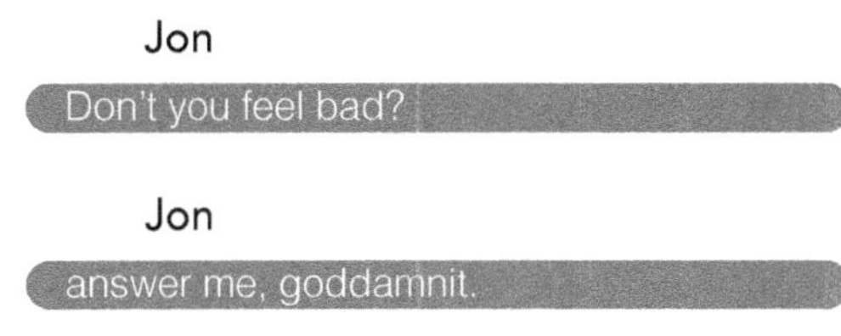


Jon

There was Barry, of course, but he… well, could be demanding. Ever since they had had sex during that Halloween party, he'd been very upfront about wanting to have sex again. He would ping Sebastián out of the blue, asking to meet—a thought that made Sebastián wish to retreat into himself.

He would never give himself over to Barry again, not by choice. He wanted all his 'friends' to shut up more than communicate with them. No, better to be left alone than be used by men who had belittled him for months. He blocked them all. *Blocked. Blocked. Blocked. Blocked.*

The only saving grace was that he had never let go of the lease at his apartment. A sign, he told himself, that meant that their relationship had never been built to last anyway. He spent time in his sad, little dwelling, cleaning up after a long year of neglect. It was like an excavation as he pulled apart the layers of his old life. He found little trinkets that felt weirdly antiquated now: poppers in his refrigerator when he had felt comfortable bringing just anyone over, and, thrown about everywhere you might expect to find trash, crumpled-up tickets for concert venues and parties. He shuddered at the more recent ones, realizing how selfish he had been not too long ago. He would have to do better.

Sebastián did his best to make the place genuinely livable. He finally removed the bed frame from its box, something he had neglected for over a year. It was nothing fancy. A standard black frame that was a pain to assemble, but once completed, it made the place instantly feel bigger. He cleaned the carpet and scrubbed away the orangish mold along the rim of the kitchen and shower faucets. To make the place more homely, he even purchased a succulent, a small, vibrant green thing he placed in a reddish-orange ceramic pot by his windowsill.

Yet, there were only so many times you could clean and rearrange the furniture in a 460 square-foot apartment before it lost its initial magic. Move a couch here. Place a shelving unit there. The process became so dull that he eventually returned to watching Netflix and tweeting his anxieties on the Internet.

"#whenwillthevaccinegethere?" he tweeted to thousands.

What else was there to do except watch celebrities embarrass themselves online and wait for the vaccine? Joe Biden had announced that all Americans would be eligible for it by May 1st, and then they could return to their lives. He could do things again. He could meet people. He would no longer be constrained by a rotation of four toxic people over and over again. Fuck James. Fuck Jon. Fuck Barry. And especially Fuck Christian. Fuck all of them.

His new obsession was trying to get the vaccine as quickly as possible. He wanted to resume his life: to get back to normal. He heard that you could simply cheat— lie about an autoimmune disorder or your weight to become eligible sooner. Sebastián had even seen someone sign up to be an Uber Eats driver on Instagram just to hop the line, but he didn't want to cut corners anymore, not this time. He would do this the right way. His nights were spent hunched over his computer with a drink in hand, pouring over his state's requirements. He was always looking for that tidbit that would help him jump the line.

"LGBTQIA+ community getting the vaccine early because of AIDS risk," read one salaciously titled article shared on Twitter.

Sebastián clicked on it, realizing its source was a complete misreading of the governor's recent executive order. Vaccine centers were being placed in LGBTQIA+ clinics for easy access. The requirements had not changed. It was hours of research wasted.

"Smokers get to jump the line," said a local influencer on TikTok.

Several clicks later, and yes, this was true. Smoking was considered a comorbidity that qualified for stage 2B, but that would be at least a month or two away. He signed up under this, but he wasn't happy about it. Sebastián wanted to get the vaccine now. He wanted to take the drug cocktail into his veins so that he could leave this tiny box he called home. It seemed more like a prison to him now than the 'cool staging area' he had thought of it as a year and a half ago.

"This pharmacy is giving away shots meant for no-shows," one Redditor posted.

Sebastián cross-referenced this with NextDoor and found that it was true. This lead did check out. He saw a recent picture of a white couple with their new vaccine cards standing in front of the store. It was giving away free shots.

He rushed out the door with only a light jacket in hand. The cool wind nipped at his ears, making them red and numb, but he didn't care. He ran to his bus stop, shivering as he hopped onto the bus's stairs right before the door closed. It took him several minutes to warm up inside. He felt like he was melting. His skin was red and puffy as he adjusted to the artificial climate inside the bus.

It was a longer ride than what he was used to. Sebastián would typically travel fifteen or so minutes around his neighborhood, but this was far. He traveled through tunnels and over hills, past emerging skylines with scaffolding, and across the river, where more lots were vacant, and the buildings were far less sleek. Metal bars were on nearly every window and door, except for the Army recruitment office, a cheap, glass box in the same building as a Subway. This was the first time Sebastián had seen an Army Recruiter in years, not since moving away from his hometown in Jersey.

He looked around and saw men and women in scrubs and construction hats, working-class people who seemed to make this forty-five-stop bus trip every day. They were Browner than in his neighborhood and seemed poorer too. Some were old with wrinkled skin and faded hair. Others looked young but just as haggard and worn out. A few had children in the mix, carrying stuffed animals or small bags with homework.

Sebastián got off for his stop, leaving him to stand and stare at the pharmacy's entrance. He had arrived in a sea of blight: no, that was a terrible way to refer to people's homes. He was in a poorer neighborhood, like the one he had grown up in. Sebastián was surrounded by two towering apartment buildings with several restaurants and a CVS on the first floor. The closest was a Chinese restaurant missing some of its letters on the light-up sign hanging above it. Off in the distance was a well-used basketball court, and adjacent to that, a playground with equipment that was breaking down. Sebastián was surprised to see here men in blue suits wearing earpieces. They stood around on the sidewalk, awkwardly waiting for Lyfts and Ubers. They must be there for the same reason.

Sebastián walked into the CVS and went to the back, to find the pharmacy.

"You here for the no-shows," asked a large woman in a red CVS shirt. She had done her eyebrows out in a way that made her stare brilliantly exaggerated yet cutting. She seemed bored by his very presence.

"Um, yes. How did you know?"

She laughed, gesturing towards his person. Sebastián made a quick look around. There were about fifteen people in the store, including staff. All of them were darker than him and poorer. His light sweater had been a Hermes wool one given to him by Christian's mom, Ashley, for Christmas. His skinny jeans were from Nordstrom. He was even wearing a Cartier watch gifted to him by Christian's grandfather, Samuel. Had he become so different in such a short amount of time? He immediately felt uncomfortable, like a big old schmuck, realizing, far too late, that he hadn't just lucked into a vaccine. He had never been to this neighborhood, and now that he had, he wanted to leave more than ever.

"Come on," she said. "I think some are left."

She started to walk forward. Sebastián stared in her direction. Should he follow? Would he? He took in a deep breath and made a decision.

# CHAPTER 34

## Mister Right

Christian was devastated when Sebastián left him, even if he had been too proud to fight for it. Their relationship had been short but so intense and memorable. He didn't know who he was anymore. After that protest, he changed his profile name a lot, hoping to find something that would fill the hole where Sebastián used to be: *Newly single, hurting, working on being ok, Looking, Nothing serious*. He finally settled on *Mister Right*, a slogan that poked at his desperation for a new partner.

Christian hadn't felt like going out that night, but was glad he'd done so. He was having the time of his fucking life. He was dancing shirtless inside an abandoned warehouse that had been converted into an underground party space. The music was thundering over speakers haphazardly strung about on pipes running across the ceilings. Strobe lights were on them, too, alongside fog machines that spouted out a haze that the lights pierced through.

Men were everywhere, mostly shirtless, with glitter smeared all over their chests. They were bobbing to the beat with drinks in hand. Christian was one of them, letting loose to the music. A hunky Australian was grinding up against him, sweaty and hot. The Australian towered from behind, holding onto Christian's hips and thrusting into him.

James was across from them, humping some twink half his age. He cast Christian a smirk, and he returned one in kind. Christian loved this moment. The feeling of being lost in a crowd of strangers was beyond intoxicating. He had been so afraid of not being let inside. The venue had demanded vaccine cards to obtain entry, and he had refused to get vaccinated because it was his goddamn right not to. He and James had ordered fake cards online, which had worked like a charm. The bouncer had given it a confused squint and then passed it back to them, having no real idea how to verify them.

Besides, it's not like the club truly cared about security. There was a long line to the bathrooms where a group of people had to be doing coke, and the weirdest man was standing in the corner in a trench coat, with a bulging gym bag at his feet, assessing the crowd with cold eyes. He gave Christian the creeps. He was clearly selling drugs or doing something else shady, and no one seemed to care.

Still, even though it had been easy to slip in here, Christian felt giddy getting away with the deception, and this was only the beginning—the first stop in a night of events he and James would try to attend. They were planning to go to every pretentious, freedom-hating gay bar on this street, the ones that had survived the recession anyway. He had placed himself in a box dating Sebastián, never sharing his opinions lest he be labeled 'stupid' or 'anti-science.' Liberals were so condescending with their bold statements and moral absolutes. He remembered all the fights he had had with Sebastián about Covid. The condescending lectures his boyfriend...

*Ex-boyfriend*, the voice reminded him.

Fine, the lectures his ex-boyfriend had given him about how stupid he was for refusing vaccines and thinking that maybe we shouldn't jab some untested science into people's arms. The late nights tossing and turning in bed as he tried to fight his instinct to cuddle his partner after a heated conversation so that his body wouldn't betray him with unearned closeness. He would inevitably wake up to Sebastián's arms draped over his side, and his resistance would instantly melt away.

Now, he could be free to be himself. Free from the judgment and the scorn of Sebastián. He looked around, taking it all in: the smiles of the crowd, the sweaty musk of hot men, and the burn of alcohol, tasting like magic in his mouth. These were the missing pieces of his life that had been suffocating him with their absence, and he wouldn't let some hysteria stop him from enjoying it. They would go to Trade next, and then another bar, before maybe capping their night at a house party hosted by Barry. He had allegedly invited dancers from a gay strip club to be the 'highlight of the party.'

### Hung AF (Barry)

they are arriving at 1 am 😈.

### Mister Right (Christian)

Awesome. I'll be there.

### Hung AF (Barry)

You better. These gremlins are thirsty.

This moment, this party, was the new normal. Hundreds of people were packed into this warehouse, crammed together so tightly that Christian thought he might become a blob of sweat and flesh. People bumped into him. They spilled their drinks on him. They kissed him. One new man ground up against his front, sandwiching him with the Australian.

Suddenly, Christian, the Australian, and this new person engaged in a transcendent three-way kiss. Christian's tongue darted between their mouths. The Australian placed his strong hands on the back of Christian's head as he pushed him into the kiss. Then, the Australian and the stranger pulled away, disappearing into the formless crowd as quickly as they had arrived.

Christian didn't care. He danced his ass off. The beat the DJ was playing was so sick, and loud, so incredibly loud and piercing. It had a bass to it that was unusual for EDM. The beat was occasionally interrupted by a pop, pop, pop. He started to get into a headspace where he phased everyone out. There was nothing else but the shifting tones of the music as it blasted all around him.

*Pop, pop, pop.*

People screamed. The beat of the music went on and on, but in a discordant way, as the DJ had left the song skipping on the same beat, which was not an artistic choice Christian could say he enjoyed. The crowd went crazy. People were frantically moving this way and that, like cats trying to escape the rain. Christian heard someone scream. The pops became louder as his friend James fell to the ground. There was a pain in his chest as someone fell on top of him. It was excruciating, like a dagger that had exploded every nerve ending in his body.

A second passed, and he heard a thump as he hit the ground. His body no longer felt like it was attached to him but deadweight, which was getting farther and farther away by the second.

The music had stopped. People were screaming, and as the world around him faded to black, all he could think about was how there was so much more to do. The world had just started to get back to normal. Christian thought of the bars he had to go to and Barry's party, and then, he thought of nothing.

# CHAPTER 35

Sebastián

Sebastián had left his apartment to escape the news. A friend had sent him a news article about how James had died, along with ten other gay men, many of whom Sebastián had seen around at clubs and parties, and he simply couldn't sit still. He had seen Christian's face in the news report, though he couldn't find any information on whether he was dead or alive, only that he had been taken to a hospital.

'In critical condition,' the article had mentioned of Christian—news that seared into Sebastián's head like a hot iron, the pain so great that it blocked out the glaring sunlight above and left him with nothing.

It was enough to make him want to scream. His boss tried to call him, and, like clockwork, Sebastián answered. The firm was short-staffed, and his boss needed him to go in that moment, but Sebastián would rather die than do that. Perhaps die was a poor choice of words? Fuck, two of his friends might be dead—because of Sebastián. In tears, he told his boss to go fuck himself. He had probably burned that bridge for good, and Sebastián didn't care anymore.

His brain simply shut down. For how long, he didn't know, but something in him broke. Nothing made sense. Sebastián stopped caring about where he was going, not thinking of anything. No hopes. No worries. The brisk spring breeze washed over his empty vessel as he absent-mindedly walked forward.

At that moment, he was a child on his mother's bed, being scolded for making his rich cousins feel bad about their nicer toys at a playdate, for making them feel uncom-fortable by his poor existence. His mother told him not to be rude, but he hadn't tried to be. Sebastián had only told his cousins how much the toys had cost because he had seen it in an ad for Nickelodeon. Those words had made them uncomfortable enough to complain to their parents about how Sebastián was 'mean' to them.

As his mom lectured him about kindness and 'not being too difficult,' the information didn't quite fit. It pushed in like a shard lodged into his chest. She was tell-ing him not to be mean, and he couldn't understand how it even applied, and yet he was expected to swallow the words all the same.

Like then, this information didn't fit. Sebastián didn't know how Christian could be dead. He had seen him, alive and well, less than a month ago. They had danced the night away before going to a McDonald's drive-thru to get fries and chicken nuggets. Christian wore the same clothes in his victim's photo: a button-up, green plaid shirt and blue jeans. Sebastián had worn a black shirt and leather pants that night, and Christian had said he had looked hot. They had talked and laughed, and then Sebastián had kissed him on the cheek, and…

Sebastián shuddered with grief. He couldn't process any of this; more importantly, he didn't want to.

"Sebastián?" called out a familiar voice.

He hadn't realized how far he had walked, mulling over his thoughts. He had journeyed halfway across town to a less scenic part of the city, and there, standing in baggy jeans and a shirt that didn't quite fit him, was Rick. The man who always showed up at the most inopportune times, awkward as ever.

"Rick? Good to see you. I didn't know you lived around here."

"I don't. I just came from a meeting at the Center," he said, gesturing to the large community center behind him. It was a building renovated in the 90s with large glass windows that made it seem like a soaring shard of glass from afar. Of course Sebastián had walked to the center. He half-remembered that many community organizations were housed there, including the LGBT Center, where ongoing meetings were constantly taking place: gay happy hours, gay networking events, anything gay, really.

It made sense for his reptilian brain to have wanted that in this moment.

"Right. I have been out of the loop with that stuff. How is the gay twenty and thirty-somethings meet-up going?"

"Oh," a laugh escaped Rick, without meaning to, "I don't go to that. I was at the trans support group."

"I didn't know you were, you know," Sebastián said, embarrassed by this sudden revelation.

"That's because you never bothered to learn anything about me," he snapped, like that answer had been building in him for some time. "Sorry, that came out wrong. I know you have recently been going through a lot with Christian and Emmett." His voice trailed off in guilt, which weirdly made Sebastián feel better.

"It's okay. We were never really nice to you. Sorry about that. We… I should have treated you better."

"Thank you. That's… I don't think I ever expected you to admit that."

"Does that mean you're becoming a girl, or are a girl, sorry?"

Rick laughed. "I'm a trans dude. Have been since before we met."

"Oh, Sorry that was super inappropriate. I'm still working out how not to be, like, a terrible person."

Rick chuckled even louder this time. "You're not terrible."

"That's sweet of you to say, but I haven't exactly been the person of the year. And I have a lot of weird anger about Christian that I haven't dealt with. I hated his guts at the end. I guess, I don't even know if he's alive, and I still hate him or hated him, to be honest, but I also love, loved him." Tears were streaming down Sebastián's face. "Sorry, so sorry. I shouldn't be dumping this on you."

"That's okay. It's okay to share your emotions with your friends."

"You still want to be friends with me? After I was so mean to you?"

"Assuming you continue not to be terrible," Rick chided. "Yeah, we can be friends. Consider it friend probation." He winked.

Sebastián wiped away the tears dripping down his cheeks. "I'd like that," he managed to blurt out.

"In fact, why don't we grab a coffee sometime? Your treat. Consider it a way for you to pay your debt back to society," Rick smirked wryly.

"Are you free now?" Sebastián asked, realizing that he had gotten what he had wanted for years: a genuine meet-cute, and it was the least interesting thing that had happened to him that day.

# Chapter

## 36

*Barry*

The party Barry had spent weeks planning, quickly turned into a wake. The news from the shooting rippled through the guests like a shockwave. The jubilant energy that not too long ago had permeated every inch of Barry's renovated townhouse sapped into agony and despair. People wept openly, and many more simply stared down at their phones in silence.

He saw the faces of those he knew flash across the screen: James and a dozen others. He felt sick. He told the DJ he hired to cut the music. It no longer felt appropriate for people to gyrate to Iggy Azalea on a day when over ten people in their community had been killed. He stood on the top of his winding staircase, which had a perfect vantage point of the crowd in the open living room below, and cleared his throat.

"I… many of you know that there has just been a shooting at a gay nightclub. Over ten people are dead." Barry paused, struggling to think of what to say next. What do you even say after that? "Many of those killed," he continued, "were people we knew, our friends, our family, our lovers." Lovers? He choked back the word as tears streamed down his face. Why was he talking about this right now? He wanted to disappear. He cleared his throat again and told himself to get it together. "I know we are hurting, but I also know there are other people out there who need our help. Maybe… we could give money?"

There was a woo from the crowd.

"Yeah," Barry went on, "we could do a GoFundMe for the victims. I know that would make me, all of us, feel better. So what do we say?"

The support was unanimous. Someone with technical expertise hastily set up a GoFundMe page, and they soon took turns plugging in payment information into Barry's desktop computer. They raised over $1,000, and Barry didn't quite know where to send it. The club? The victims? He mused this over with people in the kitchen, guests starting to drink more heavily again. They were not in a revelatory mood, but they were driven, and that feeling was even better now.

"The bar's owner, Frank something or other, they are on fire tonight," said Victoria, Barry's fag hag. She was showing everyone in the circle her phone. Frank Miller's Twitter, the man who owned pretty much every gay bar in town, was a stream of clapbacks deriding the attacks. "Oh, he was on the news today," Victoria remarked, pulling up a video of him inside a tiny box next to a news anchor on CNN.

"Our men are under attack," said Frank inside the box. He had deep, faraway eyes. "This is the definition of a hate crime, and it's not just tonight. People have been attacking the definition of what a gay man is for years. Of what gender even is."

"He's great," Barry said. "Do you think we could do a fundraiser with him? I know his PA."

"Know," Victoria repeated, performing air quotes to reference how Barry had slept with him.

"Yes, know, you jerk." He replied.

"Sure, but we might need someone a bit younger to host. You know how vain the gays can be," laughed Victoria. "And then immediately covered her mouth," realizing the comment might not be appropriate.

"It's okay," Barry comforted her. "No one is going to cancel you."

# CHAPTER 37



"**D**evastateed." Jon tweeted moments after the attack. "I don't know how i Can ever be the same."

Jon wasn't only doing it for attention. He had been utterly devastated by the loss of so many of his peers, even that conservative idiot James. He had thought there would be more time for them to catch up—for them to make up—for him to apologize. He kept thinking to-morrow would be the day he'd stop being so hard on *The Gang*$^{TM}$ for Emmett.

After all, he had been there too. He had even fucked him. Jon remembered getting down on his knees and blow-ing Emmett—all of them in a pile of men, unable to tell the difference between where someone's dick started and another one began. He remembered Emmett, though. He was the only Black man there, so his flesh stuck out in the crowd, and Jon had clung to that familiarity.

He had this distinct memory of someone in the pile coughing. Jon remembered it had maybe been James, yet no one had said anything. It had sent a momentary ripple through all of them, and then, several seconds later, the kissing and fucking simply resumed. It was a horny mass of unscrupulous people who had put that need over others' lives. Though he had never tested positive for Covid, he could have. And now this week's shooting, an event he had promised to go to but bailed on at the last minute. He very well could have been gunned down alongside James and J.J. It should have been him.

That's why this fundraiser was so important. It was an event he had put on to raise money for the victims of the attack. Barry had contacted him, telling Jon that the owner of the gay bar targeted last week, Frank Miller, had reached out over Twitter, offering up their sister location for free if Jon hosted the event.

"It'll be good publicity if an activist like you does it over me," Frank DM'd him after Barry had made an introduction.

Jon jumped at the opportunity to do something right. He had spent the last few days searching for an organization that would agree to do it at the last minute. Several had reservations about the owner, who had apparently said some not-so-great things online, but Jon had assured them that Frank was reasonable enough. Frank had agreed to offer up his space, in kind, after all… and after the year they'd all had, who hadn't said some things they had regretted?

The event was at an upscale sports bar called Catchers, which appealed to the sophisticated and sporty gay. TVs that usually played sports games hung silently on the walls, along with a healthy supply of signed bats, baseball uniforms, and other sports paraphernalia.

Jon set up the event on the dance floor on the second level. Nearly a hundred people had shown up that Saturday afternoon, cathartically mourning their friends and chosen family. A Drag Queen named Summer Camp—a local fixture—was emceeing. She wore all black, a sparkly veil obscuring her face. Summer Camp lifted it up to begin talking. "Thank you for joining us. And thank you to Catchers for hosting us. Before we begin, I'd like to offer up a moment of silence for our fallen brothers and sisters."

Summer Camp cued Jon to begin. He turned on a projector that usually played softcore porn to project the images of those who had fallen. #werememberthem was posted below each image, and the song *Blackbird* by the Beatles played in the background. Jon winced slightly every time he saw James' face. His perfectly chiseled jawline was cast eerily on the wall, like a ghost looming over those who had survived. It didn't seem possible that he could be dead too. Only two months ago, Jon had kissed those lips and gossiped over what a petty jerk he was— and now he, like so many others, was gone forever. Jon felt numb. He didn't realize until he touched his face that he was crying.

The event lasted for about an hour, as various community members gave speeches and asked for donations. They raised about $5,000 for the organization, $6,000, including the money Barry had thrown in, which one of the organization's PR people had informed him was 'a good haul.' It was supposed to go toward the hospital and funeral costs of the shooting victims, though Jon didn't know exactly how the logistics of it worked.

The only negative was that a group of 'agitators' had interrupted the event. A man in a blue hat had pushed himself to the front of the crowd, repeatedly chanting "No TERFS in the queer community" until security dragged him out. Jon couldn't believe it. He was as progressive as you could be, but he would never dream of interrupting an event this important.

When everyone finally finished saying their good-byes, the crowd started to disperse. Jon left the clean-up to Catchers' staff and headed out, already late to another fundraising event he had promised to live tweet. He rushed outside to the sound of chanting. A dozen protestors were screaming the same chant as the agitator inside.

"How does it feel to support a TERF?" shouted one of them. It was the man in the blue hat. Jon rolled his eyes, and then he saw who it was.

"Sebastián?" Jon asked, baffled. He looked slightly different from when they last saw each other in person. He wasn't keeping up appearances. Sebastián was worn down, as if he had not slept in a while. His hair was sloppy and wild. However, he also looked more energized than Jon had ever seen him. There was a determined look in his eyes as he stared Jon down.

"Jon?" he asked, also confused. "What are you doing here?… Wait, follow me."

He gestured for Jon to move out of the line of fire. The two of them walked several feet away from the protest so they wouldn't be surrounded by angry, shouting people. They were staring at each other more intensely now, and all those months came flooding back. The late-night cuddles. The arguing. The fucking. They had been so close once.

"So, what are you doing here?"

"I organized this event," Jon responded at last.

"You know the owner of this bar is a TERF, right?" Sebastián said, "He fired an employee for transitioning."

"Shit. A what now? I'd heard he was controversial to some, yeah, but I didn't hear about that."

"A Trans Exclusive Radical Feminist. Yeah, he owes her back pay. And a job. That's why we are protesting."

Jon glanced over at some of the signs the protestors were holding. They read things like 'Justice for Maria' and 'Give her what she is owed.' Many of the protestors seemed to be queer themselves, wearing the pink and light blue colors of the trans flag in the form of pins, makeup, and even one or two flags.

"Well, the event's over now, so… " His voice trailed off.

"You could join us," Sebastián said excitedly. "You disavowing Frank would help us a lot. He was using this event for cover from the bad press." Sebastián beamed at him as if Jon held the world's fate in his hands.

"Oh, well, I sort of have another event to go to."

"Oh," said Sebastián. The disappointment was evident on his face.

"I'll see you around, though," Jon added.

"Sure," Sebastián said. "I got to get back to ah, this." He gestured to the crowd.

"Bye. Good luck." Jon said.

Sebastián didn't reply, walking away. He merged into the crowd of the people who hated him. Jon felt guilty for leaving, but reminded himself that he had done well today. $5000 was a lot of money. That money would do some good.

No, he wasn't a bad person. He was a good person. He had done good.

# CHAPTER 38

*Christian*

Blackness. Darkness. For a while, Christian saw nothing. He thought he had died but then realized he wouldn't be thinking.

Sounds came back first. Ephemeral fragments at the edge of his senses. He heard the beeping of a machine. A cough. Someone said his name. He couldn't talk at all. Christian's lips were like a locked door he didn't have the key for.

Then his eyes opened. He appeared to be on a cot in what he instantly recognized as a hospital. Jon was there, slumped in a plastic chair by his bedside. He was staring down at his phone, probably waiting for some time for

Christian to wake up. How long had he been there? A day? A week? Christian couldn't say or do anything, so it took Jon forever to notice him.

It was a nurse who first spied Christian was awake, and then Jon happily looked up from his phone and made his way over. Christian couldn't understand all the words thrown in his direction. He heard the words 'attack' and 'shooting.' Jon mentioned something about a party. The one thing he heard repeatedly was Jon apologizing, but for what, he couldn't be sure.

Christian opened his mouth and found his voice was hoarse. Every word was a struggle. He said the first thing he could think of. "Easy… slut," Christian said, forgetting the nurse was next to them. "Talk… slower."

Jon slowed down the cadence of his words, and the two talked as nurses and doctors surrounded them, taking notes and running tests. Christian learned more about the attack at the nightclub: the ten people who had died; how he had been gunned down months ago; how his injuries had placed him in a coma. Jon had been at his side for over a month, waiting.

"Thank… you" was all Christian could manage to say upon learning about Jon's generosity. "Sebastián?" Christian asked.

Jon shook his head. Sebastián apparently hadn't come in for the entire time Jon had visited.

It would take days for Christian to truly process his surroundings. By then, his entire family had flown in: his mother and father, Sammie and Rebecca, his grandmother Doris and grandfather Samuel, Admiral Thomas, and even his nieces and nephews for a couple of days. He didn't know how his family had managed it, but on the first day, they were all there next to his bedside, flaunting Covid restrictions. He suspected his father or his grandfather had bribed someone. Maybe they both had.

Jon was almost immediately dismissed. "Wait, this isn't the boyfriend," his mother Ashley said as they entered, pointing to Jon, who had been pushed to the corner of the room, where he was quietly lurking.

"No, I'm Jon, just a friend."

"Well, Jon," his mom Ashley said. "Thank you so much for keeping our son company, but if you wouldn't mind. His family will take it from here."

"No… stay," Christian called out.

"It's fine," Jon said, looking directly at Christian. "I will see you later."

And with that, he was gone.

"We are glad to see you, killer," Sammie said with all the tact of a freight train.

"You were so strong, boy." the Admiral said from the back.

"Talk about conquering death," his grandfather continued.

"Oh, Christian. What were you thinking going to a place like that," his mother said, referring to the gay nightclub. Her comment stung, even though Christian knew she only meant the best.

It was hard to think as everyone was going so fast. "Guns," Christian started to say before he was immediately interrupted.

"This is why security guards in this blasted city need to be armed." the Admiral said to no one in particular.

"The police were armed," Doris scoffed. "And it took them over an hour to enter."

"There were extenuating circumstances," the Admiral quipped.

"Oh heavens, we are just thankful you are okay," Ashley deflected, kissing Christian on the forehead. "I thought I lost you forever."

Whatever magic his family worked on that first day did not work on the following ones. They couldn't all come in at the same time because of Covid restrictions, so they would file in at random times, and all Christian could do was nod and say thank you. His family spent the next couple of days providing him company throughout visiting hours, especially his mother, who would've slept in the hospital if they had let her.

One morning he woke up to the sound of his grandfather cursing someone out. The doctors hadn't told him good enough news, and he was fuming about Christian being a 'cripple.' "We are going to get a second opinion," he huffed. "Mark my words, we will beat this thing."

*You will be like this forever*, the voice mocked.

"Fuck… you," Christian whispered. He was so tired of his depression. He didn't have the energy for it anymore.

"Excuse me," his grandfather Samuel said, thinking Christian was talking to him.

"Nothing," Christian said, and with that, everyone went back to ignoring him.

Many doctors rotated in and out of his room—none of them thought he would be able to return to 'full mobility,' as they called it.

"With enough physical therapy, he'll be able to walk short distances, but he's going to require assistance for longer distances," a doctor in blue scrubs told his grandfather, speaking to him like Christian wasn't there.

Christian wanted to curse this asshole for ignoring him and treating him like a child, but he didn't have the energy. He was in incredible pain. His muscles felt like they were burning, like hot sands had engulfed his body. A doctor told him this was his new normal, and that with a regular prescription of pain meds, he would 'habituate' to it eventually. Christian didn't know how that would ever be possible.

He was discharged from the hospital shortly after that. The doctors thought he was in stable enough condition. Besides, they needed his room for more patients.

"There aren't enough beds," a nurse told his mother after she insisted on speaking with a supervisor. "Too many patients with Covid, and they need his bed," she said, pointing to Christian.

No one asked for his opinion. Most everyone ignored him. The voice would tell him this was because he was worthless, but he didn't value its opinion as much anymore. He wanted to hurt someone, and the only free target was his own mind, so he threw a lifetime of rage in the voice's direction.

*Who the fuck do you think you are?* He would demand, daring it to respond.

On particularly brutal days, he could make it whimper. The voice would tell Christian he was broken, and Christian would promptly think back at it to go fuck itself.

He didn't always succeed; some days, he still lost, but he was getting better. Or at least angrier.

*I want you to suffer like I'm suffering*, he would scream at his mind."

After days of exhausting, internal screaming, Christian was discharged from the hospital in a wheelchair, which his doctor had prescribed to him—language that he thought was both funny and sad. Shouldn't this stuff be free? A nurse had given him a quick lesson on how to use the chair and told him a physical therapist would go over it in greater detail, but he was worried. It was hard work to push the wheels forward, and after a couple of minutes, his arms felt quite sore.

Thankfully, a nurse pushed his chair on his way out of the hospital. His mother was the one who pushed him toward the car. It was awkward for all involved to get him inside it. No one competently knew how to fold his chair and place it in the trunk, leaving his father and mother to debate it for ages. His mother, embarrassingly from Christian's point of view, had to lift him from the seat and place him into the car—something he resented deeply.

When they returned to his place, Christian worried that he would wheel into his apartment and his family would see the lube and beer cans he had left scattered about the night before the shooting. He had left everything a mess—he had been a mess—but someone had cleaned up the space.

"Who… cleaned?" Christian asked.

"We paid a maid," his mother said. "It was quite the mess."

"Oh," Christian said, realizing they must have seen the mess after all.

"Her name is, I don't know, Rosa, Esperanza," his mom continued, not commenting on everything she had probably seen. "It doesn't matter. You won't have to worry about that in Connecticut."

"You… think I'm… coming back… with… you?" Christian said in a long, drawn-out struggle.

"Well, you can't exactly take care of yourself," she remarked.

"Mother… I have… a life here."

"Had," she corrected. "That reminds me, where is Sebastián?"

Christian was silent at this remark.

"Honey, I only want what's best for you," she continued.

There wasn't much to say more than that, not that he could.

He headed to Connecticut a day later, to his parent's house, which he hadn't visited since well before the pandemic. Moving through this house he knew so well in a completely different context was strange. He used to run up and down these halls, but now, every movement was a chore. He would knock over priceless knick knacks as he rolled across the halls and got his wheels stuck on luxurious rugs too thick to traverse easily.

His mother would make frustrated comments whenever this happened, usually blaming some staff person in the process. "I told her this rug wouldn't work," she would huff, or "This is why I instructed Blanca to put Doris' Christmas gifts in a box. They are far too fragile."

This made Christian feel even worse, causing him not to want to move about anywhere. He was confined to the first floor because the house was never set up to accommodate someone with a disability. There were no elevators or electric conveyors to speak of. Christian was placed in the guest wing, which was by no means terrible. In fact, it was downright presidential but spoke to how he felt here: as a guest.

He slept on a luxurious mattress that had been taken out of an elevated, wooden bedframe still sitting in the room. Except when his mom would check in on him for meals or help him go to the bathroom, he was primarily alone, left to stew on how his life had gotten like this. Christian hated this house. It's not like he would have been able to do much in the city, but at least he had known people there.

As things were, he had no autonomy whatsoever because he was relearning how to do everything. His one respite was physical and speech therapy, and even with these he was shepherded to and from suburban highrises by the family driver, always accompanied by his mother.

"You are getting so much better," she would say, like a prayer.

*Your life will be like this forever*, the voice mocked.

"Maybe you're right," Christian said, realizing perhaps for the first time that the voice wasn't his grandfather, or some other malicious entity that needed to be warded against, but his own mind, and he was scared.

# Chapter 39



Sebastián didn't know things could be this way with someone. His relationship with Christian had been so hard. Every action had been a struggle. Every conversation had been a war. He remembered the mere discussion around what to have for dinner every night had been a monumental fight near the end. Each of them would pettily bring up points and counterpoints as to why the other's decision was stupid.

Yet, with Rick, it was easier. He remembered the first time he hurt Rick's feelings, telling him that one of his ideas was stupid. He didn't even remember the comment or why he had said such a mean thing. The impulse to fight was still deeply ingrained within him. Sebastián remembered flinching, expecting a massive explosion of fury, but it never came.

"I know you are angry," Rick stated simply, probing him more tenderly than he had known for months. "But that was mean."

"Sorry," Sebastián conceded.

Rick exhaled a heavy breath. "Apology accepted."

And that was that. Rick was prone to anger easily. He had a firm sense of right and wrong but was good at channeling it. Sebastián would catch him tracing his hands with his fingers, breathing in and out with each line.

"Are you seeing a therapist," he asked bluntly.

Sebastián was taken aback by this question. "I… no. I always thought that that was for crazy people."

Rick flinched at the word crazy.

"Besides," Sebastián continued, not wanting to have to give another apology. "I can't exactly afford it now that I'm unemployed."

Rick smiled. "I think I can help with that."

Within a week, Sebastián was at the LGBT Center for group therapy. It was apparently a free service they put on every week, and Rick was a regular attendee. The room was small and cramped, with the stereotypical 1980s carpeting you see in every major government building. There was a facilitator named Bacari, who wore his hair in braids. He had an empathetic, non-judgemental expression as he listened to the queer attendees talk about their lives.

Sebastián found that he could only listen that first day. He didn't have it in him to speak. Bacari had asked him to introduce himself if he was comfortable, and he merely shook his head.

"It's okay. There is no judgment here."

In the next session, Sebastián opened up just a bit more. "My name is Sebastián. I moved here shortly before the pandemic. I'm 26. I don't really know what I'm doing with my life."

Sebastián found his voice croaking at this remark. He considered saying more but paused.

"Thank you for sharing that with us," Bacari said neutrally. "That was very brave. Would you like to tell us more?"

Sebastián shook his head.

"That is 100% okay. We can go at your own pace."

It was during a group exercise they were doing about elements of shame that Sebastián found the floodgates opening. The participants were listing their sources of shame. Bacari was writing what participants called out on a whiteboard hung on the wall.

"I'm ashamed of being assaulted," Sebastián said.

Bacari paused at this: "Thank you for sharing that. I want to focus on that if you are comfortable."

Sebastián nodded.

Bacari had compiled a list of actions, adjectives, and phrases on the whiteboard—a collection of every bad thought held by the participants in this room. "Now," he continued. "I will tell you all something that may be a bit shocking. These things don't actually trigger shame. It's our self-talk that does this. What we tell ourselves about these things, not the things themselves, that causes self-hatred."

"Sebastián, let's go with your example. And we will go around as well. What do you tell yourself about being assaulted that triggers shame?"

"That I should have known better. If only I wasn't so imperfect, this would have never happened. That I'm weak and stupid."

"Now, this is what you tell yourself," Bacari stressed. "It is not the reality. Let's focus on some of the things you said. Sebastián, it is not your fault that you were assaulted. There is no way you are responsible for that. How many people think Sebastián couldn't possibly be responsible for this?"

Everyone raised their hands. Sebastián started to cry, and he felt everything blur around him as someone asked to hug him. Yet he didn't want to be forgiven for this. He didn't want these strangers to absolve him of the mistakes he'd made.

"Stop," Sebastián shouted, gently shrugging off the person hugging him. "It's not just the assault. I have been fucking up this entire year. I stopped activism because it got too difficult. I went to underground parties when I knew I shouldn't have. I might have killed Emmett, my friend. It's all my fault. I shouldn't be forgiven. I should feel this for the rest of my life."

"That's a serious accusation. Now I want to probe that thought a little: how did you allegedly kill this person?" Bacari asked non-judgmentally.

"Well, he's not dead yet, but it's bad. I was reckless with Covid restrictions. I threw a party, and as a result, he's fighting for his life in the hospital." Sebastián was crying even more heavily now. He felt as if the world would stop if he continued focusing on this pain. All he wanted to do was feel nothing, to be nothing.

"And how do you know Emmett didn't contract Covid from work, on the street, or at a million other places? How are you specifically responsible for this?"

"Well, I don't. But I could have. It makes the most sense. I'm to blame."

"Listen," Bacari said carefully. "I'm not saying you haven't made mistakes. And it is perfectly valid to feel guilt for your actions and try to rectify those. But right now, you are surrounded by the shame that you are a uniquely awful individual. And if you continue to focus on that self-loathing, that shame, you will never be able to course correct or change. So you did some reckless things during a period when most people were going through tremendous amounts of stress."

There was laughter at this comment, and Sebastián felt weirdly more at ease.

Bacari continued: "And on top of that, you were dealing with the fallout of a traumatic event all by yourself. That doesn't make you terrible. In fact, I think you've been pretty brave. I'm going to ask everyone again. How many people think that Sebastián can be forgiven for throwing this party?"

Everyone again raised their hands.

"Now, if these objective strangers who have listened to your story think that you can be forgiven," Bacari said. "Don't you think you can forgive yourself?"

Sebastián could no longer talk, choking back the tears as he nestled into Rick's shoulder. Therapy could be a bitch.

After that session, Sebastián, feeling vulnerable and raw, turned to Rick and asked: "How are you so fucking good at this?"

"Well," Rick said, stretching out his back as he stood up from the chair. "I'm not."

"But I was a mess back there."

"It's okay to be vulnerable. It doesn't make you weak. Listen, I used to be so angry all the time. I blamed everyone for how the world treated me. And I'm still fucking angry, but I'm trying to separate when people are being shitty to me from when they cause me to remember my trauma. I'm not perfect with it, but that's fine. I don't have to be."

"I don't think I'll ever be where you are." Sebastián sighed.

"You will. Day by day, but you can't shut people out, okay?"

Sebastián nodded.

Rick typically went out with some of the attendees afterward to a tea shop to talk about… well, being vulnerable around a group of strangers. Sebastián had avoided going with them like the plague, but it was today that he decided to finally join them.

The establishment was a tea shop, a restaurant, and a bookstore. The bookstore was at the front where you walked in. The restaurant/tea shop area was in a lounge in the back, replete with comfortable sofas and chairs. Rick apparently knew most of the attendees. It was only at this moment that Sebastián realized that most of them were trans. He had been so self-involved with his sessions that he hadn't paid much attention to anyone else.

"Hey," said an androgynous-looking person in suspenders. "That was really fucking cool of you today."

Sebastián found himself almost giggling. "Thanks," he responded. "That means a lot."

"Now Rick," said an elder enby in a vest with dozens of different political pins and buttons, "are you and your, um, friend, going to the protest today? Some transphobic bar owner is trying to host a fundraiser for the shooting. They are trying to buy good press, so we will ignore how they fired a trans employee. You in?"

"Yes," Sebastián chimed in before Rick could even formulate his thoughts. "Count us in."

# Chapter 40

*Christian*

Speech therapy was going better. Christian could string a sentence together far more quickly than when he first woke up from the coma, but his voice now had a hoarser, almost melodic quality. When he listened to it in recordings, he found it was a higher pitch, as if a stranger were communicating with him. It was a peculiar sensation not being quite used to your words.

The benefit and curse of this improvement was that now his family could finally understand him. Before, they had been happy not to listen to him, shepherding him around as they saw best. Now, he was asking for things, and they didn't like it.

"Just one month… Please, only one."

He was asking his mother to let him go back into the city. Christian realized how pathetic he must sound, begging his mother to give him this, as if he were a child begging to stay up later with the adults at a party. She must have seen him like that now, but he didn't care. He just wanted to go back and get some semblance of his old life.

"I already said no. Besides, how could you afford it? You can't work right now."

"I'm not a child mother… And really?… Money? We have money."

"Your grandfather hasn't awarded you the administration of your trust yet. So no, you don't."

"We will see… about that," Christian said, turning his chair around to leave the room.

It would take over a week for his grandfather to answer his requests for dinner. He knew his mother must have communicated with him because he wouldn't agree to a private, face-to-face conversation.

"I'll see you for the monthly dinner," he replied via text, refusing to write anything else, no matter how much Christian tried to prompt him.

The dinner in question had a lot of family members coming in to see Christian for his 'reintroduction' following his coma. No one had said they were throwing a party. It was merely advertised as a dinner. However, a caterer had been hired, and the house had been decorated and thoroughly cleaned.

Hors d'oeuvres were served by wait staff as guests meandered through the house before dinner. Christian bumped into cousins and aunts he hadn't seen since before college, let alone the pandemic. He received a lot of paternalistic comments. Everyone wanted to congratulate him, especially Sammie, who thought Christian's mere living and breathing was a triumph.

"How you doing, big guy?" He asked Christian during a quiet moment when they were alone together.

"I'm good. How's Grindr?" Christian shot back, not interested in talking to Sammie at all. He wondered if that was the appropriate time to fire that salvo and realized too late that it had had the opposite effect.

The man went silent for a second. "You've never liked me very much, have you?"

"I don't have time for this, Sammie."

"First, you stole my boyfriend…"

"Are you talking about Michael? That happened over a decade ago."

Sammie ignored his comment, continuing his rant. "You've always thought yourself better than me just because I decided to man up and make an actual sacrifice for this family, and you didn't, deciding instead to live your unclean life in the city."

"God, this family is fucked up. So what am I supposed to do? Worship you because you've decided to marry a woman and fuck guys on the side?"

"Keep your voice down," Sammie barked through gritted teeth. "Some of us still try to keep up appearances and not be an embarrassment. Not that your free life has gotten you very far."

*He's making fun of the chair*, the voice stated.

*Christ, I know. Why did I ever think your jokes were clever? Now be nicer.*

"You know what, Sammie. Fine, you win. I'm sure you won't be the first repressed patriarch the Muller clan has in its closet, pun very much intended. Now I have to go."

Christian moved as quickly as he could away from Sammie and toward his grandfather Samuel, who was making court, as usual, with several of the men. "And here he is now." Admiral Thomas said enthusiastically. "We were just talking about your victory with physical therapy."

"Thank you, Admiral." Christian then turned to Samuel. "Grandfather, if I could have a moment."

"Not now," Grandfather Samuel deflected. "Join us. Have a drink."

"Of course."

Christian continued to wait for a moment of his grandfather's time. Guests would come up to him and say hello, and Christian would politely engage in a couple of sentences of conversation before wheeling back to Samuel, but the moment never came. He found that his grandfather could far more easily outmaneuver him, often positioning himself between distant cousins and over-talkative aunts that took more and more of Christian's time.

Dinner was held seated around the family's long table, which had been extended to fit tonight's many guests. It was a meal filled with mostly banal small talk, and by the time they had reached dessert, many were starting to leave. Christian was worried that he would have to wait another month to bring up this subject. And so he made a toast to all the guests still seated around him. He clang his glass with a small spoon and said: "Thank you all so very much for coming to see me. It means the world to see all your charming faces."

"Here here," several said.

"I would like to propose a topic of conversation," Christian continued. "As you can all see, I'm clearly more mobile than a month ago." There was a chuckle at this, though Christian had not meant it to be funny. "Yes, yes, well, I think I should head back to the city, but my parents disagree, and so I wanted to ask all of you for your thoughts."

The laughter died down. "Christian, we don't talk about such things at dinner." His mother barked, trying and failing to keep her voice down.

"Well, thankfully, I waited for dessert," Christian responded.

The Admiral chuckled at this and then immediately caught himself and stopped.

"I say he should go," said Doris. "Beats being stir crazy at home."

"I agree. A little independence will do Christian some good," Grandfather Samuel interjected, hoping to save himself from more embarrassment. "To new beginnings."

There was a general murmur of agreement. People were relieved that they wouldn't have to be uncomfortable after all.

After dessert, after the guests had left and only the core family members of the Muller clan remained, Samuel pulled Christian aside. "That was nasty business you pulled there, Christian. We do not air our dirty laundry like you have done tonight. That is not how we do things."

"I would not have had to do such a thing if you had merely been willing to hear me out."

"I saw no need to indulge your petulance. But fine. If you want to go back and play adult so badly. Go. But if you can't hack it there, you're coming straight home to Connecticut, where your mother can keep an eye on you."

"Understood," Christian said as his grandfather stormed off.

"We should talk about money." His father said—the first string of words he had heard from the man the entire night. His father laid out all the accounts and stipulations for how his return to the city would go. Christian couldn't quite keep up with all the details thrown at him at once, but he got the gist. They had paid his hospital bill. They would be paying for his physical therapy, the rent for the apartment, and a small stipend. "We will not be paying for this indefinitely," his father chastised. "Eventually, you will return to your job with Thomas, understood?"

"Yes… sir," Christian said. There was nothing else to say.

His immediate family stayed for a couple more days at his parent's house, bickering and arguing like it was any other weekend. Then, one by one, they left. They returned to the suburbs of Connecticut, New York, and DC. And then Christian was gone, too, back to his apartment, staring down at the people scurrying below.

He messaged Jon, the last bridge he hadn't yet burned.

Christian

I'm back in town.
Want to come over?

# CHAPTER 41



Jon was surprised to see Christian again. Christian's voice was better now, even if it retained a melodic quality to it, and they could start to have a more normal back-and-forth. Well, maybe the word normal was a poor choice of words.

"Your family is… a lot," Jon remarked. "Your mom is texting me like 24/7 for updates."

"They are. But then, so am I."

"Not like that," Jon reassured.

"I don't think you know what the hell you're talking about," Christian stated coldly.

Jon realized he had hit a nerve. He didn't know how this had gone bad so quickly. "No, I don't. Oh, Christian, I'm so sorry for not being by your side during the beginning," Jon cried. "When I heard the news of you being in the hospital, I panicked."

Jon squeezed Christian's hand. It was warm and soft. He had last touched this man's hands what seemed to be a lifetime ago. Now everything had changed so quickly.

"I was unconscious," Christian reassured him. "I think you can be forgiven."

Jon found that he couldn't stop talking now that he had started. "And for giving you such a hard time about Emmett. I was irresponsible too, and I shouldn't have pushed you away like that. The night of the shooting, when I thought you were going to die, all I could think about was that it's my fault for making you go to that club."

"No one made me do anything," Christian screamed like it had been building for some time. "I shouldn't have been such an asshole. You were right to push me away… though that might just be the painkillers talking."

"I'm the one supposed to be comforting you." Jon cried.

"Well, that's the way things go, I guess," Christian said.

Jon spent much more time with Christian over the next few days. He promised himself that he wouldn't bail on him—not like last time, but it was hard, and more than that, expensive. He was thankful Christian's family had paid for their son's hospital bill because the nonprofit Jon had fundraised for took half the money to cover their 'expenses.' The remainder hadn't even covered the costs for one victim's bill. Jon was shocked by how expensive the American medical system was. In the past, he had complained about the medical system online, but it was never 'real' to him—but now it was something affecting one of his friends.

The bills kept piling up. Neither Christian nor Jon had a car, and Christian had to go to physical therapy twice a week at an office in a sleek glass building on the other side of town. Christian couldn't easily wheel there yet, and the bus could take hours, so they ordered Ubers, a cost that his $200-a-week stipend made difficult. While his family was covering medical bills and rent, the stipend was supposed to pay for travel, food, and everything else, and it just wasn't enough.

Jon would help pay for things, but he couldn't help with much on a barista's salary, which was the only job he had managed to get after Barry had fired him. Barry had not appreciated Jon refusing to go to parties with him after starting to visit Christian in the hospital.

"You are being selfish," Barry had remarked after Jon had rejected a last-minute trip to New Orleans. "Christian isn't even awake. We should care about the living."

"He's not dead." Jon had corrected. "And it's not only him. I'm visiting Emmett too. Who I notice you haven't seen either."

Barry had scoffed.

It was their last conversation before Barry had cut ties—dumping and firing him all in one text. Money was tight now. Jon had not worried about money for over a year. He had found that if he sucked the right dick, he didn't have to think about it. However, his conversation weeks ago at the protest with Sebastián had rattled him, pausing his usual pattern of trading dick for a roof. He was with Christian now during the most inconvenient time you could be with him—after he had lost most of his money. Jon had forgotten how challenging not having money was, flashing back to that cramped room he had stayed in when he first arrived in the city. Before the bubble. Before he had met Christian. Before the pandemic.

Christian refused to ask his parents for more money. "I'm not giving them an excuse to send me home," he said fearfully one night after Jon prodded him one too many times. "They will do it."

Even so, Jon texted Christian's mom about it once after an email from his bank told him he was in the negative again. But she said no. "His grandfather wouldn't like that," she responded. "Please, tell Christian to come home. We can help him."

Jon did not reply.

As the weeks went on, he tried to help Christian in whatever way he could. An enormous task was to apply for disability. The paperwork was confusing and cumbersome, and he had so far only managed to get him on three months of short-term. The assessors claimed that even though Christian was in constant pain, he had only had a desk job before, so it wouldn't prevent him from returning to work.

"If you can move, you can work," the assessor joked.

"How is someone without help supposed to live?" Jon said after the man had left.

"Yeah, I'm learning some things aren't what I thought they were," Christian said quietly.

In some ways, Christian was easier than before. The entitled rich boy who thought that the world was fairer than it was had been slapped across the face by reality. He no longer ranted about how evil liberals and leftists were or how the answer to everything was to work harder.

"I can't believe I thought people mooched off of welfare," he remarked as the assessor closed the door. "If there is a way to do so, I would love to know because this is impossible."

But he was also struggling with getting help from others. Jon had to help Christian do many tasks now, and Christian snapped at him often, only to apologize minutes or seconds later. One night, Christian had yelled at him for being too clingy, when in reality, all Jon had done was help lift Christian onto the toilet seat—something Christian had asked for help with, only to immediately chew Jon out for it.

Christian broke down in tears seconds later. "Sorry. It's not you, and I have no right to take it out on you. Everything just hurts," he cried. "There's so much pain, and sometimes I'm so angry I want to hurt someone."

Jon kissed him on the forehead and later helped Christian make his way to the bed, where the two cuddled quietly until they fell asleep. Jon didn't know when he had moved into Christian's place. He was there at the apartment so often, helping Christian with odds and ends, that it eventually stopped being a question of whether he would spend the night.

At first, sex happened between them just as something to do. Jon felt guilty for thinking about it this way, but it was true. Neither of them was a stranger to the other's body, and it was nice to feel the warmth of Christian's tender lips on his skin. They had had sex plenty of times before the shooting, but things were different now. There was so much that had to be relearned for both of them. Christian's legs weren't mobile—they might never 'work'—but some key parts of him still had sensation. They seemed to have even more feeling than before. Jon would place his lips on the tip of Christian's member, and this small gesture would cause Christian to rive wildly with pleasure.

"Jesus, that's fucking good," he shouted.

Jon withdrew his lips to smile, before moving down to kiss Christian's balls. He cupped them with his hands so that he could kiss Christian on the mouth again without interrupting the sensation.

"Wait, stop. I'm going to cum," Christian called out.

"I want you to cum, slut," Jon said. He loved being a brat. He loved tormenting Christian, making him go 'just' a little outside his comfort zone, consensually, of course.

"But," Christian couldn't finish that sentence. He let out a giant gasp, cumming onto Jon's hands.

Later, after they had cleaned off and were cuddling, Christian proposed something. "You know, you can move in if you want," Christian said casually. "I mean officially. You pretty much already have."

"Aren't you worried things are moving too fast?" Jon questioned. "I'm poly, you know. I don't want to change that."

"Fast? My life is already so slow. It takes me more than an hour to leave the apartment, and it gives me a lot of time to think. I think my life is better with you in it. And

I don't want to change anything about you." He paused. "Besides, other guys could be fun."

After saying yes, Jon smiled and kissed Christian on the lips. He then used that man's adorably cute mouth for round two.

# CHAPTER 42

Sebastián

Rick. Elena. Christian. Sebastián had a list. It had been rotating through his head over and over again. People whom he needed to talk to: who deserved something, even if it wasn't always clear what. He had been running the list in his mind for months, but today was the day he would start it, with Rick—the easiest and most obvious.

"Would you be interested in being poly?" Sebastián asked, finally having the courage to say what he wanted.

They were both in the midst of Sunday cleaning. Sebastián was breaking down the cardboard boxes that had regularly piled up in their apartment. Well, Sebastián's apartment, but it increasingly felt like 'theirs.' Rick was cleaning the fridge, taking out all the items that had lingered there for far too long.

He took a moment to acknowledge Sebastián. "Does hot sauce go bad?" Rick asked at last, ignoring the question.

"I'm serious. We were both poly before we started dating. Don't you want to get back to that?"

"I wouldn't exactly call your last relationship a healthy example of polyamory."

Sebastián took a deep breath, trying not to let those moments return to him. The PTSD from this last year was no longer debilitating, but it still stung sometimes. An occasional nightmare would pierce through into his dreams, or even his waking thoughts, of water crashing all around him. His anxiety soared like a predator was suddenly stalking him… like he was going under. But a predator was not stalking him. He was not drowning. He would not let it hold him back from this conversation. "Okay," Sebastián breathed, "and what, we put our lives on pause because you think I have unresolved trauma?"

Rick sighed, closing the fridge door. "You think being with me is 'being on pause?'"

"Sorry, that's not what I meant. It's just… You don't get to decide when I'm healed enough to start taking risks again. It's my life, our life, and well… I didn't hate everything about being polyamorous with Christian. What about you? Is monogamy something you're interested in?"

"I guess not. You are the first monogamous relationship I've ever been in, but I grew up in a crunchy town in Oregon, and well, I've been swimming in these poly waters since before I started transitioning. I read *The Ethical*

*Slut* when I was fourteen. It's what I've wanted in life for a long time."

"So it sounds like we both want this. Then, what's the problem?"

Rick frowned at this. "You have to understand. When I met you, you were so hurt, and I guess I'm protective of you, Sebas. I don't want to see you get hurt again."

Sebastián had stopped holding the cardboard and reached out to touch Rick's hands. They were so much harder than he would have believed before dating him. Rick had callouses developed from years of herding cows on his father's farm. Sebastián continued: "I love that about you. How much you want to help people, but you can't stop me from getting hurt."

Rick nodded again. His boyish face was not smiling or frowning this time. He was staring directly into Sebastián's eyes, taking it all in.

Sebastián continued: "I love you, you know that, right?"

Rick teared up. He planted a warm kiss on Sebastián's lips, and the two of them decided to stop cleaning and work their way to the bedroom.

The next day, he called Elena. There was no use in delaying his self-dubbed 'reconciliation' tour. He was surprised when she picked up, assuming that her being angry with him had been the same thing as no longer loving him. A thought distortion, he knew. She hadn't blocked him or screened his calls. His sister wasn't a petty guy from Grindr.

"I've been a right ole schmuck," he told her over the phone when she picked up.

"Can you be more specific?" She joked.

"Elena, I'm serious. I'm sorry I haven't been around."

"Fuck you, Sebas," Elena cried, her voice cracking from tears. "You know I was getting ready to tear you a new one, and then you just apologize like that."

Sebastián found himself smiling. "Fuck you too, El."

"It's been a hard year, Sebas, you know? This last year, I've felt like I've been alone. And I could have really used my brother." He was used to her being the strong one. It was refreshing that she wasn't this once, that she needed him.

"You're right. I should have made more time. I'd like to see you and the kids next month, if you'll have me. Maybe invite the boyfriend?"

"I'd like that. So I finally get to meet the famous Christian?"

"No, a new guy. But I think you'll like him. He's…"

"Less of an asshole, I take it."

"Yeah, that."

The tour was going okay, but then there was that asshole, Christian, left. Sebastián had avoided him in the hospital. Things were too raw then. Too complicated. Yet he knew from Jon, who shockingly was not guilting him about it, that Christian had recovered enough to leave the hospital. It was time to see him again. He knew he wanted something from him, but he wasn't sure what.

Sebastián scheduled a coffee date a week later. Rick had been nervous about Sebastián doing this. "Are you sure you don't want me to come with you?" He had asked worriedly as Sebastián put on his beat-up hoodie to leave.

"Thanks, but I have to do this on my own."

And to his credit, Rick didn't fight it. He let him walk out the door, muttering passive-aggressively under his breath about breaking Christian's neck if he hurt Sebastián. Weirdly, Sebastián couldn't help but smile at this.

Sebastián and Christian met at *The Silver Spoon* on the patio where they once flirted. Over a year had passed since those desperate coffee dates. The sky was a vibrant blue, with animals and people everywhere. Christian was parked in his chair on the other side of the flimsy black table where they were situated, smiling.

"You look like shit," Sebastián said, breaking the silence.

"I feel like it." Christian laughed.

"So what's it like being, well, this," Sebastián asked, referring to the chair.

Christian flinched. "You're going to start our conversation with a bit of ableism. And I thought you were the activist one?"

"Wow, you've picked up the vocabulary and everything. Dammit, okay, let me try again."

"Nope. Sorry, you only get one. Otherwise, I get to cancel you. And privileged white men like me don't get that option very often."

"You wish," Sebastián said, rolling his eyes. "You're joking, right?"

"Yes. I'm joking. Though, given my YouTube history, you are right to be asking. God, that feels like a lifetime ago. I can't believe I've been in this chair for a little more than two months." He grimaced awkwardly. Christian looked down at his chair—as if the memories of his past life had suddenly flooded back to him.

"Sorry about that comment. That was insensitive."

"Apology accepted. God knows I owe you several apologies."

Sebastián smiled. This was going shockingly well. He had thought this conversation would be complicated, and getting here was difficult. He had started and deleted a message to Christian on text and even Grindr to no success, but nothing was holding them back now that they were face-to-face. There was no relationship to repair.

"I'm so sorry for not calling, Christian. Even though you were a class-A asshole."

"Fair," Christian interjected, slapping the sides of his chair.

Sebastián continued: "I'm sorry I didn't see you in the hospital. That was shitty."

"No, you were right to stay away," Christian echoed. "I think we should have done that sooner. I have so much to be sorry for. Emmett. Fuck. I still haven't processed that fully."

"Have you talked to him since he left the hospital?"

"I haven't. I was waiting for the right time," he said uneasily.

"You should. Don't let shame cause you to deny him an apology too."

Christian sighed. "I think I'm most sorry about not being there for you, Sebastián. You needed me in the Bahamas, and I wasn't paying attention. I should have fucking done something. Punched that actor's lights out for one."

"There's still time."

"I don't want to go to prison. I don't think I would do well there." Christian laughed.

"Wouldn't your grandfather, Scrooge McDuck, buy your way out?"

"True, though he's not exactly happy with me at the moment. They are limiting access to my trust. The one I'm not even old enough to administer yet." Christian sighed. He was trying to play it off, but the idea seemed to weigh heavily on him.

"Oh." Sebastián didn't know how to process this information. What was Christian without money? He tried to imagine him slurping down a bowl of instant Ramen noodles in a shabby studio apartment on the outskirts of town, but he couldn't picture it.

"Yeah," continued Christian. "My mom wants me to live with her and dad full time, and they aren't afraid to use financial abuse to do it. There's even talk of my brother Sammie being made the administrator for my trust. I'm getting fucked all over the place."

"Fuck. Christian. Do you have a place to stay?"

Christian gave Sebastián the biggest side-eye. "If you are suggesting what I think you are, that's not a good idea," Christian said, shutting down the possibility. "We might be able to have a conversation, but I don't think we should live with one another. Plus, I'm shit company right now. Just ask Jon. No, don't do that, he'd say I'm perfect, and just giving myself a hard time."

"But, how will you live?"

"Yeah, things are tight right now, but as Jon would say, I'm still a privileged white man who went to Yale. I have my job at the base, for the time being, anyway. Besides, I can always downsize to another apartment. One in the suburbs that is a little more accessible. It's not like Scrooge McDuck can prevent me from moving."

"You're going to move to the suburbs?"

"I will probably have to. It's for the best, anyway. I'm miserable in this city. Everything reminds me of, well, you." Christian paused. "Sorry, that was a shitty thing to say."

"Don't take this the wrong way, but are you seeing a therapist?"

"Naw, I can't exactly afford it now that my family has decided that now of all times is the moment to squeeze the purse strings."

Sebastián nodded empathetically. He again looked at the life around him—the children playing on the sidewalk, the patrons going into the cafe, some even carelessly letting their masks slip after months of fatigue. Would people forget this moment? This fear, like they had every plague throughout history? Things moved so much faster than he could have imagined.

He took Christian's hands, soft and smooth, just like they had been on that first night in Sebastián's shitty apartment. He looked at this person who felt like both a good friend and a complete stranger all in one, and smiled. "I think I might be able to help with that."

# CHAPTER 43



"And remember, you are invited to *Marx at the Movies* next Friday, if you want. We will be watching *Parasite*," Sebastián said as he walked back into the hallway with Christian moving right behind him. "Rick would love to see you again."

"Count me in," Emmett smiled, waving them off.

Christian and Sebastián had not been to his apartment—a small studio on the city's outskirts that was a leisurely twenty-minute walk away from the nearest subway stop—the entire time they had been dating, but they had come now. He guessed it was a benefit of almost dying. They had given him a list of sorries and warm welcomes.

Since leaving the hospital, he hadn't expected the flood of apologies from people, especially Christian, who, although still a little clueless, was slightly less awful. Maybe near-death experiences should be a requirement for all rich white kids with a trust fund?

Emmett closed the front door, which was a pain to close, as he had to slightly arch it upward so the lock could properly slide into place. It was taxing, and he had already tired himself out seeing his friends to the threshold. Walking even the short distance from the couch to the door had fatigued him.

Long Covid could be a bitch.

There was still so much to do. Christian and Sebastián had stopped by last minute. He had set out food for his guests, which had taken him over an hour, and now, the dishes were stacked high in his sink, and it would probably be days before he could get to them. There was the laundry, dirty clothes strewn along his bedroom floor. His cardboard boxes were bulging out of the recycling box, and now... moving them to the drop-off down the hall had become a herculean effort. His cat also needed more food, and for her litter box to be cleaned, that damn thing always needed more cleaning.

There was a clearing of a throat. Jon was still there, sitting on his worn green couch, gazing at Emmett with an amused expression.

"Are you sure those two are still not together?" Emmett joked.

"I'm sure. Though they orbit a very distinguished polycule."

"They orbit you, you mean?" Emmett laughed.

"Not just me, but yes, I'm dating Christian, and Rick and Sebastián are dating me. I'm happy to draw you a flow diagram if it's too confusing," Jon chided, leaning back on the couch, his shit-eating grin reaching peak insufferableness.

"What about Barry?" Emmett inquired as he sat down on the couch, several inches apart from Jon, relieved to be sitting down again.

"Barry is banished to the shadow realm on account of being Barry. Someone else can deal with him. I'm a little tapped out on broken white boys at the moment."

"Pot, kettle," Emmett ribbed, hoping the joke wasn't too brutal.

"Want to stir this pot even more?" Jon winked, spreading his legs further.

Emmett rolled his eyes. "And where do I fit in your river... wet... flow, that's the word, flow diagram of yours?" Emmett plowed forward inarticulately. He was out of practice with the witty banter. Brain fog did that to you.

"Well, I still love you," Jon said, deadly serious, staring directly into Emmett's eyes. "Christian wasn't the only one I visited in the hospital, you know."

"So what, you want to go back to the bubble and the mindless groupthink of Christian and Sebastián?"

Jon squeezed Emmett's hand. "The bubble doesn't exist anymore, Em, but we could."

Emmett pushed his hand away. "No, you don't get to do that." Jon tried to say something, but Emmett shushed him. "I'm not just some... some add-on you can put alongside your collection."

"It isn't like that."

Emmett stared into the eyes of this beautiful man, looking so intently at him, wordlessly, breathing in and out."

"I was alone… for months. I needed friends, and I turned to the bubble, and you all hurt me. You didn't mean to, but you did, and now." Emmett took in a deep, pained breath. Why did everything have to hurt so much? He wheezed, trying to collect himself before continuing.

Jon touched his back, rubbing his fingers softly along Emmett's spine. "How can I support you?"

Emmett started crying. "I need someone to do the dishes."

"Is that all?" Jon smirked. "I can do them right now."

"Fuck you," Emmett shouted, pushing Jon away again, harder this time, causing him to cough. "You know that's not all. I need help with everything. The dishes. The laundry. Breaking down the fucking cardboard boxes. Feeding damn Mittens. And unlike Christian, I don't have a trust fund to help me, or a you."

"I…" But Jon paused, wordless.

He got up and moved over to the kitchen. "You have me now," he said softly as he started cleaning Emmett's sink. Within three hours, he had cleaned Emmett's entire apartment.

Emmett hadn't believed Jon when he promised to come back. As the years passed, he would be pleasantly surprised.

# Chapter 44

*Rick*

Sebastián handed Rick a cup of coffee. They had just gotten back from a protest at a bank that was funding anti-LGBTQ+ politicians, and the smell of the black liquid was a pleasant gesture. Coffee was a vital component of Rick's after-protest ritual. He grabbed it and then planted a warm kiss on Sebastián's forehead. He took a large swig, taking satisfaction in the caffeine rippling through his entire body.

They had been seeing each other for a couple of months now. Initially, Rick hadn't been sure it was going to work. The first time they had attempted sex, Sebastián had violently shaken at his touch. Rick assumed Sebastián was being bigoted in that way dudes sometimes were when his guard was lowered and his pants dropped, but quickly, he learned that it had nothing to do with him. Rick had held him tightly that night and told Sebastián everything would be all right.

"I haven't felt all right in a long time," Sebastián had cried.

Rick said nothing at first, cradling him in his arms, quietly waiting until Sebastián's tears dried. "We don't have to do anything right now. You are enough."

And they didn't. Instead, they binged terrible romantic comedies for hours, debating fan theories until well into the night. It took weeks—light-years in gay years—for them to do anything more than kiss, and Rick didn't mind it. It had been worth the wait. Sebastián was now a regular boy pussy connoisseur. Rick had even recently pegged Sebastián with a giant rainbow dildo he had affectionately anointed the Rancor. He was a nerd at heart, after all.

It surprised Rick when Sebastián and Christian made peace. It was even more of a shock when Sebastián floated the idea of him and Rick dating Christian's boyfriend, Jon, who was also in a poly relationship. It felt complicated, but Sebastián explained that things were better now.

"Christian and I are better friends than we were ever boyfriends," Sebastián remarked. "Also, Jon has a nice dick. You'll like it."

Fair enough, and he was indeed enjoying it.

Besides, Rick could deal with complicated. Sebastián was sweet to him, doing things like bringing him coffee without being asked. They had visited his sister Elena recently, and part of Rick was worried that things were moving too quickly, but he had to remind himself that he was happy. That there was no proper speed for a relationship and that right now, this was enough. That seemed to be his position on a lot of things these days—take what the world gives you, but never settle. Always demand more, and give others grace when they show they can.

The protestors had settled around a table in the city's only openly identified queer coffee shop. Ain't that a mouthful? They were of different races and ethnicities, all trans, except for Sebastián, who was performing the role of the token cis. He seemed to take on this role happily, doing his best to be a helpful ally. He had pulled out a pad of paper and was jotting down notes as the group planned what they would do for their next protest.

Later, after all taking rapid tests, some of them planned to go to his apartment and have sex. Rick would feel the many hands of his trans brothers and sisters. Sebastián and Jon would, too, for that matter, often bringing Emmett along in tow. But on the rare days Christian came with them, Sebastián and he never seemed to interact sexually. They only occasionally clasped each other's hands as they made love to others—a fragile reminder of a relationship that no longer existed but still lingered in both of them.

But first, they had to decide their next target.

"Maybe the mayor's office or a corporation's headquarters?" floated a protestor.

"Or that transphobic reporter's house," another suggested.

Rick smiled to himself. He loved how activism made him feel less alone. He liked the camaraderie he felt now in this instant. He made a mental note to file this moment away for whenever the shame of the past became too much to bear. Whenever he thought about how he had transitioned so late in life, how Rick had not been involved in politics until his late twenties, or how they might all have to go back inside again because of this new strain called Delta.

In those dark moments of self-hatred, he told himself he would think about these radical queers gathered around this table with their masked faces, joking about the shitty state of the world and how badly they wanted to change it. Right now, he could trick himself into believing that change was possible, and that was enough.

# ACKNOWLEDGMENTS

The work of a novel is never the result of one person, even a self-published one such as this.

I, of course, have to thank my wonderful partner, Arty, who has been a constant source of inspiration, support, and edits. I would love to give a shoutout to my sisters, my parents, both in blood and law, as well as to my wonderful friends, especially Shauna whose conversations were quite useful in holding onto my vision. Without them, this trans-enby would have never finished a novel. I am eternally blessed to have them in my life, especially my jelly belly, Arty.

I also want to give a warm set of thank yous to my fellow editors over at *After the Storm Magazine*. Building out that futurism magazine has allowed me to develop my voice and become a more confident writer. I hope we will have many more years together, challenging what the future can look like.

I would not be here without the fantastic developmental edits of A. Knight, whose insights helped me finetune this novel into what it is. I would like to thank the designers David Colón and Brady Moller, who helped with the book's cover and layout. I likewise want to thank my beta and sensitivity readers: Nicole Neuman, Kat Lewis, and Jessica H. As a writer there is always a risk I will miss something, and I did my best to try to get as many voices as possible, which was not always easy with a self-published novel.

All of these people are who helped make the work you have read today possible. I am grateful for their assistance.